Bound to
Her Blood Enemy

by

Tora Williams

This is a work of fiction. Names, characters, places, and incidents are either the product of the author's imagination or are used fictitiously, and any resemblance to actual persons living or dead, business establishments, events, or locales, is entirely coincidental.

Bound to Her Blood Enemy

Cover Art by *Debbie Taylor*

The Wild Rose Press, Inc.
PO Box 708
Adams Basin, NY 14410-0708
Visit us at www.thewildrosepress.com

Publishing History
First Tea Rose Edition, 2018
Print ISBN 978-1-5092-2076-2
Digital ISBN 978-1-5092-2077-9

Published in the United States of America

Dedication

In memory of my dad
and rainy days in Welsh castles.

Chapter One

April 1146

A hunting horn echoed around the walls of Redcliff Castle. Heart hammering, Matilda picked up her skirts and hurried toward the huntsmen by the gate. They were about to set out. This could be her last chance. One moment alone. With any of them. That was all she needed.

One of the men turned. She stopped, her fists bunching in the soft wool of her gown. Saints preserve her! It was her guardian. How had he got here so fast? She could have sworn she'd seen him enter his wife's chamber.

She dropped into a curtsey. "Sir Reginald, I didn't realize you were joining the hunt."

"Come to wish us luck, have you?" The knowing glint in his eyes sent a chill down her spine.

She drew a deep breath. She'd come this far; she couldn't give up now. There might still be a way to get what she wanted. "And a safe return." She risked a flirtatious glance at the nearest huntsman. "I hope to see our guests unscathed at the Easter feast." Please God, let him take the hint and seek her out when he returned.

The nobleman looked her up and down, his eyes lingering on her breasts. "It would take a catastrophe to keep me from your company."

Matilda wiped her palms on her skirts, fighting queasiness. For the first time she doubted her ability to keep up this charade. If only Sir Reginald had invited pleasanter men to Redcliff.

A rattle made her turn her head. A beggar, bent double beneath his ragged cloak, shuffled toward them. He held out a wooden dish containing a few coppers. He shook them again.

"Alms for the poor, my lady?" The hood shadowed his face, but he spoke in the reedy, tremulous voice of the old or infirm.

Before she could reply, the huntsman who had just spoken stepped between them. Matilda cried out in shock when he lashed out at the beggar, striking the poor man in the face and knocking the dish aside.

"How dare you address a lady? Stay away from her, you cur."

He raised his arm again, but Matilda flung herself between them. "Stop! Don't hurt him."

The huntsman lowered his fist and stepped back, giving her a stiff bow. "As you wish, my lady. But if I were you, I'd throw him out. No good ever came of inviting vermin into a house." He mounted his courser.

Sir Reginald moved as if to follow but turned back to Matilda at the last moment and seized her arm in a bruising grip. "You're playing a dangerous game," he said, his voice as smooth as butter but with an edge of malice. "If I ever catch you making sheep's eyes at one of my friends again, I'll have you flogged. Understand?"

Matilda nodded, pressing her lips together to keep them from quivering. Sir Reginald gave her one last hard look before he released her and joined the other huntsmen. She watched, rubbing her arm, as the men filed out of the gateway. As they descended the causeway leading off the sandstone escarpment that gave Redcliff its name, she had a mad impulse to dash out of the gates herself. It was a futile dream. The man on the gate threw a wary glance in her direction. Sir Reginald would have given him strict orders concerning her. No doubt her guardian would also have a word with the nobleman during the hunt. He would warn him off, just as he did all the men who crossed her path.

The gates creaked shut, and she turned to leave. The beggar still scrabbled in the mud for his coins. "Are you hurt?" She tried to examine his face to see if he was bleeding, but his hood obscured her view. "That was a brutal blow."

He fended her off and turned his head away. "I've taken worse."

"Maybe, but I'd like to help." She grasped his hood and pulled it back, revealing a shock of chestnut hair and the strong, angular face of a man no older than thirty. She recoiled with a small cry, her pulse racing.

Her first thought was to run, but the man grasped her wrist while with the other hand he covered his face again. In a low voice he said, "Don't give me away. I won't harm you, but Sir Reginald would see me hanged."

Matilda darted a swift glance about the bailey. The guards on the gate had their backs to her, watching the departing hunt. The workmen who had come to see the hunt off were drifting back to their various bothies around the edge of the bailey. No one had noticed her unmask the beggar.

"An honest man wouldn't need to disguise

himself," she replied. "Why should I care if you are caught?"

"If that was the case, you'd have called for help by now."

She couldn't deny the truth in that. Her fear of him was balanced by the possibility that he was the answer to her prayers. As long as Reginald Fitzjohn didn't know the man was here, he couldn't stop her enlisting his help.

"Who are you?" she asked. "What are you doing here?"

"The bailey isn't the place for this conversation."

Of course not. She forced her whirling mind to come up with a solution.

"Come with me to the stillroom," she said finally, raising her voice to ensure the guards heard. "I'll tend your cut myself." Then she added in an undertone, "We'll be alone there, but within earshot of the armorer. I'll scream if you make so much as a threatening move."

The man nodded, and she led the way to the keep and down the stone steps to the undercroft.

Once in the herb-scented stone chamber, she turned to the stranger and drew in a sharp breath. "Merciful saints! How did you manage that?"

"Manage what?"

"I could swear you're a whole foot taller."

His lips twisted in a wry smile. "People see what they expect most of the time. Wear rags, and they dismiss you as a beggar." He pulled his cloak closer about him and appeared to shrivel before her eyes.

She crossed herself, startled. But as her eyes became accustomed to the dim light, she saw the man was indeed only bent double beneath his cloak. Now she came to look closely, she saw the outline of broad shoulders and a muscular back. He straightened again. Blessed saints, how had he managed to conceal his height? Her face didn't come any higher than his chest. She ought to avert her gaze, but she stared, fascinated, at the thin rag he wore as a shirt. Or, rather, it wasn't the shirt that fascinated her, but the firm muscles beneath. She had to press a hand to her stomach to still the curious fluttering within.

"Sit there," she said, indicating a stool beside the lit brazier. Maybe she would be less flustered if he wasn't looming over her.

She busied herself with lighting the tallow candles ranged on the wooden table to supplement the light slanting in from high windows in the vaulting. Then she gathered a flask of strong wine, a jar of comfrey ointment, and a soft cloth from the shelves on the back wall before turning to the stranger.

He had thrown back his hood and was watching her, his hazel eyes gleaming in the reflected light from the brazier. For a moment she froze, her fingers tightening upon the jar. What was it about this man that caused her wits to scatter? She set the flask and jar upon the bench but kept hold of the cloth, needing something to occupy her hands.

"We're alone now, so tell me who you are." She fought to keep her voice steady. No easy task, when her examination of the bruised cut below his eye forced her to take in the strong lines of his cheek and jaw.

"My name is Huw ap Goronwy."

"You're Welsh?"

He smiled. A crooked smile that spread a curl of

warmth through her belly. "You're quite safe. I ate my fill of Norman maids last night."

She'd been too flustered to pay attention before, but the musical lilt of his accent summoned happy memories from her childhood. "I didn't mean it that way. My mother was Welsh." That must be why he had this strange effect on her. He reminded her of the yearning gap in her life. Relieved, she uncorked the wine.

"Was?"

"She died when I was five." Matilda tipped a little wine upon the cloth and dabbed at the cut, wincing at the pain she must be inflicting.

Apart from a slight tightening of the jaw, Huw gave no sign of discomfort. "And your father?"

"Dead the following year." The desolation of those days came back in a rush, but at least it served a useful purpose. It reminded her that men were unreliable. She would attempt to enlist Huw's help, but she wouldn't make the mistake of trusting him.

She reached for the ointment, only to gasp when Huw gripped her wrist.

"Hold—you're Reginald Fitzjohn's ward?" There was an odd look in his eyes that she couldn't read.

"Yes. What—?"

He let her go. "You're Matilda Comyn."

A shiver of unease trickled down her spine. "How do you know my name?"

"I keep my eyes and ears open."

"That's no answer." Suddenly she was afraid. Not the same fear she held for Sir Reginald, but the fear that came when standing on a precipice, knowing one misstep would send her plunging into the unknown. She moistened her lips which had grown dry. "You still haven't told me why you're here. Give me a reason why I shouldn't turn you in."

"Even if I tell you, what guarantee do I have that you won't turn me in anyway?"

"Because I'm no..." She stopped. This wasn't how the conversation should be going. So far, she'd learned his name, and that he was Welsh. She'd as good as told him her life story. Trying to get information from Huw ap Goronwy was like wrestling with eels.

"There's no guarantee. You'll just have to trust me."

"I trust no one."

This was getting them nowhere. "You're right. I could turn you in." She stabbed a finger up toward the main body of the keep. "There's any number of men up there who would be very interested to know why a Welshman is here, disguised as a beggar."

"What's stopping you?"

"In case you hadn't noticed, Sir Reginald and I are not on the best of terms. If he caught you and found out I'd spoken to you, he'd punish me. So, believe me, I want you to stay hidden."

Huw's face darkened. "He beats you?" It gave her a thrill to hear the concern in his voice. It wasn't something she was used to from a man.

"Only when..." She caught herself. She was doing it again. Giving him information when he volunteered none. "That's not your concern."

Huw shifted on the bench as she was speaking, and his cloak parted. The tunic underneath was just as ragged, but a glint caught her eye. Before he pulled the cloak closed again, she caught a glimpse of a dagger at his hip. Although its ornamentation was simple, the quality of the workmanship was clear. No ordinary man would bear such a weapon. A suspicion of the truth formed in her mind, and she grasped it. Anything to break through this man's reserve.

"You're Owain Gwynedd's man, aren't you?" She'd heard rumors that the king of Gwynedd was seeking to reclaim the lands taken by the Normans, taking advantage of the chaos in England.

A muscle jumped in his jaw, betraying him.

"That's it." Her voice, which she had kept pitched low, now rose in excitement. "You're here as his sp—"

"Quiet!" He clamped a hand over her mouth and spoke in an undertone. "Do you want to get me killed?" He glanced over his shoulder toward the open doorway, his body tense. Matilda forced her breathing to calm. If he'd wanted to kill her, he would have done so by now.

The sound of the armorer whistling, accompanied by the rasp of whetstone upon iron, drifted into the room. Huw relaxed and loosened his grip. "Promise to keep your voice down, and I'll let you go."

She nodded. His reaction had dispelled any doubt about the rightness of her guess. The plan that she had been turning over in her mind was looking ever more possible.

He removed his hand from her mouth, and she stepped back, rubbing her arm.

"Did I hurt you?"

She shook her head. She picked up the jar of ointment and fumbled with the stopper, fighting the urge to speak. Two could play at this game. This time he was going to talk, and she was going to listen.

One corner of his mouth tilted up. "Very well," he

said. "You're right. I am the king of Gwynedd's man."

"And you're"—she dropped her voice to a murmur—"spying out the Norman strongholds for him?"

He nodded.

"Is that why you're here at Redcliff?" She frowned. Redcliff was a few miles east of Shrewsbury. Not far from the Welsh border, but surely not close enough for the Welsh to have a claim.

"Not in this instance, no."

"Then why are you here?"

"I came to find you."

****

The jar slipped from Matilda's fingers, clattered upon the wooden table, and rolled off the edge. Huw caught it and set it down without shifting his gaze from Matilda's face.

"Me?" Matilda's face was all wide, blue eyes. Odd that devil spawn should look so innocent. "Why me?"

"Because you could be useful." He mustn't give too much away. He would wait to see what more she volunteered about herself before he revealed his hand.

"I don't see how," she said. "Sir Reginald never tells me anything. And now I'm not even allowed outside the bailey."

"Why's that?"

To his frustration, she clamped her lips shut. She picked up the jar, removed the stopper, and dipped her fingers into the ointment. "It's comfrey, for your bruise."

Huw nodded and tilted his face, allowing her to smooth on the ointment. He would have to be patient with her. She was as skittish as a newborn foal, and no wonder, considering how Fitzjohn treated her. His interest had been roused from his first sight of her, when she had marched across the bailey, armed in all her finery, radiating tension. And that was before he'd learned she was the girl he'd been sent to find.

Prickles of pleasure coursed through his flesh at her light touch. The ointment might be soothing, but having her lean close—so close he caught the scent of honeysuckle rising from her skin—was anything but.

Concentrate! he told himself. But it wasn't easy when his task involved him with a girl whose full, tempting lips and alluring curves reminded him how long it had been since he had last bedded a woman. Only one thought kept him from pulling her close and stealing a taste of those lips: she was a Comyn. It was enough. Just. And yet…

She was starved for love. He'd stake his favorite horse on it. How could she be otherwise, as the ward of a whoreson like Fitzjohn? And that was her weakness. If he paid her some appreciative attention, she'd do anything he asked.

"That feels better." He indicated his bruised cheek. "Thank you." He looked around the vaulted room, taking in the shelves crammed with pots and bottles and dried herbs hanging from hooks on the ceiling. "Is this all your work? If so, you've a great deal of skill for one so young."

A tinge of rose touched her cheeks. "I spend all the time here that I can."

"Away from Fitzjohn, you mean?"

She nodded. "But he encourages my work. Says a girl ought to learn the art of healing to become a good wife."

Huw leaned back and regarded her thoughtfully. "And has he found a husband for you yet?" It was unusual for a high-born girl her age to be still unmarried, now that it occurred to him. She looked to be about eighteen or nineteen.

To his surprise she went pale. For a moment he thought she wasn't going to answer, but then words tumbled out in a rush. "When I turned fourteen, I thought this hell was about to end. He would choose me a husband, and I would be free." She paused. "From him, anyway. But that was five years ago. At first, I wondered why he was delaying. I thought it was because he wanted to keep the revenues from my land."

"But something changed your mind," he prompted when she paused again.

She looked down at her hands. Her veil swung forward, obscuring her face. "I learned two months ago that his wife was ill. Dying." She raised her head and looked him straight in the eye.

Huw shivered.

Her face wore no more expression than a stone effigy. "When she dies, he'll take me as his wife."

Understanding dawned. "To keep your inheritance."

She nodded. "When I found out, I made plans to escape. But I made the mistake of confiding in my maid. She told Sir Reginald, and I've been confined here ever since."

Now her look of desperation as she'd approached the hunting party was explained. "That's why you tried to speak to that huntsman earlier," he said. "You wanted to enlist his help." With her golden-blonde beauty, there would scarcely be a man breathing who

11

could resist her. God knows he would have been hard pressed himself, if it hadn't been for the taint of her Comyn blood. "But would you really have married one of them? I doubt you'd have been any better off."

Her lip curled. "Never. Once free, I was going to slip some poppy syrup into his drink and make good my escape."

Interesting. He would have to watch her carefully. She wasn't nearly as fragile or helpless as she appeared.

"Where would you have gone?"

"To appeal to King Stephen and ask him to choose me a husband who wasn't Fitzjohn."

"You would have far more freedom with a Welsh man." No. What was he thinking? The last thing the Welsh needed was to pollute their bloodlines with Comyn blood.

Remember why you're here, he told himself. This was the same as any other task for the king. He must see it through and not be beguiled by a beautiful face. Above all, remember she wasn't to be pitied.

Matilda rose and cleared the table. "I don't know much about Wales, I'm afraid. I remember some of the tales my mother used to tell me, though, about mountains and waterfalls. I'd love to go there one day."

Now Huw saw his way to completing his mission. And it would be so much simpler if she believed the idea was hers. "You still have family in Wales."

"I do? I don't know much about my mother's family. I know she had a brother, but if she told me anything else, I was too young to remember."

"You didn't know your mother was cousin to the king of Powys?"

Matilda froze in the act of returning the flask and

jar to the shelf. After no more than a couple of heartbeats, she placed the goods down with deliberate movements and turned to face him, her eyes shining. "Do you think the king of Powys would help me regain my inheritance—Coed Bedwen?"

Coed Bedwen. The merest mention made his heart contract. "I couldn't say," he replied.

"But it used to be part of Wales, didn't it?"

"Part of Gwynedd, yes." It was only his years of playing a role that enabled him to keep the emotion from his voice.

Or maybe his skill failed him, because Matilda gave him a searching look. "Have you been there?"

"Never." Although he'd seen it. Many times. His father had made sure of that.

"But you're going back to Wales, aren't you? You could take me with you. To my family."

And there was his victory. "In fact, King Owain instructed me to invite you to his court. He would be able to contact your family for you." It hadn't been an invitation, more an instruction to bring her at any cost, but Matilda didn't need to know that.

She gave him a long look. "I can't imagine what he can want with me."

He shrugged. "Once I've freed you from Redcliff, you can ask him yourself."

Because even if Huw knew, he wouldn't tell her. And she'd better not think he was going to help her regain Coed Bedwen, either. Because Coed Bedwen was his.

Chapter Two

Matilda climbed the steps from the stillroom, the glass phial in her bodice digging into her breast with every movement. The moment she left the shadowy stairwell, she glanced about her, fearing her guilty secret would be plain for all to see, but she needn't have worried. All around the bailey, men and women were strolling to the great hall for the Easter feast. Two days ago, the smells of roasting venison that wafted from the outdoor roasting pits would have set Matilda's stomach rumbling, but now it was cramping with dread.

She slipped around the back of the stables. This being Easter Sunday, the stable yard was deserted. The only sounds to be heard were the occasional snorts and whickers from the horses inside.

She blew out a breath and leaned against the wall, pressing her fingers against the rough wood. She didn't think she'd been seen. As long as Sir Reginald hadn't noticed her slip away early, there shouldn't be a problem. Huw might do this sort of thing every day, but she prayed this would be her last time. And she hadn't even got to the difficult bit yet.

A light step jolted her upright. She pressed a hand to her breast.

"Did you get it?" The deep, lilting voice was Huw's, but the tall, hooded man who strode into view surely couldn't be him. He was dressed in a knee-length tunic and close-fitting hose. The color was drab brown, but the wool was finely woven and the leather belt that cinched the tunic at the waist was clasped with a silver buckle that no ordinary man would wear. There was a kidskin bag slung over one shoulder.

Then she lifted her eyes to his face and saw Huw's angular face, a frown scored deep between his brows. Below his eye was the bluish bruise and scabbed over cut she had treated yesterday. Her fingertips tingled at the memory of smoothing salve along that finely sculpted cheekbone.

Her heart pounded an erratic beat against her ribs.

"Did you get it?" he repeated.

"I…yes." She pulled out the phial of poppy syrup to show him before tucking it back into its hiding place. She drew several deep breaths. What had been so straightforward when they had discussed it yesterday now seemed fraught with danger.

He must have seen her fear, for his gaze hardened. "Are you sure you can do this? If I must make alternative plans, I need to know now."

His doubt pricked her ire. She lifted her chin. "I can do it, Huw. Trust me."

"Don't use my name; I'm not Huw tonight." Before her eyes, the lines on his face softened. It was as though the stern, harsh Huw had disappeared and in his place stood a man with a teasing glint in his eyes.

Matilda edged away from him, her pulse racing. Blessed saints, who was this man?

She opened her mouth to say—what? She had no idea. But before she could make a sound, Huw spoke again. Even his voice was different—higher and with a slightly affected French accent. "Tonight, I am Aimeric the troubadour, who has played for King Stephen himself. And the Empress Maude. Music takes no sides."

He pulled back his hood, revealing the shock of chestnut hair that until now had been hidden. He swept into a low bow, although he kept his eyes fixed upon hers.

"I...why didn't you come as the beggar again?" Not the most intelligent of questions, but her wits had scattered to the four winds.

"It wouldn't do for the beggar to be seen again around here. I attracted too much attention yesterday. Besides, a beggar would have no business talking to a lady such as yourself."

Huw drew a breath, as though to say more, but then he stiffened, his eyes widening. Matilda was about to ask him what the matter was when she heard it— footsteps approaching. Whoever it was would round the corner of the stable before they had time to hide. Her stomach twisted in sick dread.

Huw grasped her shoulders and pressed her back against the wall. Her shock at the liberty he was taking snatched away her cry of shock before it could leave her throat.

"Put your arms around me," he murmured, his lips close to her ear. "Now!"

The command jolted her from her daze, and she pressed her hands against his back. Her heart beat erratically, although whether from fear of discovery or the unfamiliar feel of a man's hard body pressed against hers, she couldn't tell.

"Now smile. Pretend you haven't a care in the world." Huw's warm breath caressed her cheek.

16

Understanding dawned, and she tilted her head to gaze into his eyes and forced her frozen features into a smile. She darted a quick glance over his shoulder and saw one of the stable lads stroll into view. She sagged in relief; such a lowly servant wouldn't feel it his place to report her to anyone.

However, as one fear faded, another grew. She became aware of Huw's closeness. His power. His maleness. One of his hands was curved around the nape of her neck—large hands, with a steely strength in his fingers. No doubt he could snap her neck with ease.

Her mind screamed at her. What was she thinking, putting herself in this man's power? Hadn't everything that was wrong in her life been caused by men? He had said he would take her to King Owain, but men had made promises to her before they hadn't kept. Fitzjohn had promised to take care of her when King Stephen had granted him her wardship, and her father…

She swallowed back bitter bile, and her mind veered away from that thought, clutching at anything to keep her from remembering the words that had haunted her for years.

I'll always be there for you.

No! Think about something else. Anything else.

Unfortunately, it was hard to marshal her thoughts into any kind of order with Huw pressed so close to her. His face filled her vision. Her fingers itched to trace his angular jawline and dip into the dimple in the center of his chin. The heat of his hand against the small of her back spread through her body and pooled in the pit of her belly. Her chest felt so tight it was a struggle to draw breath.

She had to put some distance between them. Now,

before her mind lost all rational thought.

Another glance over Huw's shoulder showed the stable lad disappearing through a doorway.

"He's gone," she said.

Huw stepped back. It was a good thing she had the wall at her back, or her trembling legs might not have held her up.

"Did he notice us?" Huw asked.

"I don't think so." Matilda studied his face. All the softness had vanished, replaced by the now familiar frown. And just for an instant she thought she saw a flicker of something more. Anger? Distaste? It was gone—or concealed—before she could be sure of what she had seen.

A trickle of unease ran down her spine. She knew nothing about this man. Every instinct warned her that escaping into the wilds of Wales with him was foolishness in the extreme.

Every instinct bar the one that had thrilled at the feel of his body against hers.

She pressed her fingers to her temples. She needed space to think. "It's time to go to the feast," she said. "I can't be late. Sir Reginald would want to know where I've been."

Huw nodded. "We mustn't be seen together; you go first. Remember not to talk to me or give any sign that you know me. Make your move when the dancing starts. Wait for me by the gates. I'll be there as soon as I can."

I'll be there… I'll always be there for you.

Feeling sick, she hurried across the bailey to the great hall. It wasn't too late to back out of this plan. She could report Huw to Fitzjohn. That might earn her enough trust to give her another chance to make a break for freedom alone. Without the need to depend on a man.

An idea struck her, and she slipped down the steps to the stillroom. If Sir Reginald had missed her, she wanted him to think she had been there. As luck would have it, the first person she saw as she emerged a second time from the stairway was her guardian. He was dressed in his finest clothes, obviously on his way to the great hall.

Sir Reginald scowled at her. "Where have you been?"

She pointed down to the stillroom. "I wanted to check I had the ingredients for a remedy I thought would help ease your wife's pains." It wasn't entirely untrue—she had done that before going to meet Huw. Along with fetching the poppy syrup.

He gave a curt nod. "Well, see that she gets it later. She's sleeping now, and you must take her place at the high table in her absence."

Matilda let out a shaky breath. Thank Heaven she hadn't raised Fitzjohn's suspicions. That still left the way open to her escape tonight if she decided to go through with it. She bowed her head in a show of meekness and allowed Sir Reginald to lead her into the hall.

The great hall was already crowded with people jostling for space at the lower tables. Everyone stood and bowed in respectful silence while Sir Reginald walked down the length of the hall toward the high table upon the dais. The hall was decked for the Easter festivities. Dazzling white linen cloths covered the tables, set with gleaming silver goblets, jugs, and platters. Bunches of daffodils competed with the blazing candles upon the high table. The huntsmen and women in the wall paintings danced in the flickering firelight.

The riot of light and color was in complete contrast to Matilda's mood. She took her seat at the high table and clenched her hands in an agony of indecision. What should she do? Stay with Fitzjohn, safe for as long as his wife lived, or take her chances with Huw?

Servants came into the hall bearing trays heaped with roasted venison, goose, and boar, sending a murmur of appreciation around the tables. The air of anticipation, as the priest stood to bless the meal, was almost overwhelming. Before he had even finished the "amen," Sir Reginald seized the closest dish to him, and a ripple of chatter started up again.

A hauntingly beautiful melody rang out. Matilda looked to see where it was coming from. She couldn't suppress a gasp when she saw Huw standing to the side of the high table, his head bent over an instrument cradled against his shoulder. It looked like a lyre, only it was played with a bow. She watched, a thrill trickling down her spine, as his long fingers coaxed a tune out of the strings that had even Sir Reginald transfixed.

Who was he, really? If she hadn't met him before, she would never have believed he was anything other than a minstrel. And a gifted one at that. Was the Huw she had met just another disguise? Could she, knowing how men used deceit and trickery to achieve their own ends, put her life in his hands? She sent a silent prayer up to the heavens.

Holy mother Mary, I beg you, show me a sign, set my feet on the right path.

****

Huw let his gaze wander around the hall as he played. The feast had hardly begun, yet most of the revelers, Fitzjohn included, were drinking heavily. Good. He'd be less likely to notice when Matilda drugged his wine.

Matilda. He did his best not to look at her, remember how it had felt to hold her close. How was it that this daughter of a family touched by the devil should be so beautiful?

He struck a wrong note, sending a jarring discord up into the soot-blackened rafters. He recovered himself quickly; a glance around showed him that everyone was too busy with their food to notice his music.

Everyone except Matilda. She was looking at him, frowning. A surge of irritation coursed through his veins. She was a Comyn. To his mind, that was the same as saying she was a monster. How dare she sit there, picking at the food servants had toiled for days to prepare? If it hadn't been for her family, he would be lord of Coed Bedwen and hosting his own Easter feast today. The temptation to fling down his crwth and leave the castle there and then, abandoning her to Fitzjohn, nearly overcame him.

But he couldn't disobey his king. He remembered Owain's words when he had sent Huw to Redcliff: "The anarchy in England won't last forever. And when it ends, the victor, whoever that may be, will look to Wales. If you can bring me Matilda Comyn, we have a chance to strengthen Gwynedd against whatever storms may come."

A voice whispered in the back of his mind. *Once out of Redcliff, you will have her at your mercy. You could fulfil your oath.*

He silenced it. Owain Gwynedd might have many faults, but his love for Gwynedd and its people was what had kept Huw loyal to him all these years. If Matilda Comyn was so important to the king, he would do his utmost to bring her to him. He had waited this long; he could wait a little longer before taking his revenge.

And maybe in that time he could find a way to ignore the fire that flooded his veins every time he looked at her.

When the final notes of his song died away, even Sir Reginald applauded. "Come and sit beside me and have a drink," he invited. "A reward for your music."

Careful to stay in the persona of Aimeric, Huw accepted the drink he was offered and sat on a low stool beside Sir Reginald's chair, doing his best to keep his face in the shadows. He felt the first twinges of unease. He hadn't expected Fitzjohn to pay him much attention. On the one hand, talking to Fitzjohn could provide him with vital information, but against that, it would make life difficult if he ever needed to spy out a place where Fitzjohn was again. He might be recognized.

"You've picked a strange time to visit England." Sir Reginald twisted his silver goblet this way and that so the gems studding its base flashed in the candlelight. "I would have thought you'd prefer the peace of your own land."

Huw shrugged. "What can I say? I like to travel. Besides, there seems to be a tenuous truce holding at the moment. I haven't met any resistance on the road." That was probably because he travelled heavily armed and by stealth, but there was no way he would admit to that.

Sir Reginald snorted. "Maybe things are quieter, but only because Stephen and Maude have bled this country dry between them. I've been forced to pour huge amounts of my income into funding Stephen's war and for what? I've barely enough money to run Redcliff now. I would have had to abandon it if it weren't for"— he shot a glance at Matilda—"certain revenues available to me through my ward."

Huw knew exactly what he was talking about: Coed Bedwen. That was why he couldn't afford to give up his wardship of Matilda. He needed the revenues from Coed Bedwen. If Matilda married another, then her husband would receive her inheritance, leaving Fitzjohn with a large shortfall. He almost felt sorry for the man. Almost.

He stayed to talk to Sir Reginald for as long as he could bear, but as the man had no information of interest to him, he excused himself at the earliest opportunity and picked up his crwth. The meal was ending, and any moment Fitzjohn would call for the dancing to start. That was Matilda's signal to make her move. He needed to be ready.

With every nerve and sinew as taut as the strings on his crwth, he struck up a new tune and prowled the length of the hall until he could see out of the door. Thank Heaven: the sun was setting at last. The last golden rays shone through the clump of oak trees lower down the escarpment, and long shadows crept across the bailey. It would be dark within the hour, giving him the cover he needed to carry out his plan. He made his way back up the hall and stood near Matilda.

He caught her casting a wary glance his way. Her

face was pale, and she was gripping her goblet so hard he was sure the gems must be cutting into her fingers. She better not be having second thoughts. One way or another, he *would* get her away from Redcliff tonight, but it would be so much easier if she came willingly.

She looked lost. Alone. He couldn't help empathizing. He had developed his reliance upon himself because as a spy, there was no one else for him to depend on. If he made a mistake, he was on his own. But as a woman, Matilda should have a whole host of people supporting her. Her parents, then her guardian, followed by a husband and children. But her parents had died, her guardian had failed her badly, and as a result the husband and children she should have had weren't in her life.

By all the saints—stop this now! If he allowed himself to feel pity for a Comyn, he would be lost. He thought of his grandfather and all the Welsh men, women and children who had died because of her devil-spawn grandfather. He would do all in his power to obey his king and bring Matilda safely to him, but once his mission was complete, he would be free to fulfil his vow.

He finished his song and was about to start another when Fitzjohn clapped his hands. "Time for the dancing to begin." The people cheered, and the minstrels who had been idle during Huw's performance picked up their instruments. A merry blend of pipes and lyre, underlain by the insistent pulse of a drum, filled the hall.

Huw, who hadn't taken his eyes off Matilda, saw the color drain from her face, and she swayed slightly. Her attendant was looking at the minstrels and clearly hadn't noticed Matilda's sudden weakness.

Snatching a wine cup from the table, he leaned across and gripped Matilda's arm.

"Some wine, my lady?" He pressed the cup into her hands. As their fingers brushed, he felt as though sparks had leapt from the fire and shot through his flesh. Judging from the sudden color that flooded her face, she had felt it too.

It was just the tension and anticipation. Nothing more.

Matilda snatched the cup from his hands and took a deep draught. "Thank you," she said when she put it down. To his relief, she looked much stronger.

But he couldn't risk her faltering. Not now.

Glancing to either side to make sure no one was looking, he leaned closer and took her arm in a firm grip. He hissed into her ear. "You must eat. A sparrow couldn't survive on the amount you've had today, and we've a long way to go."

Indignation kindled in her eyes, but to his satisfaction, she picked up her knife, cut off a piece of venison, and popped it into her mouth. Belatedly he realized he was staring at her lips while she chewed. Full lips that would tempt even a saint. And he was no saint.

A wave of heat washed over him and pooled in his groin. Hellfire! This was a danger he hadn't reckoned on when he had agreed to come here—the distraction a beautiful woman could provide. And he couldn't afford to be distracted. Not when it could cost him his life.

Drawing a deep breath, he looked around the room. Most of the revelers were gathered at the far end of the hall, following the intricate steps of a circle dance. No one was watching him or Matilda.

Good. His moment of inattention hadn't cost him anything, and he would make sure it didn't happen again.

From the corner of his eye, he noticed Matilda pick up a wine jug and turn to her guardian.

"I ought to attend to your wife," she said. "See if she needs anything."

Fitzjohn gave a curt nod and waved her away.

Huw watched her disappear through a doorway behind the dais. His heart sped up as it always did when the action was about to start.

He packed his crwth into its bag and slung it over his shoulder. He was ready. All he could do now was pray Matilda didn't falter.

Chapter Three

Matilda clutched the jug to her chest the moment she was through the door. This was it: the moment to determine which path to take. Should she bide her time in Redcliff, waiting for an opportunity to escape alone, or should she risk going along with Huw's plans? Her heart yearned to make a bid for escape tonight, but her mind shied from putting herself at the mercy of yet another man. A spy. A man who lied for a living.

Her head buzzed with chaotic, conflicting thoughts. She'd hoped the peace of the sickroom would help her think, but the potential consequences of each decision loomed large, and Huw's voice clamored above it all, urging her to hurry. Holy Mother, help her! If only she could calm her mind enough to think.

She wasn't helped by the nagging feeling something was amiss. It was some time before realization dawned. The chamber was silent. Deathly silent. In the past days, it had echoed with the rasping breaths of the sick woman.

On quaking legs, Matilda approached the bed. The shutters were closed, but a scattering of candles cast a golden glow on the still form huddled in the blankets. There was not the slightest movement. Not even a whisper of breath.

Fitzjohn's wife was dead.

And if Fitzjohn had his way, before the poor

woman was cold in her tomb, Matilda would take her place.

Numb with shock, she placed the wine jug on the table and reached down to close the sightless eyes.

"God grant you peace," she murmured. The peace she could never have known in her marriage.

Then she sank down upon the stool beside the bed and buried her head in her hands. She was faced with a stark choice between two men: one she knew and one she didn't. Both dangerous. She could either escape tonight with Huw or accept her fate as Fitzjohn's wife. If she didn't leave tonight, she wouldn't get another chance.

And she could bid farewell to Coed Bedwen. The only place she'd known happiness.

In the end it was no choice at all. If there was any chance of regaining Coed Bedwen on her own terms, she had to take it. As much as she dreaded putting herself in the power of Huw ap Goronwy, it was better to risk death at his hands than the certainty of misery with Fitzjohn.

She looked at the corpse, her eyes brimming with tears. "Forgive me." She pressed a hand to the lifeless chest and murmured a brief blessing. "I know I should wash you, anoint you, summon a priest. But I think this is the sign I prayed for. I have to leave—now—before Sir Reginald learns of your death."

She crossed herself, then rose, all doubt gone. "When I am mistress of Coed Bedwen, I will have masses said for your soul."

There was no time to linger. She pulled the phial of poppy syrup from her bodice and poured the contents into the wine jug. Just before the last few drops drained out, she jerked her hand back as a thought struck her. She looked at the amount left in the tiny glass container. Even if there wasn't enough left to put a man to sleep, it would certainly disorient him for a while.

She replaced the stopper and tucked the phial back into her bodice. She picked up the jug and strode from the chamber, her nerves singing. Maybe she had more options than she'd thought.

Sir Reginald looked up when she approached the high table. "How is my wife?"

"Resting peacefully."

Sir Reginald's cup was empty, so she filled it to the brim, praying her shaking hands wouldn't give her away. Even though she had held back the last drops of the drug, there should still be enough to send him to sleep for some hours. Enough time to ensure she and Huw could put several miles between them and Redcliff before the chase started.

She took her seat, her muscles rigid with tension. Where was Huw? Her heart lurched when she saw him standing near the door, his eyes fixed on her. His brows rose in a silent question. She gave a single nod. He slipped through the doorway and disappeared from view.

A snore next to her drew her attention back to the high table. Sir Reginald's head was nodding, his eyes closed. The blood pounded in her ears, and her chest felt tight. It was time.

She picked up the jug and rose from her seat. She half expected Sir Reginald to tell her to sit down, but he didn't stir. She strode down the hall, picking up two pottery cups from one of the lower tables as she passed. She made no attempt to conceal them, and no one challenged her. It was as Huw had said when they had discussed their plan in the stillroom: *act with confidence and no one will stop you.*

She didn't look back, but the point between her shoulder blades itched. Any moment now, surely she would hear Fitzjohn's shout. But no one stopped her. She entered the bailey and drew a gasping breath of cold air.

Twilight had fallen, and the first pale stars glimmered above her. A few people milled about in the bailey, but if Huw fulfilled his part of the plan, they shouldn't be a problem. She strained her eyes in the dim light, searching for him by the storeroom where he should be, but she couldn't pierce the shadows. If she wanted to escape, she would have to trust him. Just as he would have to trust her.

She made her way to the gates. Even though it was a feast day, Sir Reginald had left two guards here. The only way out of Redcliff and to freedom was past them.

They were seated on a bench beside the gate, playing knucklebones by the light of a pair of torches set in sconces on either side of the gates. As soon as they saw her, they stood.

She did her best to smile brightly as she approached, despite her pounding heart. *Act with authority,* Huw had told her when they had planned this. *You'll be most convincing if you yourself believe that Fitzjohn has ordered you to bring wine to the guards. Play out the scene in your head. Hear his voice. Smell the wine on his breath. Convince yourself it's the truth. Then you'll believe you have the authority to give the wine to the guards, and they will sense that conviction and accept your words without question.*

She took a deep breath and did as he suggested. She saw herself back in the hall, heard the music and laughter, breathed in the scent of roasted meat, felt the acrid burn of woodsmoke in the back of her throat. And to her great surprise, she heard Sir Reginald snap out his order.

She raised her chin and marched up to the guards. "Sir Reginald told me to bring you this." She placed the cups on the bench. As she poured wine into the first cup, she opened her mouth to explain further, but then shut it, remembering what else Huw had said.

Don't give too much detail. That's the way inexperienced liars get caught. If they ask you'll have to elaborate, but I wager they'll be too grateful for the wine to question you.

She handed the first cup to one guard, who accepted it with a grin.

"Good health to you and Sir Reginald." He put the cup to his lips.

She could hardly believe it had worked. Trembling with relief, she poured wine for the second guard, to find that there was only enough for half a cup. It was too late to mix more; pray God it was enough.

Both men drained their cups. Matilda collected them with a smile and walked away, but only until she was out of sight. She stood in the shadows and waited, listening to the men's chatter, fighting to steady her breathing. Their speech was getting slurred. Or was it her imagination? Dear God, how did Huw cope with this tension, day after day?

Worse than the tension, though, was the lying. His advice rang in her ears: *Convince yourself it's the truth.* Was that how he lived his whole life? Acting a part so convincingly he almost believed himself to be that person?

Was he playing a role with her now?

She shivered. A man like that could make her believe he had her best interests at heart, when all the while he was leading her into danger. Her only comfort was the phial concealed in her bodice.

When the opportunity arose, she would use it and continue her escape alone.

A soft grunt drew her attention back to the guards. Straining her eyes for the slightest indication they were still alert, she crept out of the shadows until they were in view. Both were slumped across the bench. As she watched, one of them broke into rumbling snores.

There was no time to lose. She backed away and gave a low whistle—her pre-arranged signal to Huw—and pressed herself into a corner, out of sight from anyone in the bailey, but able to see out. Five painful heartbeats later, a figure broke away from the shadows surrounding the storeroom and ran toward her. Although it was by now too dark to make out his features, she could tell from his height and figure that it was Huw.

He joined her in her corner, pressed against her side to stay in the shadows. He murmured into her ear, "The fire's set. It'll flare up in no time. As soon as the alarm's raised, make for the gate." Just as she had waited for the guards to fall asleep, she waited in strained silence. It was hard to concentrate with Huw pressed so close she could feel the hard contours of his muscles through the wool of his tunic. Her heart was beating so hard, he must be able to feel it pounding against him. It was the tension that made her heart race so. Nothing to do with Huw's nearness. It was unthinkable for her to desire a man she couldn't trust.

She caught her breath as a flicker of red light lit up the storeroom window. Any moment now…

With a start she realized she was gripping Huw's arm. The instant she let him go, there was a shout from someone in the bailey: "Fire! The storeroom!" Everyone turned to look.

Huw hissed in her ear. "Now!"

They scrambled to the entrance. Huw unbolted the wicket, set into one of the large, oaken gates. As he did so, Matilda watched the people in the bailey, praying under her breath. If anyone looked their way, they would be clearly lit by the torches. The next few moments were vital. If they were seen, all would be lost.

She sobbed with relief when the creaking of the hinges alerted her to the opening of the gate.

"You first." Huw stabbed a finger toward the narrow opening.

She sprang toward the gap, only to freeze when one of the guards groaned and sat up. He rubbed his eyes and blinked at the escaping pair.

"Troubadour," he mumbled. "Come to sing us a song?" Then he slumped back across the bench.

"Move!" said Huw, then when she couldn't seem to get her legs to obey her, he shoved her through and followed her out onto the causeway. As soon as he'd pulled the gate shut behind them, he grasped her arm and steered her down the steep, winding track at a run. By this time the moon had risen—a silver disc, visible through the latticework of the oaks' upper branches. It was only three days before full, so provided enough light to guide them.

"He recognized you," Matilda gasped. "When he wakes, he'll tell Sir Reginald."

"Only if he remembers. And even if he does, Sir Reginald won't know where to look for you. He only knows me as Aimeric the troubadour, remember."

Even so, Matilda shuddered at the thought of Fitzjohn hunting her down. She was out of the castle, but not free of him yet.

"Where *are* we going? I mean, I know you're taking me to King Owain, but we won't get there tonight, will we?" It struck her how little she knew of Wales, even though she had lived all her life on its borders. Huw had told her that King Owain was at Aberffraw, but she had no idea how far it was or how long it would take to get there.

"I have a camp hidden in the woods only a mile or two from here. My horse is there." There was a pause. "You do know how to ride a horse, don't you?"

"Of course." Although how she would manage in her best gown was a problem that hadn't occurred to her before. The skirts weren't full enough for her to ride astride. Not without hitching them up and revealing her legs to mid-thigh. The heat of a blush climbed from throat to face as she contemplated revealing that much flesh to Huw.

Clearly unaware of her embarrassment, Huw continued, "We'll ford the Severn north of Shrewsbury and cross into Powys. Even if Fitzjohn discovers you missing tonight, he won't be able to follow you into Wales. I know of a deserted farmhouse where we can spend the night."

That brought her to a sharp halt. "Alone?"

Huw tugged her arm, urging her to keep walking. "You have my word I won't touch you."

She had no answer for that, but allowed Huw to lead her to the foot of the escarpment without another word. She had walked into this with her eyes open. Had as good as begged Huw to take her with him. But at no point had it occurred to her that it would mean spending the night alone with him.

Once they reached level ground, Huw steered them north, skirting the edge of the settlement that had grown up in the shadow of the castle. Bypassing the village's ploughed strip fields, they entered dense woodland. An owl hooted, its mournful sound echoing Matilda's feelings. All her hopes had been fixed on making a good marriage, of reclaiming Coed Bedwen through her husband, and being lady of the place where she had spent her only happy years. But if she were known to have spent the night alone with Huw, who would want her?

This obviously hadn't occurred to Huw. Perhaps Welsh customs were different. Whatever the reason, she had no intention of spelling it out to him. The thought of explaining that people would assume he had taken her virginity made her want to curl up in embarrassment.

A flare of anger burned in her heart. Of course Huw wouldn't consider such a thing. It was another example of how men had made decisions on her behalf all her life without considering the deeper implications to her. Their only concern was their own ends.

Which begged the question: why was she so important to King Owain that he would send his spy to fetch her?

Whatever the reason, suddenly Matilda didn't want to find out. If the king of Gwynedd had a plan for her, she wanted no part of it. She wanted to be mistress of her own destiny. She would use the remaining poppy syrup to escape Huw, then go to the king of Powys. He was a cousin, after all. Hopefully with him, she could set her own terms.

It wasn't long before she heard a soft whinny. She must have walked through the woods in a daze because now they were in a clearing where a horse on a long tether stood beside a trickling spring.

Huw frowned at her. "You're not exactly dressed for riding."

"You don't suppose Sir Reginald would have been suspicious had I arrived at the feast wearing my riding gown?"

He ignored her sarcasm, simply saying, "You'll have to sit in front of me."

He swung into the saddle in one fluid move and then pointed to a nearby tree stump. "Stand up there."

As soon as she was balanced, he trotted up and grasped her around the waist, pulling her up until she was cradled in the crook of his left arm, sitting partly across the saddle and partly across his thighs.

Her worries about spending the night alone with him paled into insignificance. The sheer intimacy of their position made her face burn.

However, once they started moving at a brisk trot, she clutched at his shoulder, fighting to keep her balance.

Huw tightened his hold on her. "Trust me," he said. "I won't let you fall."

And strangely, she did feel safe. Pinned between

his arm and his broad chest, she knew the only way she could fall was if he let her go. Considering the trouble he had taken for her, he wasn't going to do that.

As there was nothing she could do at the moment to effect her own escape, she should conserve her strength.

Bide her time.

****

Huw blew out a breath when they crested a hill, and the moonlight showed him the thatched roof of the cottage at its foot. It wasn't the most difficult or dangerous journey he had made, but he had never been so glad to reach his destination.

They hadn't been on the move for long before he had felt Matilda relax against him as she drifted to sleep. He tightened his grip to prevent her head from lolling uncomfortably, and was struck yet again by the irony of being forced to protect his enemy.

She was unaware. At his mercy. It would be the work of a moment to thrust his dagger between her ribs and throw her body into a ditch. No one would know. He could tell Owain they'd been ambushed by outlaws, and she'd been killed in the fight.

Maybe then the mocking words his great-uncle had used to taunt him all those years ago would be silenced.

He looked down at her face, innocent in sleep. The moonlight bathed her in a silvery glow, an angel in stained glass.

God's blood! He couldn't do it. Not like this. The need to fulfil his oath burned hot in his belly, but even so, he couldn't kill her in her sleep. There was no honor in that.

A sneering whisper seeped into his mind, saying

that already she had beguiled him, weakened him. And it was true, he was torn, struggling to reconcile this Matilda with the image of the Comyns he'd lived with all his life. Could an ugly soul truly reside in such a beautiful body? The honeysuckle scent of her skin, the softness of her breasts against his arm, the glimpse of a slender ankle peeping out beneath the hem of her gown... Only a dead man could fail to be moved by a woman who looked like Matilda Comyn.

Yet even the Devil could appear in fair guise. He would do well to remember that. He had a lifetime's experience of ignoring his desires. He could do so now.

He would watch her carefully, because sooner or later her Comyn blood would tell. And he would be ready.

He halted the horse beside the house and shook Matilda's shoulder, maybe a little more roughly than necessary. "Wake up. We're stopping here for the night."

She jerked awake and pulled herself more upright, then looked around, her eyes wide. "Are we in Wales?"

"Yes. This is Powys. It won't take long to reach Gwynedd tomorrow."

"And Fitzjohn can't find us here?" She looked around as though expecting armed knights to spring out from the trees.

"If he got a full dose of the poppy, he won't be awake enough to notice you gone until tomorrow, let alone send out a search party for you."

She turned her face away from him and clutched onto the saddle boss. "Good. How do I get down?" There was a tremor to her voice. Odd. She hadn't struck him as nervous before. Maybe she was still half asleep.

He refused to let her fear move him. He couldn't afford any weakness where she was concerned.

He put an arm around her waist and helped her slide down to the ground. Then he dismounted and tethered the horse to a post. "Make yourself useful," he said. "Go inside and light a fire. I left some basic supplies and set some kindling in the hearth when I came past on the way out." He unslung his saddle bag and pulled out his tinder box, which he tossed to her. "You'll find a flint and steel in here. I'll join you once I've taken care of my horse."

By the time he joined Matilda, a fire was blazing in the hearth in the center of the room and a scattering of smoky rushlights cast a golden glow on the crumbling wattle-and-daub walls and the two straw pallets, which were the only furnishings. Matilda sat on one pallet, hugging her legs, her chin resting on her knees. A cup stood on the beaten earth floor next to her, together with a plate of bread and dried meat. She had left the same for him beside his pallet.

He pulled a blanket from his pack and handed it to her, then retired to the other side of the fire with a blanket of his own. All the while Matilda remained unmoving, eying him with an unwavering gaze, as though waiting for something.

Huw felt uncomfortable, as though she was stripping him bare, layer by layer. Needing a distraction, he picked up his cup and swallowed half the contents in a single draught.

At once, Matilda's shoulders relaxed, and the watchful tension drained from her face. His senses instantly came alert. He recalled the tremor in her voice when she had replied to his comment. What was it he had said?

Hellfire! *If Fitzjohn had got a full dose of the poppy*, he wouldn't be awake to search for her. Did that mean she hadn't used it all?

He took a cautious sip of his wine and rolled it around his mouth. It was a rough drink, mixed with honey, but now he was concentrating, he detected a distinct bitter aftertaste.

He sprang to his feet, knocking over his cup upon the rotting rushes. Curse the devil-spawn to Hell! She had tried to drug him!

The floor rocked beneath his feet. Funny. He didn't remember boarding a ship. The remains of the wine spilled out onto the floor, swirling, eddying. It was a whirlpool, threatening to swallow him whole and spit him out onto a cold, rocky shore.

No. That wasn't right. *Think!*

It was Matilda. There she was. Regarding him with those wide eyes. Not an angel any more. No, by God. A cornered leopard, poised to spring.

He split into two men. One intoxicated, the other lucid, but trapped in a dream where all his movements were heavy, sluggish.

Matilda was going to escape. He had to stop her. He clung to that thought, willed himself to stay awake.

****

Matilda watched Huw, her heart pounding. Had he drunk enough to fall asleep? He swayed and clutched at the wall, then staggered to his knees, falling onto his saddle bag. Maybe he wouldn't fall asleep, but he was certainly disoriented.

It was time to act. She could be on his horse and away from here before he could stumble after her.

She rose to her feet. Not taking her eyes from him for an instant, she edged toward the door.

More swiftly than she would have thought possible, Huw sprang after her. Her breath coming in sobs, she ran for the door. Her fingers scrabbled at the latch, and she just managed to pull the door open when strong hands seized her around the waist and yanked her backward. Her feet caught in the hem of her gown, and she tumbled, hitting the floor with a painful bump. Before she could recover from her daze, Huw grasped her wrists. She struggled but couldn't pull free.

"Devil spawn! Think you can outwit me?" His voice was slurred. She was amazed he could stand, let alone overpower her.

He stooped and with an ease that made her gasp, picked her up and carried her across to the wall. There, chinks of moonlight revealed gaps in the wattle-and-daub paneling, exposing one of the main support pillars.

"Have...tie you up." He wrapped a strip of leather around her wrists—the strap from his saddle bag. Cold realization washed over her. He must have noticed the taste of the poppy syrup and exaggerated his intoxication to throw her off guard.

"Not s'comfble as bed but...can't have you runnin' 'way if I...fall sleep."

He wrapped the strap several times around the pillar and tied it. The moment he stepped back, she jerked on the strap, hoping to free it, but the leather scored deeply into her flesh without the knot giving way even the smallest amount. She slumped to the floor and bowed her head to her knees. Her last chance of freedom was gone.

She heard Huw's uneven footsteps cross the room,

followed by the creak of the door. A moment later the splash of water reached her ears. There must be a water trough outside.

She raised her head when she heard his soft tread return and the click of the latch as the door closed. He was leaning against the door, water glistening on his hair and face, watching her with the concentration of a hawk seeking its prey.

"Not a stained-glass angel anymore," he said, his voice still a little slurred. "Knew you'd show your true nature, given time."

"What do you mean?"

He waved away her question and stumbled across to his pallet, where he sat down in an inelegant sprawl.

"Why'd you do it?" he asked. "I was helping you escape. Thought that was what you wanted."

"What I wanted was to be free of men who make decisions for me without considering my wants or needs."

He chuckled, taking Matilda by surprise. It was the first time she had seen him smile. If he had been handsome before, even with the perpetual frown lines, now he was…beautiful. There was no other word for it. Her pulse, which had only just settled from the escape attempt, sped up in an uneven tattoo.

"So you were going to run out, alone, into the night?" He laughed harder. "What would you have done if you'd met a band of outlaws? Sat them down and invited them to a nice, civilized drink of poppy juice? Even if you'd lasted the night, where would you have gone? You don't know anyone here. You don't even know where we are."

A blush burned her face. Even inebriated, he made

good sense. It was interesting, though, to see him in this state, his defenses down.

If he could relax enough to laugh in front of her, what else might he reveal?

Maybe she could salvage some good from her failed attempt. This was probably the one chance she would have to get the truth from Huw. If she could discover more about him, about his plans for her, she hadn't used the last of the poppy syrup in vain.

"I decided I'd rather take my chances alone, than risk finding myself in the same situation as in Redcliff. What does King Owain want with me? Why won't you tell me?"

"Because he refused to tell me." Huw shook his head. "He's always explained his reasons before." The words burst out, and Matilda knew this was no lie. This was Huw, unguarded. Vulnerable.

An uncomfortable knot formed in her stomach, hard and cold. It felt wrong to use Huw's state to her advantage. Hadn't she just railed against men who used her to their advantage? Would tricking him into blurting out his secrets make her no better than them?

No. This was different. Her life could be in danger, and she needed to know what she was facing in Huw's company.

"Are you close to the king?" She groped for the words that would release the information she sought.

"He trusts me, confides in me. Has to, considering the work I do for him."

"Surely you must have some idea why he wants me?"

Huw shook his head. "Just told me it was for the good of Gwynedd." He laughed and in a sing-song chant repeated, "For the good of Gwynedd." It was as though he was repeating a lesson learned from a young age.

He picked up his cup and frowned at it. "Empty."

He tossed the cup upon the floor and folded his arms behind his head. "I can guess why he wants you, though. He must've made a deal with Powys about you."

Matilda's mouth went dry. "Because I'm related to the king of Powys?"

Huw nodded again. "Has to be. He wants to strengthen ties with Powys by marrying you to one of his nobles."

Matilda bit her lip. She should have expected something like this. To be passed from one man to another.

"Why so sad?" Huw asked. "You must have known you would have to marry. Better a Welshman than that Norman goat's arse, Fitzjohn."

Despite herself, Matilda giggled. No one had ever used crude language in front of her before. And the way Huw had said it, "Norman" had been by far the worse insult.

Yet how could she explain? "I know I have to marry. I just wish that for once, I could have some choice. All my life I've had to live with the consequences of some other man's decisions. And it's never worked out well. I know I could choose better for myself."

"Who would you choose?" Huw's voice was mocking. "A hero straight from a minstrel's ballad? A gallant knight to rescue you from Fitzjohn and fight to reclaim your inheritance?"

"Only if he does me the favor of widowing me in the process. Then at least I'd have the chance to run my life my own way. And keep Coed Bedwen." She gave the strap another savage tug, but it refused to give. "Better still, let me marry a man burning to go on crusade or a long pilgrimage. Then I would have Coed Bedwen with no chance of the king marrying me off to some other grasping monster."

Huw's eyes narrowed. "Coed Bedwen. So that's all you want." There was an undertone of dark malice in his voice that made her shiver.

She licked dry lips and nodded.

"Well, you'll never have that."

Sick dread washed over her. "What do you mean?"

"The king has already promised it to another."

"Who?"

He laughed. "It's a big secret. Mustn't tell you."

She sat up straighter and raised her chin. "We'll see about that. Coed Bedwen is mine. I'll—" She stopped. She was doing it again. Even under the influence of the poppy syrup, Huw had managed to get her to give him more information about herself. This wasn't how this was supposed to go.

"What about you?" she asked. "Are you married?"

His lips wrenched in a bitter twist. "There's no place in my life for a woman. I have nothing. Just danger, lies, and secrets."

A log crackled on the hearth, sending up a shower of sparks. There was a brief flare of flame, casting a red glow over Huw's face. Matilda winced when she saw the bleak expression on his face. Then the flames faded, casting his face back into shadow.

"Nothing," he said again.

"Why do you have nothing?" she asked. "You're King Owain's trusted man. He obviously values you. He must reward you." For some reason, even though he'd tied her up, forcing her to sit on the filthy rushes, she felt the need to comfort him. It must be the healer in her, unable to see someone hurt or broken without wanting to fix them. And Huw, she sensed, was broken deep inside.

"Oh, he pays me well, but not with the thing I want. Not yet."

"What's that?" Her breathing quickened as she sensed that she was getting close to what drove him.

"My family's holding, the *llys*—manor—and the lands that went with it. It was lost in my grandfather's time."

"How?"

Huw picked up the wine skin and emptied it into his cup. "The usual story. The Normans wanted it, so the Normans took it. They killed my grandfather. They would have killed my father too, even though he was just a boy, but a servant helped him escape. He went to live with his uncle, but what he'd witnessed twisted him. He never forgot what happened."

He took a deep draught of wine and was talking with no need for Matilda to prompt him.

"He never forgot the home he had lost. When I was growing up, he was forever telling me about it and how it was my rightful inheritance. He would often take me to climb a hill from which we could see the *llys* where he had grown up.

"Then when I reached my majority—that's the age of fourteen in Wales—he took me up the hill again, but this time he made me promise to do everything in my power to take back our lands from the Normans and avenge myself on the man that had taken it."

"How was that possible? Surely he would have died by then."

Huw gave a feral smile. "Oh, we have long memories here in Wales. Our blood feuds are passed down from one generation to the next."

Something about that smile unnerved her. This was a side of Huw she didn't want to explore. Not alone at night, miles from help.

She changed the subject. "Tell me how you ended up in King Owain's service."

"My father died not long after that day on the hill. The day of his funeral, my great-uncle…made it clear I was a burden. Not welcome. I decided the only way to get my land back—to obey my father's last wish—was to fight for Gwynedd and earn the notice of the king. So I left and went to the King of Gwynedd—Owain's father—and asked to be taken into his service.

"Not long after, Owain noticed me entertaining my fellow soldiers by mimicking various well-known members of the household. I thought I was going to be thrashed into the next world, but instead he said he could find a use for someone of my talents. He did, too."

He drained his cup, then smiled the same chilling smile. "And soon…soon I'll get my lands back. A reward for fetching you."

So, Huw, too, was using her to suit his own ends. She shouldn't be surprised; it was only what all men did.

But the lurch of disappointment told her she'd hoped Huw would be different.

Chapter Four

Huw awoke to the stillness of predawn. He massaged his temples. Why did it feel like a blacksmith was trying to hammer his way out from inside his head?

His eyes focused on the cup beside his pallet, and he groaned.

Matilda. The poppy syrup.

He looked across the room. The last glowing embers of the fire showed Matilda, huddled in the angle of the wall and floor, her tied hands held awkwardly on her knees. Her head lolled on one shoulder, and she was breathing the deep, even breaths of sleep. She would probably ache all over when she woke up.

He ruthlessly squashed his twinge of sympathy. He couldn't afford any weakness where she was concerned. He had let his guard drop for one moment yesterday, and look what she had done to him.

Truly, she had proved herself a Comyn in more than name.

He needed to clear his head. Leaving Matilda to sleep a little longer, he rose and went outside. He might as well ready his horse.

He had just tightened the girth strap when the memory of his slurred conversation hit him.

God's nails! He had half a mind to take that accursed woman back to Fitzjohn. They deserved each other.

He strained to remember all he had said.

Please don't let him have mentioned Coed Bedwen and the blood oath. He rested his aching head against the horse's flank, willing his swirling memories to form up in some kind of order. What a fool he had been! *Trust no one.* That was the motto he lived by. Yet all it had taken was a pretty face, and he had been lulled into leaving her alone, giving her the opportunity to drug him.

Gradually the memories resolved themselves. Some of the cold, leaden weight in his chest eased. He hadn't revealed his link with Coed Bedwen.

Nevertheless, in one night, he had revealed more of himself to her than he had to anyone save Owain. In his world, information could be a deadlier weapon than a sword. He might just as well have handed Matilda his knife and bared his chest for her to strike.

And if she thought he would hold her in his arms on horseback again all day, fogging his senses with her soft body and enticing honeysuckle scent, she was in for a shock.

He clenched his jaw and strode back into the cottage. His saddlebag was still lying beside his pallet. He rummaged through it and pulled out a tunic, undershirt, braies and hose that he'd had no occasion to wear on this trip. Then he flung them at Matilda's sleeping form before unfastening the leather strap from the pillar.

"Get up," he said, his voice hard.

Matilda stirred and tried to sit up, only to look at her bound wrists with a scowl. "You'll have to help me," she said. "My legs have gone to sleep."

He grasped her elbow and hoisted her to her feet.

Then he bundled the clothes into her arms.

"Untie me," she said.

"You lost the right to an easy journey when you drugged me and tried to escape."

"I can't believe you're going to take me to your king, tethered like a dog!"

"You took advantage of my kindness yesterday. I won't make the same mistake today." He indicated the clothes. "Put those on. We'll make faster time if you're wearing something more suitable than that gown."

She looked down at her wrists. "How am I supposed to do that with my wrists tied? Besides, I need to…" Her cheeks glowed crimson.

He pinched the bridge of his nose. "Very well. I'll untie you. There's a bucket in the corner you can use." She drew a sharp breath, but he spoke before she could get a word in. "And I'll wait outside. But remember this: Fitzjohn will be scouring the countryside for you. If you try to escape again, I'll leave you for him to find."

She paled and nodded. She didn't have to know he was making an empty threat. Owain would use his guts for bowstrings if he let Matilda go.

****

If anything, riding with Matilda behind him was even worse than when he'd had her draped across his lap. When he'd decided to dress her in his clothes so she could ride astride, he hadn't considered how it would feel to have her thighs pressed outside his and the slender length of her body against his back.

What witchcraft did she possess to make him so painfully aware of her at every moment? What was it about her that slipped past his defenses where other women had failed? Part of him wanted to punish her for her Comyn blood; the other part wanted to pull her off the horse and tumble her right there in the open.

By the time they crossed into Gwynedd, he was simmering with suppressed need and irritation. Even the hills and streams of his homeland failed to soothe him the way they usually could.

Matilda herself had been silent for most of the ride. Probably nursing her resentment over being tied to the saddle's cantle. Let her complain to Owain if she wanted to; he didn't care. At least by that time she'd be the king's problem, not his. The king's and whichever poor unfortunate he'd chosen to marry her to.

And the burn in his chest was simply because he'd bolted down his noon meal of bread and dried beef too fast. Nothing to do with jealousy at the man who would take Matilda to his bed. It was impossible for him to desire her. He would be happy to be rid of her.

"How much farther are we going?" Matilda spoke in his ear, jolting him from his thoughts.

He pointed to a rugged hill crowned with a stand of trees. "The royal *llys* of the *commote* we're travelling through lies at the foot of that hill. We're staying there tonight."

Her sigh of relief tickled his ear, sending a shiver through his flesh. "You mean I'll be sleeping in a real bed?"

"You'd be sleeping in a dungeon if I had my way." There were no dungeons, but she didn't have to know that. "In manacles. I—"

The sound of hoof beats cut short his words. He wheeled around, looking for the source of the noise, and saw a group of about twenty horsemen approaching

51

from the south.

He drew his knife and reached around Matilda to sever the cord binding her hands to the cantle. "If I shout 'run,' make for the *llys* and don't look back."

Matilda rubbed her wrists with a gasp. "It's not Fitzjohn, is it?"

"I doubt he could have got here so fast, even if he knew where to look. Still, it's best to be on our guard."

Then he spied the standard one of the horsemen carried and the tension drained out of him. "Thank the saints! It's King Owain."

He reined in his horse and waited for Owain to reach them.

"Huw. I was hoping to intercept you," the king said. Then he cast an appraising eye at Matilda. "I take it this is Matilda Comyn."

Huw sketched a hasty bow. "It is. What are your orders, my lord?"

With a jerk of his head to the north, Owain said, "You and the lady will accompany me to the royal *llys*. I've brought someone who's anxious to meet her."

Then he kicked his heels, urging his horse into a trot. For a few moments, they were surrounded by mounted men, who eyed them as they guided their steeds around them, churning up clods of earth. One man caught Huw's attention. He was russet-haired, with a careworn face. He eyed Huw and Matilda with an intensity that made him uneasy. Huw couldn't recall having seen him before, and he knew everyone in Owain's service. Was this the man who wanted to meet Matilda?

He joined the back of the group, relieved he had untied her before anyone had seen her bindings. He didn't want his king to know how she had caught him off guard.

However, as they neared the *llys*, he found he wasn't worrying about his lapse in concentration so much as his instinctive reaction when he'd thought they were in danger. His first thought had been to protect Matilda. Why, when his whole purpose in life centered around avenging his family on the Comyns? What was wrong with him?

He ground his teeth. The sooner he delivered Matilda into the king's hands the better. He obviously needed to separate himself from her, to forget her courage, her beauty. Forget how she lit a fire in his flesh. Only then could he pursue his oath with renewed vigor.

When they arrived at the *llys*, Owain ordered Huw and Matilda to a meeting in the great hall once they had refreshed themselves.

After a quick wash in the chamber he had been allocated, he found Matilda in the courtyard, hesitating in front of the doors to the hall. She was wearing a borrowed gown of cornflower blue that matched her eyes. It was simpler than the costly bliaut she had worn yesterday; even so Huw thought he had never seen a woman more beautiful, and he despised himself for his weakness.

He gave her a thin smile and gestured toward the door. "Time to learn your fate."

They found Owain seated on the dais, the russet-haired stranger beside him. Huw studied him as they approached. He wore no insignia, but his calf-length tunic, made of fine quality burgundy cloth with golden embroidery around the neck and hem, indicated this was a man of status.

"This is Gruffyth ap Rhys," said Owain. "I invited him to join us, because he has an interest in the outcome. He's a cousin to the King of Powys, and Matilda's uncle."

Huw heard a gasp next to him, then Matilda stepped forward. "Uncle Gruffyth," she said, a hesitant smile forming. "I remember Mama telling me about you, how much she missed you."

Gruffyth took her hands. "It's good to meet you at last, child. When I heard your father had died, I wanted to take you in, but King Stephen handed your wardship to Fitzjohn before I could act."

"No doubt to keep the Comyn lands under English control," put in Owain. He gave a grim laugh. "But with God's help, we're going to take it back."

He addressed Huw and Matilda. "Since Coed Bedwen is on the border with Powys, I have negotiated with the King of Powys. He has agreed that I may keep it under my control, in return for a share of the ransoms. Gruffyth here has agreed to strengthen my force with men of his own."

Coed Bedwen! Huw clenched his hands into fists. Surely Owain couldn't have betrayed him after all his years of loyal service. Matilda had to be here because of her relation to the king of Powys. Not to snatch away his birthright.

He opened his mouth to speak, but Matilda got there first.

"So you agree I have a right to the land?" she said. More a statement than a question. God's breath! Her arrogance made him seethe.

Owain made a placatory gesture. "You certainly

have the right to make a claim. Gruffyth is here to represent your interests."

Huw narrowed his eyes. He was familiar with his king's tactics. The matter had already been decided, and from Owain's expression, neither he nor Matilda was going to be happy with the outcome.

Chapter Five

Matilda raised her chin. Despite his misgivings, Huw had to bite back a smile. He recognized that sign. It meant Matilda was about to display her stubborn side. Thank God it was no longer his problem.

She took a step closer to Owain. "My lord, with all due respect to my uncle, he's only just met me. How can he represent my interests when he doesn't know me? I can represent myself."

Owain waved her to a chair on his left, gesturing to Huw and Gruffyth to sit as well. "If this business was straightforward then maybe I would agree."

Matilda perched on the edge of her chair, looking as though she was about to spring up and start pacing. "It is straightforward. I'm the heiress of Coed Bedwen. It belonged to my father and his father before him."

"And before that it was Welsh. It belonged to Gwynedd. Did you consider that?"

Matilda opened her mouth then shut it again, frowning. Huw would have found the situation amusing, if it weren't for his gut-twisting anticipation of what Owain must be about to reveal. He had kept his own link with Coed Bedwen from her because however good an actor he was, he wouldn't have been able to conceal his hatred of the Comyns. Matilda would never have consented to accompany a man who had vowed revenge on her family.

"But that was years ago," Matilda said in a small voice. "In my grandfather's time."

Huw couldn't let that pass without comment. "The Welsh have long memories. It's time you learnt that if you want to live here." Feuds were passed down from one generation to the next. Huw had been weaned on tales of her grandfather's atrocities, and his oath was branded on his heart. It was all he had left. Its fulfillment the only way to prove his worth.

Owain shot him a glance and a slight shake of the head. Huw leaned back and crossed his arms. If the king wanted to deal with Matilda in his own way, Huw was only too glad to let him. It would be a relief to hand her over to her relatives and have nothing more to do with her. A treacherous voice in the back of his mind whispered that he would miss her. She challenged him, roused his interest in a way no other woman had ever managed. He swiftly quelled that thought.

The king turned his attention to Matilda. "There's another issue you should be aware of. By Welsh law no woman can inherit land."

Matilda bunched her fists in the folds of her skirts, her knuckles white. "What are you saying? That you had Huw bring me here only to tell me I have no rights at all in your land?"

"Not at all. Your uncle claims you as kin. I'm merely pointing out that you *do* need him to represent your interests."

Matilda leaned forward. "But why did you bring me here? If you wanted to seize Coed Bedwen, you could do it without me."

Owain gestured to Gruffyth. "You're best placed to answer this."

"I suggested it, my dear," said Gruffyth. "I was made aware of your predicament—that Fitzjohn had put off finding you a husband so he could continue to take revenues from Coed Bedwen. On my recommendation, the king of Powys has agreed to ally with Gwynedd to take back Coed Bedwen. It's in both our interests. Gwynedd regains lost territory, and Powys gains a buffer from Norman incursions in that part of our territory." Matilda's uncle glanced at the king. "As well as a substantial payment for our services, of course, and an agreement to cease raids across our borders."

Huw was impressed that Owain had managed to get what he wanted for a relatively small return. But Owain usually got what he wanted.

"Where do I fit into your plan?" Matilda asked.

"I was coming to that," replied her uncle. "As your nearest kin, it is my duty to find you a husband. And I've secured you one that will seal the alliance between Powys and Gwynedd and at the same time allow you to remain in Coed Bedwen."

Oh, no. Not this. Not him. Huw could swear he heard the crash of a cage door slamming shut. Trapping him.

He drew a shaky breath. "My lord—"

But Owain cut off his protest with a blocking hand.

"You see there is a man loyal to me who has a genuine claim to Coed Bedwen," the king said to Matilda.

"And you want me to marry him." Matilda looked resigned but not displeased.

Huw felt sick.

"That's correct. He's strong enough to hold Coed Bedwen against the English. And it's high time he sired some heirs."

That gave Huw a jolt. He had a sudden image of him holding a child with Matilda's wide, cornflower-blue eyes. Of Matilda in his arms, kissing him. In his bed.

He scrubbed at his eyes as though he could erase the images that way. There was no place for a woman in his life. He had nothing to offer her.

He bit back a groan as he remembered saying exactly that to Matilda last night. Then other words forced their way into his head, leaking out from the darkest recesses of his memory.

You are nothing.

"When will the wedding take place?" Matilda's voiced recalled him to the present.

Never, if he had anything to do with it. The moment he was alone with Owain, he would do all in his power to change his mind.

"In a week," Gruffyth answered. "You must be married quickly—Fitzjohn is bound to be searching for you. While I don't believe he would find you here, so far from the English border, I don't want to risk you falling under his power again. Once you're married, he'll no longer have any claim on you. We've agreed the marriage will take place here. My wife and I will remain here with you until then."

"Who am I to marry?" asked Matilda. "And when do I meet him?"

Huw tensed.

Owain pointed to him. "You already have. It's Huw ap Goronwy."

The blood drained from Matilda's face. A rainbow of emotion flickered in her eyes. Huw couldn't read them all, but some were plain. Confusion, anger, betrayal.

Unless he could talk Owain out of this madness, it was going to be an unhappy marriage.

****

Owain gave Huw a glare that could have turned the glowing charcoal brazier to ice. "Are you telling me you refuse to marry her? Against my direct orders?"

Owain's scribe walked into the side chamber where Huw had cornered Owain after the meeting. He halted, looked from Huw to the king, then turned around and walked straight out. Huw would have laughed had there not been so much at stake.

He returned Owain's stare without flinching. "Yes. I won't marry her. God's nails, Owain—this is Matilda Comyn. You know what her family did to mine. You know about the blood oath."

Owain strode over to the desk that occupied most of the space in the room. He selected a scroll from the pile that threatened to topple to the ground and waved it in Huw's face. "This is a petition from a Rhys ap Howell, asking for justice after his son was murdered by Rhodri ap Llewelyn."

He snatched up another scroll, sending the others tumbling to the floor rushes. "And this is from Rhodri ap Llewelyn, accusing Rhys ap Howell of murdering his father." He flung the scroll back upon the table. "These cursed feuds have to end, Huw. They're tearing Gwynedd—all of Wales—apart."

"But I swore an oath. I—"

"There are other ways to settle it, as you well know, Huw. You can accept a blood price."

He knew. But the vow he had made to his father

promised blood. "I can't—"

"What else is it, Huw? It's not just the blood oath. There's another reason. When you turned down other heiresses I found for you, I thought it was just because of the life you led, but now I'm not so sure. Why do you resist marriage?"

"It is because of my life. I survive from one day to the next, not knowing how many more I will see. What kind of life is that to offer a woman?"

But that wasn't the whole reason. A woman would get too close, discover the truth that he had buried deep down.

You are nothing...

And Matilda, after only two days, had managed to get closer than anyone before.

"You will find that women are stronger than you give them credit for. Besides, you will no longer be my spy, but lord of Coed Bedwen. No, Huw, you can't argue your way out of this one. My mind's made up."

Owain picked up the cloak that was slung over a chair and wrapped it around his shoulders. "It's getting late. We can talk more in the morning."

He swept out of the room.

Huw chased after him. King or no, he wasn't going to let Owain out of his sight until Huw had dissuaded him.

****

Matilda lay curled on the bed in her guest chamber, hugging a blanket. She couldn't cry. Maybe she would feel better if she could.

In her head, she saw again the moment when King Owain had revealed the identity of her intended husband. The claimant to Coed Bedwen. Huw.

She closed her eyes, attempting to block the memory. But nothing could shut out the sense of betrayal. She had confided in him, told him about her hopes of regaining Coed Bedwen. He had listened to her, soaked up all her information.

He had used her. He was no different from any other man. He was not to be trusted.

And now they were to wed.

She was no fool. She had always known she would need to marry to hold her land. But after a life of being let down by the men she had depended on, she needed a husband she could trust.

She had said nothing to Huw. Just calmly excused herself, saying she felt unwell, and returned to her tiny guest chamber. She would need to talk to him soon. And her uncle. But not tonight. She couldn't face him yet.

Snatches of conversation drifted in through the windows, the creak of heavy doors, footsteps. Slowly the light faded.

A knock at the door. Matilda sat up, her heart pounding. "Who is it?"

"The maid, my lady."

A middle-aged woman entered at Matilda's bidding, carrying a lit taper. "I've come to light the candles, my lady. And to ask if you wanted me to bring you any food, or if you were going to take your evening meal in the hall."

"I'm not hungry, thank you." They must eat later here. Back in England the main meal was at noon. First their different laws and now this. How long would it take her to get used to the customs here? "I'm rather tired. I think I'll go to bed."

"Let me help you with your gown."

Once the tallow candles glowed in their niches, picking out the painted vine leaves on the plastered walls, the maid helped Matilda strip to her shift and combed out her hair. Then she left. Matilda removed her shift and climbed into bed.

The candles burned lower, but sleep evaded her. Thoughts of Huw filled her mind. She had escaped from one man who had used her to achieve his own ends, only to be handed over to Huw.

Who had also used her.

Should she talk to her uncle? Would he intercede for her?

No. Why would Gruffyth be any different from any other man in her life? They had all let her down. Right back to her father.

She clamped the heels of her hands against her eyes, trying to banish the memories associated with her father.

I'll always be there for you…

She leapt out of bed, pulled on her shift, and picked up her hose and shoes from the chest at the foot of the bed. A walk outside would clear her head. She considered putting on her gown but dismissed the idea. She would never be able to manage the lacings. However, along with the gown, she had been loaned a woolen cloak. She rummaged in the chest and pulled it out, then wrapped it around her shift. She crept out into the courtyard.

The chill breeze slapped her cheeks the moment she stepped outside. Everyone must have retired for the night, for the courtyard was deserted. The moonlight showed her a stone seat in a corner. She sat there, breathing in the peace. The only sounds were the occasional stomp and whicker of a horse in the stables and the distant yelp of a fox.

A creaking door startled her. Golden candle light streamed out from a small chamber adjoining Owain's great hall for a moment before being quenched. Low voices approached. Blessed Virgin, here she was dressed in little more than her shift, and there were men coming. She huddled back into the shadows.

She could just make out the dim figures of two men approaching, one chasing the other. The pursuer caught up with the first man and grasped his arm. "You must reconsider." She recognized the melodic tones of Huw. Her pulse started racing.

The men stopped not far from her. Both were cloaked, but she would recognize Huw's graceful form anywhere. She was in a quandary. She didn't want to eavesdrop, but neither did she want to be seen in this state. Least of all by Huw.

"I can't believe you'd ignore something entrenched in our laws." Huw spoke in Welsh, but Matilda could follow most of what he said.

"I hardly need you to remind me of the law."

Oh, holy Mother! That was King Owain. She fought to keep her breathing silent. If she was caught listening in to a king's conversation... She shivered. There was no knowing what the consequences might be.

Owain continued, "And it sounds like you need reminding of the *galanas*." *Galanas?* That word was new to her.

Huw spat out a string of more unfamiliar words, but she needed no translation.

Owain sighed. "My duty, by law, is to protect Gwynedd. And this marriage is vital to my plans."

Marriage? Then Huw must be objecting to her. Even though she balked at the idea of their marriage, it rankled to think Huw would be so against it—against her—that he would dare to defy his own king.

"There must be plenty of nobles in your court who would be glad to marry her and provide you with the alliance you need. I don't see why it has to be me."

"The deal with Powys is for Matilda and Coed Bedwen together. And you're the man I need to hold Coed Bedwen, even if it wasn't yours by right. Look."

Owain sat on a bench a stone's throw from Matilda's and drew his dagger. He bent down and scratched into the ground with a sweep of his arm. "This is the border between Gwynedd and England and this"—he made a smaller movement—"this is the *commote* of Coed Bedwen. Currently in English territory. See how it takes a bite out of Gwynedd? Without it, our lands north of Coed Bedwen are surrounded by English territories on two sides rather than just one. It makes us vulnerable. If not for their civil war, you can be sure the English would do their best to take another chunk, and then another. Until our border's a good ten or twenty miles further west. With Coed Bedwen under our control, our whole border is stronger."

Matilda listened in fascination. She had been so caught up in her own desire to return to Coed Bedwen, it hadn't occurred to her there were larger concerns to consider.

Owain continued, "The strife in England won't last forever. When it's over, the Normans will look to extending their borders again. I need us to be strong, against the day when that happens. And I can trust you not to be taken in by their lies. There are very few men whom I trust as well as you. And you've only got to look at what's happened farther south to see the havoc the Normans can wreak when they turn one Welsh lord against another."

"You can take Coed Bedwen without aid from Powys. You have the strength. There was no need to force me to marry."

The words, spoken in Huw's melodic voice, wrapped themselves around Matilda's heart and squeezed. Force him? Then he must truly find her repugnant. Men didn't pass up the opportunity to marry an heiress for no good reason.

With a swift movement that made Matilda gasp, Owain stabbed his dagger into the ground near Huw's foot. She clamped a hand to her mouth and prayed the men hadn't heard her.

"Only a fool would think we are strong enough to hold out against England alone," said Owain.

Matilda slowly relaxed. If either man had heard her, she was certain they would have shouted out a challenge.

"We need to make alliances," Owain was saying. "Powys is strong, but already it's crumbling at the edges. And if Powys falls then Gwynedd is exposed. This marriage is vital to strengthening the ties between us and may prevent Powys from turning to England."

Matilda was surprised at the passion in his voice. And humbled that she could be the key to Wales' survival. She was new to the country, but she cared about it deeply—it was the last link between her and her mother. And her only surviving family was Welsh.

Her Norman kin had failed her. It was time to throw in her lot with the Welsh. Even though Huw didn't want her, she would honor the agreement to help Wales.

"I can trust you with this," Owain said to Huw finally, "because I know you feel the same way. You can look beyond your own interests and do what is right for Gwynedd. And ultimately Wales."

Huw sat with a bowed head and said nothing. Matilda counted twenty painful heartbeats.

Finally, he spoke. "In that case I'll go through with it," he said. "For your sake and for Gwynedd."

But not for hers.

Owain rose to his feet and Huw followed. They both walked away toward the cluster of buildings on the far side of the courtyard. Matilda drew a shaky breath and was about to rise, when she heard Owain's soft laughter.

"You know, you make it sound like a sacrifice, Huw. But she's a beauty. I wager she'll soon find ways to make you forget her tainted Comyn blood."

Huw groaned and made a comment, but she couldn't make out what he had said. Then the two men parted and entered different doors.

Matilda hugged her stomach, feeling sick. It was Owain who had spoken of her tainted Comyn blood, but it had the sound of a quote. And there was only one man he could have been quoting.

So that was what Huw truly thought of her. He'd hidden it well, but she'd seen for herself how skilled an actor he was.

Tainted Comyn blood. Of course. If Huw's family

had held Coed Bedwen before hers then her grandfather must have seized it from them.

Oh, holy saints above! The words Huw had spoken about his family crashed down upon her. Then her grandfather had been responsible for his grandfather's death. She swallowed against the sudden ache in her throat. No wonder Huw despised her. How could she hope to overcome such enmity?

Chapter Six

The next morning Matilda was awakened with a start by the maid entering her chamber. After returning to her bed last night, she had been unable to sleep. The words "tainted Comyn blood" had rung in her ears over and over again, first in Owain's voice, but gradually changing to Huw's. The candles had burned down to stubs before sleep finally overtook her.

Heavy-eyed and aching, she struggled to reach a decision, but it was hard to concentrate while the maid laced her gown and braided her hair. Was it better to avoid Huw or seek him out? While she shrank from speaking to him, they were to be married in a week. They must talk sometime, so it would be best to get it out of the way quickly.

"Do you know where I can find Huw ap Goronwy this morning?" she asked the maid once her hair was arranged into two long braids down her back and her veil pinned in place.

"I expect you can find him in the hall with the king," the maid replied. "Your uncle will be there as well."

Reflecting that it would be better to see Huw in the company of others, she hastened across to the hall.

She found that the maid had been correct—Huw was standing beside the central fire. With him were the king, her uncle and a short woman who looked to be in

69

her late thirties. Just like the other women she had seen at the *llys*, instead of a veil, her headdress consisted of a length of linen wrapped closely around her head. A tendril of dark hair escaped at her left temple.

Gruffyth looked up and smiled. "I hope you're feeling better this morning." When she nodded, he reached out to take the hand of the dark-haired woman, giving it a tender squeeze. He drew her closer to Matilda. "This is my wife, Gwenllian. You must excuse her for not greeting you. She only speaks Welsh."

Matilda smiled at Gwenllian, glad to have a distraction from Huw, who had not taken his eyes off her ever since she had walked into the hall. "I am glad to meet you, Aunt," she said in Welsh.

Gwenllian's somewhat stern face was transformed by a broad smile. "Welcome, Matilda," she said. "It is good to have a new member of the family." Then she turned to her husband and Huw. "You didn't tell me she speaks Welsh."

Huw frowned. "I had no idea."

Matilda gave him a tight smile. "You didn't ask."

A soft cough drew her attention. "I think we had best give these two a chance to talk," Owain said. "I'm sure they have much to discuss."

"Thank you. Yes, we do," said Matilda, not turning her gaze from Huw.

****

Matilda had obviously recovered from the shock of yesterday's announcement.

"When did you learn Welsh?" Huw asked her in that language. It was strange. Even though he knew of her Welsh kin, until now he had firmly associated her with the Normans. It came as a shock to remember she was equally Welsh. It brought her closer to home. Made her less easy to despise.

"My mother always spoke Welsh to me." She stumbled over some of the words, but her accent was good. "After she died I...I always felt closer to her when I spoke or thought in Welsh. It was as though she was there, listening."

Her eyes filled with tears, and he turned his head away. He didn't want to see her sorrow or remember she had lost her family, too. He couldn't afford to feel pity for her, acknowledge she was a woman who suffered the same griefs, joys, and fears as any other.

"It will come in useful when we take Coed Bedwen," he said. Best to concentrate on practicalities, not imagine molding her slender body to his, kissing the tears from her cheeks.

She gave a harsh laugh. "Coed Bedwen. Even now, is that all you can think about?"

"What else is there?" He certainly wasn't thinking about tasting her lips, teasing them into a smile. No. She was a Comyn. He mustn't forget his oath. He forced his face into an expressionless mask and faced her.

She had blotted away her tears and was standing straight, her chin up, face composed. "Our...our marriage, for a start. We should discuss it."

"What is there to say? I already know your thoughts on the matter. You want me to die or journey to the Holy Land. Believe me, I have no intention of doing either."

Matilda winced. "So you haven't forgotten that."

"I rarely forget anything. You can be sure I'll check my food and drink very carefully from now on."

71

"I'd never—"

"But you did." He rubbed his temples. Tried to ignore the beguiling scent of honeysuckle. "All I want is Coed Bedwen. As the king has made it clear the only way I can achieve that is through marriage to you, then marry we must. However, don't expect me to succumb to your underhand tricks next time—I'm on my guard now. Coed Bedwen is mine, and I intend to keep it."

She tilted her head to one side, studying him with narrowed eyes. "Why is Coed Bedwen so important to you?"

She spoke in Welsh, but Huw answered her in French. He needed to remember she was Norman. A Comyn. It was harder to do that when they spoke Welsh. "You know why. You managed to get me to explain at length when you drugged me with that damned poppy."

She shook her head. "It was important to your grandfather and father because it was their home." Her steady gaze bored into him, stripping away his outer layers, probing for his soul. "Why is it special to *you*?"

He wiped damp palms on his tunic. He must be standing too close to the fire. "I don't understand. You know the answer—my vow to my father." And thank the saints that even drugged, he had withheld the true nature of the vow, had only said the vow was to win back Coed Bedwen.

"But your vow was just taking on your father's burden. Here's why Coed Bedwen is special to me—it was my childhood home, the last place I was happy." Her voice took on a wistful tone.

She turned away to face the fire, hugging her arms to her chest. "It was so beautiful. I used to love standing on the walls with my mother, listening to the birdsong, watching the river and the trees swaying in the wind. My mother could name all the hills we could see stretching away into the distance, and would tell me stories of the fair folk that lived inside them, feasting and dancing."

Huw swallowed. "My mother used to tell me those stories, too. Before she died." Then he wished he could have eaten his words. The last thing he needed was to feel empathy for her. It was already hard enough trying to match his knowledge of Matilda with the Comyns of his father's memory. He didn't want to think too closely about how similar their childhoods had been, both having lost their mothers at a young age.

Matilda turned to face him, tears glistening on her cheeks. "Now you know what makes Coed Bedwen special to me. What about you? Not your father or grandfather, but *you*?"

"I…" But he had no answer. Coed Bedwen was too wrapped up in his oath. If he took that out of the picture, what did Coed Bedwen alone actually mean to him?

He was saved from answering by Owain, who strode up and clapped a hand on his shoulder.

"Please excuse us, my lady," Owain said. "I must speak with Huw alone." He turned to Huw. "It's time we discussed your scouting mission to Coed Bedwen."

Huw nodded and followed Owain to the same chamber where he had spoken with Owain the day before. But he couldn't tear his thoughts from Matilda's question. Why was Coed Bedwen so important to him? Without his oath, what did it mean?

Then another thought halted him in mid stride.

Without his oath, what was *he*?

His great-uncle's sneering voice echoed in his head.

You are nothing.

****

Matilda watched, chewing her lip in frustration, as Owain led Huw through a doorway behind the dais. A wave of anger shot through her. She had just opened her heart to Huw, explained why Coed Bedwen meant everything to her. Yet when the king asked him to discuss Coed Bedwen, had Huw suggested she join them? Of course not. All her life, decisions had been made affecting her, that she'd had no say in whatsoever. And so far, she had suffered as a result. Well, no longer!

She picked up her skirts and marched after the men. She didn't knock or even hesitate at the door. It was time they realized she wouldn't be lightly dismissed. She found herself in a small room, containing a few chairs around a lit brazier. Shafts of sunlight slanted through high windows up near the rafters, one of them pooling upon a litter of scrolls upon a scribe's desk. This must be where the king conducted his business whenever he was in residence.

Huw and Owain had just taken their seats, but they sprang up when she entered.

"Whatever you have to say can wait until we're finished," Owain said, frowning. "Huw and I have important business to discuss."

"Anything concerning Coed Bedwen is my business, too. And as I'm the only person in this room who has lived there, I'm surprised it didn't occur to you to ask me to join you." The last time she had been there had been when Sir Reginald had moved the household there for a short time five years ago, but she wouldn't admit to that unless pressed.

"You should include her, my lord. She does have a point."

Matilda hadn't expected Huw's support. She flashed him a brief smile but was met with a frown. Maybe he was just humoring her.

Owain considered her with narrowed eyes for a few heartbeats, then pointed her to a chair. "Very well. Do you have any suggestions you'd like to make at the start?"

The skepticism in his voice pricked her into an angry response. "Yes," she said. "When Huw goes to spy out Coed Bedwen, you should send me with him."

****

Huw nearly choked. "That's a ridiculous suggestion. You can't possibly—"

But to his disbelief, Owain interrupted, "What intelligence do you think you could provide over and above what Huw could find?" He sat back down and eyed her as though sizing up a young warrior.

"My lord, you can't seriously be considering this. It's madness!" Huw half expected Matilda to laugh and say it was a joke, but she remained standing, facing Owain, her chin up, fists clenched at her sides.

He sat with a jolt. Holy Mother of God, she was serious. The thought of having Matilda with him in a dangerous situation made him go cold. Not because he feared for her safety, of course. But he couldn't trust her not to do something foolish that would endanger them both.

And she was a potent source of distraction. If he

had been beguiled by her allure on their two-day journey here, how much worse would it be spending a week or more alone with her?

Then just for an instant he saw Matilda's eyes flicker. It was a look that said she had acted on impulse and was only now realizing what she was letting herself in for. Good. Maybe she would come to her senses and back down.

But Matilda drew a deep breath and with a steady voice said, "As I mentioned, I have inside knowledge of Coed Bedwen. And with all due respect to Huw, he is Welsh. I am half Welsh but was brought up a Norman. I understand them as you do not. I also have contacts in the village who could help me get into the castle."

She seemed to be making up her words as she went along, but annoyingly they made good sense. The part of his mind that was always assessing a person or situation, even when he wasn't spying, approved of her ability to think quickly and come up with workable suggestions. But he did his best to shut out those thoughts.

He opened his mouth, but Owain got in first.

"I've never sent a woman to do something so dangerous before. Why should I do so now?"

Huw relaxed. Finally, the king was seeing reason.

"*Because* I'm a woman. Women can pass unnoticed where men get questioned." She pointed to a jug of mead that was on a low table in the corner. Three horn cups were beside it. "Those weren't there when I came in. Who put them there?" She gave Owain a challenging smile.

It was time to put an end to Matilda's fantasy. She would thank him later. "A red-headed maid came in

76

through the side door just when the king asked you what intelligence you could offer above mine," he said, enjoying the wide-eyed gaze she turned upon him. He sent up a prayer of thanks that he had caught the movement in the corner of his eye and glanced across in time to see the maid. "She placed the jug and two cups on the table, then dashed out and brought back another one."

Matilda swallowed, and a flush crept up her throat. Huw would have felt sorry for her if he didn't know she was better off staying safe with her uncle whilst he went to Coed Bedwen. Alone.

"There is little that escapes Huw," said Owain, his lips quirking. "However, I must point out that I didn't notice the maid."

Huw's gut felt as heavy as if he had just swallowed a lead weight. "This is preposterous. You can't seriously be considering this?"

"You have to admit, she makes a good point," said Owain. "Few men possess your talent of observation; she's right about that. And men don't take such care to guard their tongues around women."

Matilda's face split into a triumphant smile. Now it was Huw's turn to clench his fists.

"I haven't agreed to your request yet," Owain said to Matilda. "I need time to think about it. Leave me. Both of you. I'll let you know what I decide."

Huw stood, bowed, then grabbed Matilda's arm and marched her out of the room and into the hall.

"What do you think you're doing?" He kept his voice low, aware of the eyes that turned their way. "This isn't a game. You could get yourself killed."

"I don't know why you're getting yourself worked

up about it then. It would be a lucky escape for you if I did. You'd get Coed Bedwen without being tied to a wife you despise."

Huw grimaced. "Do you honestly think I want to undertake a dangerous mission with a woman I can't trust not to drug me?"

"You dare talk to me about trust when you didn't tell me about your claim on Coed Bedwen?"

A rustle of skirts and a waft of rosewater announced a new arrival. "I think you should save this conversation until you're somewhere more private, don't you?"

Huw was on the point of telling the woman it was none of her concern, when he realized it was Matilda's aunt, Gwenllian. Gruffyth stood at her elbow.

He was saved from answering when Matilda got there before him. "Don't worry, Aunt, we have nothing more to say to each other. I'll await the king's decision in the courtyard."

She swept out, leaving Huw to face the black looks of both Gwenllian and Gruffyth.

"Would you care to explain what that was about?" Gruffyth asked.

His frown deepened as he listened to Huw's explanation. "Then you had every right to challenge her." Gruffyth tore off his cloak and flung it across a bench. "If this is the kind of madness that results from being brought up in a Norman household, I'm relieved none of my children have ever set foot outside Wales."

"I'll go and talk sense into her." Gwenllian went after her niece.

"I doubt it'll work," Huw said. "She's the most stubborn woman I've ever met. Once she's got hold of an idea, there's no talking her out of it."

"You've only known her a short while, yet you can really claim to know her that well?" Gruffyth asked.

"I…yes, I believe I do," Huw replied.

Gruffyth left him to follow his wife and Matilda. Huw remained in the hall, reflecting on just how well he did know Matilda. Of course, in his line of work, it was a necessary skill to be able to read another person from only a few clues. But with Matilda, it was deeper than that. She had managed to worm her way under his skin until he was aware of her at all times. Even now, he found himself imagining what she would be doing in the courtyard. Pacing perhaps, her chin lifted in that stubborn tilt while she ignored the advice her anxious aunt and uncle were probably pouring into her ears.

How had that happened? He had never had a problem with keeping people at a distance before. What was it about Matilda that was different?

It must be their families' fraught shared history. He had been painfully aware of her from the beginning, studied her. In doing so, he must have let down his defenses. And he had to admit, Comyn or no, the way she had stood up to Owain showed courage. For the first time, it occurred to him that his admiration for her went deeper than mere physical desire.

No! He clenched his fists. He would not let this happen, couldn't question the rightness of the blood oath. It was the only thing that gave his life any purpose. He ruthlessly squashed all his softer feelings.

He was torn from his musings by the creak of a door opening behind him. He turned to see Owain approaching.

"Where is Matilda?" Owain asked.

"Outside, my lord. Have you made your decision?"

"I should tell you both together."

"Tell me now!" Hugh snapped, before adding a belated, "my lord."

Owain gave him a level look. "I've decided to let Matilda accompany you."

Huw stepped up to Owain and reached for the neck of his tunic, only just jerking his hand back in time. He'd been sorely tempted to shake the king by his throat until his teeth rattled. "You can't—" he began, but Owain cut him off with a curt gesture.

"I can. And for one very good reason, above and beyond the ones we've already discussed."

"And that is?"

"In the eyes of many of Coed Bedwen's inhabitants, Matilda is the rightful heiress. The reason I've held back from retaking Coed Bedwen—and much of the other lands the Normans have seized—is that we don't have the strength to take their castles by force. But if the folk within them can be persuaded to revolt…"

Huw didn't know whether to laugh or cry. "You want her to be a figurehead. A rallying point for a rebellion."

"Think of the bloodshed it will save, Huw. Not to mention how it would limit destruction. Do you seriously want to take possession of a castle we've been forced to reduce to rubble?"

It made sense, he couldn't deny it. Too much sense. "You didn't dream this up just now, did you? You've planned this all along."

"It was always a possibility. I made up my mind when she came storming in here like an avenging goddess. You can't deny she's got spirit. She's got the strength to inspire people to rally to the cause."

"And I haven't? My family has the older claim to Coed Bedwen."

"The Welsh would rally to you, I have no doubt of that. But most of the folk there came after the Comyns took control—they're English. They'd be more likely to stomach Welsh rule if they had the assurance that Matilda was to be their Lady."

Huw's simmering anger boiled over. "What of my oath? Would you have me renege?"

Owain scowled. "This is more important than your own personal feud. If you can't live with that, I'll find another man who *is* prepared to put aside his personal issues in loyalty to me."

Huw took a breath. He couldn't afford to see Coed Bedwen in the hands of another man. He bent his head. "I hold my loyalty to you above everything, my lord."

"Good. Then go and inform your lady of my decision."

"At once, my lord."

But he didn't meet Owain's gaze. Because if the king thought this marriage would prevent Huw from fulfilling his vow once he'd regained Coed Bedwen then he was in for a shock. Nothing was more important to him than his vow.

****

"Matilda, you must listen to sense. This is..." Her uncle pinched the bridge of his nose. "It broke my heart when I heard your mother had died. I can't lose you too."

Matilda couldn't look him in the face. She bent down, making a pretense of picking a fresh leaf of spearmint that was beginning to show pale green spring shoots. She had come to the herb garden, secluded behind its wattle fences, to be alone, but it hadn't taken her aunt and uncle long to find her. Her uncle's distress shook her, but for all that she regretted the impulsive outburst that had led to her offering her services to Owain, she couldn't back down now. Not in front of Huw.

"It's in the king's hands now," she said. "I must abide by his decision, whatever that is."

Gwenllian spoke, her voice grim. "I think we're about to find out." The crash of the wicket gate slamming shut accompanied her words.

Matilda straightened up to see Huw storming down the paved walkway. His face was set in hard lines.

Gruffyth hurried up to him. "The king has agreed?" he asked, his voice strained.

Huw nodded, and Matilda was surprised that her overwhelming feeling was one of relief. Although why that should be when it involved going into danger, she couldn't say.

"I did my best to talk him out of it," Huw said, "but he had good reasons for his decision." He cast a frown in her direction that made her stomach knot. She hoped his anger with her would die down, or working with him, let alone being married to him, would be a trial.

"I'd like a word alone with Matilda now, if you don't mind," he said.

Gruffyth sent a doubtful glance in her direction, but then said, "Come, Gwenllian. The least we can do is leave Huw to see if he can succeed where we have failed." He pressed a hand into the small of his wife's back and led her away.

As soon as the gate clattered shut behind the pair, Huw said, "You've got what you wanted. I hope you won't regret it."

"I hope so, too," she said. "But I had to offer."

"Why?"

"Everything important that's happened to me is down to decisions made by men—my…my father, King Stephen, Fitzjohn…and look at the misery they caused me. From now on, I've decided to take control of my life."

"Even if that puts you in danger?"

"Women have died at the hands of men in their own homes. I'd rather face death head-on than have it creep up on me unawares in a place where I should be safe." She did her best to keep the tremor out of her voice, although her stomach knotted at the prospect of what lay ahead.

"In that case you'll be happy to learn Owain's chosen you as the figurehead for a revolt. We plan to take Coed Bedwen from within. You'll have all the danger you want."

Matilda's mouth went dry. Was Owain mad? She had no experience of leadership. Did she possess the ability? And the courage?

Huw was watching her, a frown biting deep beneath his brows. Clearly, he didn't believe she had. She raised her chin. "I think the king is a wise man. I hope you'll agree that we need to work together closely. Unless we do, we're both at risk."

"Of course. But understand this: I'm in charge. You'll obey me without question. And no acting without consulting me first. Agreed?"

His eyes bored into hers, as hard as flints.

Argument would be futile.

"Agreed."

****

Their uneasy truce lasted through the days that followed. Most of her time was taken up with preparations for the wedding. Gwenllian had been shocked to learn Matilda had escaped Redcliff with only the gown she had been wearing. Therefore, she had taken it upon herself to provide new ones. Most of Matilda's days were spent in Gruffyth and Gwenllian's guest chamber, embroidering hems, listening to the chatter of Gwenllian and her ladies. This did have the advantage of improving her Welsh. And as much as she knew she and Huw should be discussing their mission, she was relieved to have an excuse to stay away from him. She couldn't be easy in his presence. The day was drawing nearer when she would be his wife. And yet again, she would be at the mercy of his decisions.

The only time she saw him was at mealtimes.

"Has the king decided when we're to leave?" she asked him at dinner, two days before the wedding. The silence between them had become so unbearable that speech with him was the lesser of two evils.

"The morning after the wedding," Huw said.

Matilda lowered the piece of bread she had been about to eat and placed it on the table. Suddenly her stomach felt too tight to eat. The morning after the wedding immediately made her think of the night before. Their wedding night. She had tried hard not to dwell on that. Gwenllian had taken her aside only that morning, told her what to expect. Hinted at the pleasure to be found in the marriage bed. Matilda found that hard to believe. She hated the thought of being naked in front of Huw, with nowhere to hide. Of being vulnerable. She couldn't imagine ever trusting a man enough to willingly allow him to use her in that way.

Yet the church forbade her from denying her husband his rights, and right now she needed all the protection that God and His saints could offer.

"How far is it?" she asked. If she filled her mind with practical issues, she wouldn't have to think of lying with Huw.

"Less than a day's ride from here. Your uncle has agreed to accompany us for most of the way, but we'll have to travel the last few miles on foot. Arriving on horseback would draw too much attention to ourselves. Anyway, it's good that you'll have a bit more time to get to know your uncle and aunt."

Matilda looked over to where Gruffyth and Gwenllian were sitting, enjoying a performance by Owain's bard. As she watched, Gruffyth whispered into his wife's ear, and she laughed, then took hold of Gruffyth's hand, twining their fingers together.

To Matilda, brought up in a Norman household, their public intimacies should have been shocking, but she was curious and cast several glances in their direction. She had never witnessed such tenderness, such ease in a couple.

Next to her, Huw reached forward to pick up his wine cup. She studied his fingers, long and slender, yet she knew from experience how strong they were. With a sudden jolt in the pit of her belly, she imagined weaving her fingers through his in the same way her aunt and uncle were doing. She could almost feel the heat of his hand in hers, the roughness of his thumb circling her palm.

She snatched up her wine cup and took a deep draught. It was impossible. She and Huw could never be that comfortable together. She clutched the cool silver cup tightly, trying to rid her hands of the burning sensation. She would never be able to trust Huw enough to relax and welcome his caress.

Yet in two days they were to be married.

Chapter Seven

Matilda wished she could press her hands to her stomach to try to ease the fluttering within, but when she lowered her arms, Gwenllian scolded her.

"Stand still, dear, or we'll never get these lacings right."

"I don't know why we take so much trouble over dressing a bride," said another lady, one of Gwenllian's attendants. "The groom is always too busy imagining her without clothes to notice what she's wearing."

"Ah, but the art is to assist the groom's imagination," said another, giving a sharp tug to the lacings, further tightening the gown beneath Matilda's breasts. She said something else which Matilda didn't follow, because she was unfamiliar with the Welsh, but from the giggling it must be yet another joke about the wedding night.

A night she dreaded.

Yet after that evening where she had allowed herself for the first time to imagine the feel of Huw's hand in hers, whenever he was near, her heart would give odd thumps, coupled with a spreading warmth in the pit of her belly.

And now, with all this talk of the wedding night, her chest felt so tight, she could hardly breathe. The women must have laced her gown far too tight.

After much fuss and discussion, Gwenllian stood

back and looked Matilda up and down.

"There. You can put your arms down now, dear. Let me see how it looks."

Matilda obeyed, wishing she could sit. She was feeling lightheaded because she had not managed to eat anything all morning. That was definitely the reason. Nothing to do with the images of Huw that wouldn't leave her.

Gwenllian walked around her, pausing here and there to straighten seams and remove loose threads. Now Matilda knew how a horse must feel, being groomed for the market. "I knew this color would suit you," Gwenllian said, tugging one flared sleeve into place. "This wine-red wool brings a lovely warm glow to your skin. The moment I saw you, I knew this cloth would make the perfect wedding gown. I just wish there was more time to prepare." Her aunt ran a finger across the embroidered gold flowers around the neckline with a sigh. Then she picked up the girdle that was embroidered to match the trim on the neckline and hem, and wrapped it twice around Matilda's hips before knotting it. "This would look so much better if we'd had time to sew on some seed pearls."

"It's exquisite," Matilda assured her, forcing her frozen features into a smile. "I couldn't have hoped for such a beautiful gown even with months to prepare. You've worked wonders."

Gwenllian hugged her, then picked up an ivory comb. "Let's get started on your hair," she said. "It's a good thing brides wear their hair down—I don't know how I'd manage styling hair as long as yours. I swear it reaches your hips." Matilda had already noticed that Welsh women wore their hair much shorter than

Norman or English women. Gwenllian's hair was only chin-length.

Matilda's hair was a shimmering fall of golden silk by the time a soft knock sounded at the door. One of Gwenllian's ladies peered inside. "It's time to leave for the church, my lady."

Matilda stood, folding her arms across her stomach. All warmth fled.

This was really going to happen. She was going to marry Huw. Until now it had seemed like a dream, unreal. Now it hit her that there was no avoiding it—within the hour she would be wed to a man who despised her.

Tainted Comyn blood.

The women gathered around her, all smiles and laughter as they fastened a necklace of garnets around her throat and placed a matching circlet upon her brow, both borrowed from her aunt. Then together they walked out into the courtyard, where Gruffyth awaited them.

He gave her an approving smile. "You look lovely, my dear. Now come, we mustn't keep them waiting."

Taking her arm, he led her through the gates and down a rough pathway to the church. Trees and thatched dwellings passed by in a blur. All she could see was the knot of folk by the church door, Huw in the center, towering over the rest.

He was looking her way, although it was still too far to make out his expression. She doubted it would be happy. They might have come to a grudging truce, but Huw had made no secret of his reluctance to marry.

She wanted time to slow down, but all too soon she was facing him, her uncle placing her cold hand into

Huw's warm one. At first she couldn't find the courage to raise her eyes, but when she did, Huw didn't look so much angry as startled.

He gave her a tight smile, then they turned to face the priest. A gentle breeze stirred Matilda's hair, blowing strands of it across Huw's face. The lightheaded sensation returned. If it wasn't for Huw's firm grasp, she felt she could float away. She repeated her vows, hearing her own voice, but hardly aware what she was saying. She searched Huw's face as he placed a gold ring studded with garnets onto the priest's open book, but she could see no sign of happiness there. No sign of emotion when the priest slid the ring onto her finger. The kiss Huw planted on her lips was as cold as the stone walls, his repugnance a crushing weight upon her chest.

With a heavy heart, she walked through the church doors, still holding Huw's hand, and knelt at the altar to hear their first Mass as husband and wife. While the priest's somber chant echoed from the vaulted ceiling, she cast glances at the man beside her. Huw. Her husband.

His mouth was turned down and deep lines furrowed his brow. Not the expression a bride dreams of seeing on her new husband, but she couldn't blame him. She doubted she looked any happier.

Huw looked up and met her gaze. Her stomach swooped. She was immobile, unable to look away. This was the first time she'd allowed herself to look at him properly. She took in the sweep of his thick lashes, the flecks of green and gold in his eyes. The way they studied her in return, drinking in every detail. His frown lines deepened, then his gaze dropped to her mouth.

Heat flooded her face, and she tore away her gaze, focusing on her clasped hands for the rest of the Mass.

They returned from the church and went straight to the great hall for their wedding feast. They sat side by side at the high table, sharing a trencher, but although Huw picked the tastiest morsels from the serving dishes for her, she could hardly swallow a thing. Owain's great hall glowed with golden candlelight and the deeper scarlet and crimson blaze of the central fire. The air throbbed with the joyful ripple of a harp, and they were surrounded by laughing voices. But they themselves were silent.

Matilda's nerves were as tightly strung as the bard's harp. Every now and again her hand would brush Huw's, or she would feel the press of his thigh against hers, and crackling awareness sparked through every fiber of her being. What was happening to her? If only one of them could say something, maybe the air would weigh less heavily, stop humming with unspent lightning. But all she could do was watch his hands where they cradled his goblet. Hands that had every right to do with her as Huw pleased.

The bard finished one song and started another. The haunting chords merged into the very same song Huw had played in Fitzjohn's great hall. She closed her eyes. She had to say something now to break this painful silence. Anything.

That was when it struck her.

"You haven't introduced me to any of your friends," she said.

"You've met Owain," he answered, starting as though disturbed from a dream.

"But Owain's your king. What about friends you

grew up with?" She searched the faces of the men present, looking for any she thought would be likely candidates.

Huw shrugged. "There weren't any. What about you? Isn't there anyone you wish you could have with you today?"

"From Sir Reginald's household?" She shook her head. "He made sure any companions were ones who would report my every movement to him. I spent most of my time trying to avoid companions, not seeking them out."

Huw's mouth twisted. "It seems we have more in common than we first thought. We both prefer to be alone."

"Yet we have to find a way to work together if we want to retake Coed Bedwen."

"It's quite simple—do as I say, and there won't be a problem."

A spike of irritation stabbed her in the gut. "You might be the one who's spent years as a spy, but Owain chose me because I know Coed Bedwen. Don't let your animosity blind you to my usefulness."

To her surprise, Huw didn't strike back with a barb of his own but set his cup back on the board with a sigh. "You're right. You have my word I'll listen to you. But you must trust me and let me have the final say."

Trust. She picked up a piece of bread and slowly tore it to pieces. "You know I find trust difficult."

"And with good reason, I grant you. But this will only work if we can rely on one another. We'll probably have to work separately, but I'll be there for you if you get into trouble. I need to know you'll do the same for me."

I'll be there for you.

Matilda swallowed down bitter bile. What had she got herself into? She stumbled to her feet with no idea of where she was going, she just knew she had to get away.

Before she could make a move, a commotion broke out among the revelers.

One man raised his cup with a cheer. "Looks like the bride is in a hurry to get to the bridal chamber." Judging from his flushed face, he had downed more than his share of the wine. "Time for the bedding revels!"

To Matilda's dismay, the cry was taken up by others, and soon it was clear they wouldn't be quieted. A group of men surrounded Huw and swept him out of the room, some of the jokes they shouted made Matilda's ears burn. She didn't have time to wonder where Huw was being taken, however, for Gwenllian and her ladies approached.

"This is earlier than I'd expected, but I suppose we can be grateful we got through the feast without any broken heads," her aunt said, taking her arm.

Pressing her hands to her stomach to ease the churning within, she allowed the women to lead her from the hall. She walked blindly, only becoming aware of her surroundings when she saw they were in her guest chamber. There was a glowing fire in the brazier and the large, canopied bed had been strewn with blossoms and herbs.

"It's my own secret mixture of herbs," said a dark-haired woman as she tugged at the lacings of Matilda's gown. "It's guaranteed to ensure the conception of a son. You'll have a swollen belly come harvest time."

Despite the heat from the brazier, goose pimples rose on her skin. She shivered. She wasn't ready for this, needed more time. Would it hurt?

"There'll be maids weeping across Gwynedd tonight," another woman said. "I'd be tempted to cast aside my Dafydd for a tumble with Huw ap Goronwy."

That gave Matilda pause for thought. From what these women were saying, not only was there pleasure to be found in the marriage bed, but Huw was considered particularly desirable. She had spent so much of her life being wary of men that she hadn't paid attention to their attractiveness.

There wasn't time to ponder the effect Huw had on women, though, for the sound of male laughter and singing approached.

Her pulse sped up as the women hurried to undress her, all the while offering advice on the best ways to give Huw pleasure, while ensuring her own. Finally, she was left standing in her shift while they combed her hair and anointed her with rosewater.

Fists rapped at the door. Giggling, the women stripped Matilda of her shift and hustled her into the bed. The linen sheets were cold against her naked flesh.

The door burst open and the men tumbled in, Huw in their midst. The women squealed in protest, but it sounded half-hearted.

Peering over the bedcovers, she saw the women leave and a priest step forward. Sprinkling the bed with holy water, he prayed God's blessing on the couple, then he left. She watched as the men began to strip Huw of his clothes. Her eyes newly opened to his potential desirability, she studied him, willing herself to feel something. Anything to help her through the night.

There was much to admire, now she came to look. She already knew he was strong, but now, as the men removed his tunic, his undershirt did nothing to hide the breadth of his shoulders and narrowness of his hips. The ties on his shirt were undone so it gaped open, offering her a glimpse of sculpted muscle and whorls of dark hair.

Her mouth went dry. Although she hadn't lost her fear of what was to come, a thrill of anticipation accompanied it.

Once Huw was stripped to his undershirt and braies, he managed, with much scuffling and cursing, to oust the last of the men from the room.

He slammed the door shut. They were alone.

The blood pounded in Matilda's ears.

She expected him to come straight to bed; instead, he paced over to a table in the corner, upon which stood a jug of wine and two goblets. Matilda's heart hammered, admiring the play of muscles in his calves and thighs that were visible through his fine linen braies.

She sat up, tugging the sheets to her neck, and took the cup her offered her. The pounding in her chest became painful when he stripped off his shirt and braies. She lowered her eyes and took a gulp of wine, but not before she caught a glimpse of sleek, firm flesh. The mattress dipped as he slipped into bed beside her.

Then Huw spoke, his voice making her jump. "Don't look so afraid. I won't hurt you."

She raised her eyes to his face and saw not the distaste she had half feared, but a look that she could have sworn was confusion. But she must be wrong. Huw always knew what to do.

"We neither of us have made any secret that this marriage is against our wishes," Huw continued, his voice gentler than she had ever known it. "We're both in this for Coed Bedwen, and I won't do anything to risk losing it."

"Nor will I," she replied, wondering where he was going. This seemed a strange conversation to be having on their wedding night.

"I've been thinking what you said about trust earlier. I realize I need to show you that you can trust me. So I won't touch you. Not until you're ready."

She doubted that was a hardship, considering his distaste for her, but she bit back the retort to that effect. This was what she wanted. Why question his motives? Besides, the stresses of the day had worn her down; she couldn't face an argument.

"I appreciate that," she said finally.

"Then we've got a long journey ahead tomorrow. We should get some rest."

But as she settled back in the bed, along with the relief that washed over her, she was aware of a nagging, hollow feeling in her chest. She did her best to shrug it off, dismiss it as tiredness.

She couldn't possibly be disappointed.

****

A pale light was just seeping through the cracks in the closed shutters when Huw gave up the attempt to sleep. He slipped out of bed, careful not to disturb Matilda, and pulled on the laborer's clothes he had placed there the previous day.

The candles had burned out, but there was just enough glow from the brazier to make out Matilda's slight form beneath the blankets. She was lying on her side, her hair fanned out upon the pillow. The blankets had slipped from one shoulder to reveal silken flesh and the curve of one breast. She looked vulnerable, peaceful, as she never looked when awake.

It had been hours before her breathing had slipped into the deep, even rhythm of sleep. He wondered if she had been as affected by his nearness as he was by hers. He had burned with the knowledge that her naked flesh was only a hand's breadth from his. There was nothing stopping him from pulling her into his arms and taking what he had desired almost from their first meeting. Nothing except his oath.

He was torn. Two men. One was burdened by the need for revenge, the other was overcome by an unexpected tenderness for the woman beside him. And he wanted to give her pleasure. Hear her soft cries, feel her slender body arch beneath him, see the rapture on her face as she surrendered herself to him.

Saints preserve him! He strode over to the table, poured himself some wine, and swallowed it in a single draught. They had a long way to travel today and a raging arousal wasn't going to help.

He poured another cup and returned to the bed. She looked so peaceful. Innocent.

Could she truly be held responsible for the sins of her grandfather?

He reached out a finger toward her bare shoulder, fighting the urge to rip aside the blankets and take her there and then.

In the next instant, he jerked his hand away. Hellfire! He mustn't forget his oath! He couldn't falter now, not when he was so close to regaining Coed Bedwen. Not to mention that he'd only last night promised Matilda he wouldn't touch her. It was the only way he'd been able to think of getting her to trust him.

It was vital to win her trust if they were to have any chance of succeeding in their task. That was far more important than slaking his lust. And it could only be lust—nothing more. It was inconceivable that he should have any softer feelings toward a Comyn.

He paused a moment, willing his pounding heartbeat to slow. Then he spoke. "Time to wake up, Matilda."

She stirred, and her eyes blinked open. She sat up and the sheet slipped farther down. He handed her the wine cup and turned away hastily. There was only so much he could take before he gave in to his baser urges. He saw her shift on the chest at the end of the bed, so he flung it at her. "Get dressed. We leave today, and there's a lot to do."

There was the sound of rustling, and then came the pad of her feet on the floor rushes.

"I trust you slept well," she said, her voice blurred with sleep.

Hinges creaked, and he looked round to see her bending down, rummaging in the open chest. Her shift outlined her firm, rounded rear.

Bloody hellfire! What was Owain thinking of, sending her to Coed Bedwen with him? How was he supposed to concentrate? Ever again.

"Well enough." The lie stuck in his throat, but what was he supposed to say? *I didn't dare relax for a heartbeat, for fear that I'd forget myself and ravish you, even though everything in my upbringing forbids me to feel that way about you.* "How about you?"

"Perfectly."

So they were both liars.

There was awkward silence, broken when Matilda gave an exclamation of disgust as she pulled a bundle of wool from the chest. "I can't believe I have to wear this. It's the color of dung." She sniffed it and wrinkled her nose. "Smells like it, too." It was the costume that had been provided for Matilda to wear to Coed Bedwen, that of a laborer. After all, turning up dressed as a high-born Norman was hardly the way to pass unnoticed.

Glad of a distraction from the tension between them, Huw said, "Maybe it will look better on." It had been on the tip of his tongue to point out that she could have her choice of fine gowns if she'd rather stay behind, but he stopped himself in time. That could only lead to further argument.

She pulled a face but drew the garment over her head. There were no lacings at the side to mold it to her body from hip to chest, nor did the sleeves flare out from the elbow to give tantalizing glimpses of wrist and forearm with each gesture. Instead it hung in a shapeless tube down to the floor. She pulled out the cord belt that went with it and tied it around her waist. It didn't look any better, but the belt hitched up the gown so the hem didn't drag on the floor.

They both looked at one another, and Huw could swear there was an audible snap as the tension broke. They burst into laughter at the same time.

"If only I could have got married in this, maybe we would have had more to say to each other," Matilda said finally, wiping tears from her eyes.

Huw smiled. "And denied me the sight of you in

that red gown? It would have been a crime."

Matilda gave him an odd look.

"Did I say something wrong?"

She shook her head. "I was just thinking that we get on well together when we're not fighting over what we want."

She made a valid point. Together they'd achieved her escape from Redcliff with far more ease than he'd thought possible. For a moment he allowed himself to imagine what their life could be like were there not blood between their two families.

"How about this?" he said. "We'll call a truce for the entire time we're in Coed Bedwen. We'll leave our unhappiness about our marriage behind. And as to how we manage Coed Bedwen together…and *if* we can…we'll make those decisions when it's ours."

Matilda looked at him thoughtfully, then a half-smile tugged the corners of her mouth. "Agreed. A truce. On one condition."

"What's that?"

"I need you to be completely honest with me. No lies. If I'm going to be able to follow your orders, you must be open with me. If you can't, I'm going to my uncle to tell him to withdraw his support."

He had no choice. Not when he was so close to achieving his dream. "Agreed."

But his promise left him feeling exposed. Vulnerable. He didn't know how he would cope being alone with Matilda with no lies to hide behind.

He drew a deep breath and pointed to the door. "Then let's go and reclaim Coed Bedwen."

But once that was accomplished, the truce would be at an end.

Chapter Eight

They broke their fast on barley bread and smoked herring. When they left the hall, their horses were already being led from the stables.

Her uncle strode up, dressed for the journey. "Good morning. I took the liberty of saddling horses for you both." He frowned at Matilda. "It's not too late to change your mind, you know. You'd be more than welcome to stay with me until Coed Bedwen is back in Welsh hands. You don't have to do this."

Matilda put her hand on his arm. "I do, Uncle. This is the right thing to do if my presence can prevent a long siege." Although she was aware of Huw by her side, probably praying that she would agree with Gruffyth.

They mounted their horses and set off. Riding with her uncle's party, they made good time. Hills, woods, and streams flew by. Matilda rode with her aunt, which meant enduring her subtle probings concerning her wellbeing after the wedding night. She knew Gwenllian was only being kind and wanting to offer advice, but Matilda had no intention of confiding in her. She needed to concentrate on the mission, on Coed Bedwen. Everything else was a distraction.

The problem was, she was riding directly behind Huw. And now she had forced herself to admit to her stirrings of attraction, it was becoming more difficult to ignore the effect he was having on her. No matter how much she tried to recall the layout of the castle and village of Coed Bedwen, all she could do was admire his lithe grace on horseback, his long, strong legs, the coppery glint of his hair in the sunlight. With the result that her insides were quivering and a slow, delicious heat spread through her whole body.

All in all, it was a relief when Huw called a halt. "This is where our paths diverge. Matilda and I must continue on foot."

She experienced a pang of apprehension as they stood watching her uncle's party depart. From here on they truly were dependent on each other. Now their truce would be tested to the limit.

They were standing at a place where two valleys met. Gruffyth's destination lay along the valley to the south and west. Coed Bedwen was farther east.

Huw pointed to a wooded hill on the southeastern horizon. "We're going that way," he said. "We'll stop to eat and discuss our plans when we reach the top. Coed Bedwen is only about six miles from here, so there's no risk of running out of daylight before we get there."

He set off at a pace that had Matilda gasping with the effort of keeping up. No wonder he didn't expect them to talk whilst walking. It took them an hour to reach the hill, first following the high banks of the stream, then cutting across open land.

As the land began to rise, Huw's pace quickened, much to Matilda's disbelief. She stumbled behind him, panting and clutching her sides. She didn't even have the breath to ask him to slow down. For what felt like an eternity they climbed, Matilda not taking her eyes off Huw's back. It was only her determination that kept her going. She plodded on, fighting the urge to scratch her arms, which itched from the coarse wool of her tunic.

They were about three quarters of the way up when Huw turned. His expression was remote. For a moment he looked through her. Then his gaze sharpened, and he hurried down and took her arm.

"Forgive me. I was lost in a dream. I wasn't thinking of you at all."

"I could see that." She didn't have the breath to utter the stream of insults that had been brewing for the duration of their march, but she glared at him, letting her eyes do the talking.

"We'll stop here for a few minutes to let you get your breath," he said after an awkward silence. He removed his cape and spread it on the grass. "Sit down here," he said. "You look exhausted."

Matilda collapsed upon the cape with a groan and fought to regain her breath. Huw stood with his back to her, gazing eastward. She followed the direction of his gaze, and her eyes fell on a line of trees like a caterpillar on a round hill a few miles distant.

"I think I know where we are now," she said when she'd recovered enough to speak. "I've never approached Coed Bedwen from this angle before, but I remember seeing that hill against the skyline from Coed Bedwen. If I'm right, we should be able to see the castle once we reach the top of this hill."

"That's right. You get a fine view of the whole area. My father used to bring me up here. He"—Huw glanced back at Matilda—"he wanted me to see where my family had come from."

Now she understood why he had been ignoring her. This place must be a sharp reminder of his family's loss at the hands of hers.

"I…I hadn't thought how hard it must be for you, to be in the company with a Comyn in this place," she said. "I'm sorry I put you in this situation."

To her surprise, Huw came and sat next to her, his sternness fading. "In truth, it was Owain's intention all along. Your insistence forced his hand into announcing it sooner than planned, but it's him I blame for you being here, not you."

At least Owain saw her worth. And as for Huw…well, she would just have to throw all her energy into their mission until he was forced to appreciate her. To give him his due, he was being more open with her now. It seemed he took their truce seriously.

She rose. "We should move on; there's no time to waste." Then with a sidelong glance at him, she said, "You could have pretended you wanted me here, though."

The corner of Huw's mouth quirked. "What—and break my promise of complete honesty? I'm afraid insincere flattery wasn't in the terms of our truce." He picked up his cape and put it back on. "Now let's get to the top."

Matilda couldn't hold back a reluctant smile. With lightened spirits, she continued the climb. If Huw could let down his guard enough to tease her, maybe he would eventually overcome his dislike of her. It made her even more determined to prove herself.

And if that meant struggling to overcome her natural distrust of men, she would. It wouldn't be easy, but as Huw was obviously trying to fulfill his side of the bargain, she would do her best to trust him in return.

Huw set a less demanding pace this time, but even so, it didn't take long to reach the top. The slope became less steep higher up, and Matilda found it much easier to stay with him.

The hilltop was dotted with rocky outcrops with tufts of springy heather in between. Lower down the far slope were the slender, gray pillars of the birch trees Matilda remembered from her childhood. Beyond them, at the bottom of the valley, a haze of wood smoke hung over a huddle of thatched roofs. Coed Bedwen. And beyond the village, on high ground rising toward a river cliff, was the castle. Even though it was still a long way off, the bulk of the keep at the highest point was clearly visible, the sandstone appearing blood red against the dark clouds that were rolling in.

"I can't believe I'm here at last," she breathed, drinking in the sight. "I remember gathering bluebells with my mother in those woods. There were so many of them, it looked like the trees stood in a misty blue lake. I can't see bluebells now without thinking of my mother." Tears pricked her eyes. She could almost smell the sharp, sweet scent of the bluebells, hear her mother's silvery voice raised in song as they gathered armfuls of the flowers to decorate the great hall for her birthday feast.

"Bluebells are my favorite flowers," her mother had said, "because the woods were thick with them the day you were born. Every time I see them, I thank God for giving me my greatest gift: you."

Matilda blinked away the tears. A few short days later, her mother had sickened and died. That day among the bluebells was her last happy memory. She missed her mother. Yearned for the warmth and security of her love.

Huw sat upon a flat rock. "Use your memories to spur you on," he said. "From now on you're going to have to endure rough conditions and hard work. If ever you feel like giving up, think about those happy memories and use them to inspire you to continue."

"What happy memories do you use?"

His face grew hard. "I don't have any. I intend to make them."

He patted the rock beside him. "Sit down. It's time to make plans."

Matilda hesitated, then sat next to him. Instantly she became aware of a crackle of energy between them. What was happening to her?

In the woods below, she heard the hollow tapping of a woodpecker and a faint green haze draped the bushes. The air was heavy with the surging energy of spring. That's what affected her. Nothing to do with Huw himself.

Huw reached in his pack and produced a bundle wrapped in oilcloth and a wineskin. "We can eat while we talk." He opened the oilcloth to reveal a large crust of bread and a chunk of cheese. He tore the bread into two and handed her half and then pulled out his knife and cut her some cheese.

"We need to agree on our approach before we get to the village," said Huw between mouthfuls. "Once we're there, we'll be the subject of gossip from the ale house to the tannery. That's always the way with strangers. If our story isn't convincing, we'll be discovered before nightfall."

Huw's words acted like a pail of icy water upon

her. One false move and they could end up in the hands of the castle guards. The punishment for spies involved torture and usually death. Maybe as a woman she could expect leniency, but there would be no such hope for Huw.

She took a deep breath. "We'll need a good reason to stay in the village. The first thing to do is to contact the villagers and tell them we're looking for work. Once we get to know them we'll be able to assess which ones are likely to join a revolt."

Huw snorted. "It's a good thing Owain let you come. I'd never have thought of that myself." He picked up a twig from the ground and twirled it between his fingers. "And what reason shall we give for leaving our home? People will be bound to ask."

"We could say our village was struck by fever and so many died that the survivors were forced to abandon it."

Huw raised his eyebrows and gave an approving nod. "You think fast. That's good."

She felt a rush of pleasure and instantly despised herself. She was behaving like a lapdog, craving approval from her master.

"We must do our best to avoid being separated," said Huw. "You'll have to change your name; a Norman woman would never be wandering the countryside in the company of a Welshman. From now on you're Mallt *ferch* Gwilym."

Matilda, daughter of William. At least that was no lie. She prayed she would be able to cope with remembering all the others.

"Lying is a sin." She hadn't meant to speak her thoughts, blushed when she heard her voice.

"Don't...don't you fear eternal damnation for what you do?"

Huw gave her a long look, then pulled a whetstone from the pouch at his belt and sharpened his knife with long, measured strokes. "It's also a sin to steal and murder, yet the Church didn't protest when the Normans killed my grandfather and took his land. I don't believe God will punish me for trying to prevent that happening to others."

Matilda winced, grateful that at least he'd said "Normans," not "Comyns."

"Forgive me; you're right," she said. "I may be half Norman, but I'd hate to see more of Wales fall under Norman rule."

Huw smiled. "We'll make a Welsh woman of you yet."

A Welsh woman. Matilda put her hand to the braid that swung over her shoulder. And saw a way to persuade Huw she was serious about her task and wouldn't be a hindrance.

"If I'm to be a Welsh woman, there's one more thing we need to do before we go down to the village."

Huw raised his brows. "And that is?"

"Cut my hair."

****

It was true; Matilda's hair was far too long for it to pass as a Welsh style. So why had he not suggested a cut himself?

"You could just pin it on top of your head. If you wrap your veil around your head in the Welsh style, no one would be any the wiser." And then she would still have that silken fall of hair the color of winter sunshine. *The tresses Huw longed to bury his fingers into.*

The hand holding his whetstone slipped, and he only just managed to avoid slicing a finger open. Hellfire! What malevolent spirit had whispered that thought into his ear?

"I would know the difference, and I want to do this properly." She raised her chin. "When we were escaping Redcliff, you told me I had to believe I was the person I was playing if I wanted to be convincing. I have to do this if I'm to believe."

She reached up and untied the linen coif she wore in her guise as servant. Her fingers trembled. "I want to get Coed Bedwen back, whatever the cost. I want to reclaim my happy memories." She dropped the coif to the ground. "I want to walk amongst the bluebells and feel close to my mother. To her love. My hair is a small price to pay."

Cracks formed in Huw's convictions, threatened to shatter them. Try as he might, he was finding it harder than ever to see Matilda as a Comyn. He saw her again as the courageous maid that had drawn his eye right at the start. The one that had marched directly into trouble to take control of her fate. Before he had known she was a Comyn.

"You're right," he said, his voice little more than a husky whisper. "Here, let me do that."

He unfastened the strip of leather that bound her braid. Just this one time, he would give in to his desire. He unraveled the plait and carded his fingers through her hair, reveling in the weight of it, the silken slide through his fingers. Then he knelt behind her and continued to comb her tresses until they were a swirling, gleaming curtain around her shoulders.

One of his hands slipped, and the tips of his fingers

brushed the nape of her neck. Her shoulder tensed, and she caught her breath.

"Do it now. Please."

His heart twisted when he saw her fists clenched at her sides. For a Norman woman long hair was a symbol of her high status. Her determination to crop it for the sake of their task filled him with admiration.

All thought of who she was disappeared. She was simply a woman making a brave gesture and he was overwhelmed by the need to comfort her. "You have beautiful hair, Mallt, like spun sunshine." His voice sounded hoarse in his own ears. "Cutting won't change that."

By all the saints, it wasn't her hair alone that was beautiful. Not just her face and figure either. No, it was the woman within. The woman who had lost everything she held dear and suffered cruelty for much of her life, yet hadn't given up hope. Hadn't abandoned her intrinsic goodness.

He struggled to close his mind to her qualities, but his regard for her won out. Her obvious sorrow over her mother made him wish she could take joy in the bluebells of Coed Bedwen once again.

With trembling hands, he picked up his knife and began to cut. As each strand of hair fell to the ground he felt his own convictions crumble. Did anything link her to her grandfather besides her name?

The rasping saw of severing hair filled the silence, making him wince. Strange it should affect him so when he had killed many men without flinching once. Soon the ground was covered with tendrils of gold. Matilda's hair no longer reached to her hips, but fell around her face in a chin-length cap. It framed her face, emphasizing the exquisitely chiseled nose and cheekbones and the full curves of her lips.

Lips he had an overpowering urge to kiss.

He sheathed his knife, backing away. Only last night he had promised not to touch her. He couldn't afford to throw away what little trust he had earned by giving in to his desire, no matter how much he burned for her. "There. I'm finished."

Matilda turned to face him, running her fingers through her hair, pulling a face when they reached the blunt ends. "Well, no one's going to believe I'm a Norman now. How do I look? No, don't tell me; I don't think I need to know."

"You look like a true Welsh woman." In fact, with the sunlight turning her hair into a glowing halo, she still looked like a stained-glass angel.

She gave a twisted smile. "I never thought I'd hear you say that. I thought I'd always be a Norman outsider to you."

"Is that how you feel—an outsider?" He shouldn't be surprised. After all, he had hardly made her feel welcome.

She looked down at the village below. "Coed Bedwen is the only place I've ever felt at home. The only place I want to live. That's why it's so important to me."

He stood beside her and looked down, remembering her challenge to him from before the wedding—forgetting why it was so important to his father, what made Coed Bedwen special to him?

He still couldn't answer. It was too tied up in his oath. Without that, it had no meaning.

"It's important to me as well," he said, in denial of

his uncertainty, defying her to disagree.

Matilda glanced sideways at him. "Huw, is it true that my grandfather killed yours?"

"That's what my father told me."

"I'm sorry." She spoke so quietly he could hardly hear her voice above the din of the birds shrilling warnings of the coming rain. Nevertheless, each word struck his heart, piercing through the protective armor that years of hardship had placed there. "I'm sorry your family suffered at his hands. I know winning Coed Bedwen back won't undo the harm done, but I hope it will ease the pain in your heart."

She placed a hand on his arm with a hesitant smile. It was only the lightest of touches, but the jolt reverberated through his body.

"I...thank you," he said. He had to turn away so she wouldn't see the sudden tremble of his mouth. The beliefs his life had been based on were crumbling, and without them he didn't know what he was. But he could deny it no longer: she might bear the same name as her grandfather, but that was the only thing they shared. Her heart was true, not the blackened, cursed stone that he'd been taught to believe lurked in the breast of every Comyn. At last he allowed himself to admit the truth that should have been clear to him from the start: she was innocent of the crimes committed by her grandfather.

He could never hurt her.

It took a moment to compose his features before he faced Matilda. "It's time to move on; it's going to rain soon."

Matilda nodded and turned away, her eyes downcast. She must have expected him to say more, but he was at a loss for words.

She picked up her coif and tied it closely around her head, tucking her shorn hair inside. Huw watched her for a moment, then looked down at Coed Bedwen once more. A chill seized him. This was the very spot where his father had forced him to swear his oath. The oath that had given his life purpose. Meaning. Oh, he knew he could never harm Matilda as it demanded. Owain, curse him, had probably realized that all along. But without his oath to sustain him, what was he?

Mocking laughter rang in the back of his mind and he heard his great-uncle's voice. *You are nothing.*

"Is something the matter, Huw? Did I say something wrong?"

He started and turned to find Matilda waiting for him, her coif neatly bound.

He forced a smile. "Nothing at all. Come, it's time we went down to the village."

But his great-uncle's voice followed him down the hill.

A narrow path led off the hillside, growing steeper as it approached the birch wood. They were forced to slow down for fear of tripping. To make matters worse, the dark clouds had soon covered the sky from horizon to horizon and a light rain began to fall, making the path slippery underfoot.

They were about to enter the woods when Matilda slid and would have fallen had not Huw caught her around the waist. He let his arm linger, enjoying the feel of her in his arms.

For a moment, Matilda relaxed against him, and he breathed in the scent of honeysuckle. His hand slipped from her waist to the flare of her hip. It felt so right to hold her, protect her.

She tensed and pulled away. "I can manage now."

Huw loosened his hold but took her arm instead of letting her go. "If you fall and hurt yourself, it would ruin all our plans."

Now that his eyes were opened to her innocence, it was as though he was seeing her for the first time. Although he regretted the loss of her beautiful hair, he had to admit her new style suited her. With it bundled beneath her veil, it allowed him to see the elegant lines of her long neck and the set of her shoulders. He followed the sweep of her throat from where it appeared beneath the neck of her gown, up to the angle of her jaw and the shadowy hollow behind her ear. A sudden urge struck him to trace the line with his fingers and follow with his lips. Heat swept through him as he imagined placing his lips just below her jaw, tasting her flesh and feeling the flutter of her pulse.

The surge of desire drowned out his great-uncle's voice. It was still there tickling the back of his mind, but he refused to listen.

"It's going to take longer than I expected to get down to the village." Matilda's voice shook, almost as though she, too, was affected by their closeness.

"It will be too late to ask for work. We must find shelter for the night as soon as we get there. Otherwise we're in danger of having to spend the night in the woods." Focus on the important issues, he told himself, not the voice, nor the pulsing heat Matilda's presence sent through his veins.

With a supreme force of will, he managed to thrust aside all thoughts except those directly involving their mission.

They had just entered the woods when Matilda stopped dead, nearly tripping Huw. "I have an idea." Matilda's face was lit with excitement. "My old nurse married the tavern keeper in the village. After her husband died she carried on running it alone. She'd take us in, I'm sure of it."

"But she'll recognize you."

"She'd never give me away." Her voice was firm. "She was the sweetest, kindest soul. Besides, she's Saxon. I'm sure she'd welcome the chance to see the Normans gone from Coed Bedwen, just as much as the Welsh would."

Huw frowned. "I agree she would be useful, and a tavern would be a good center for organizing a rebellion. But we must be careful. We can't be sure she won't betray us. We'll watch her for a day or two until I'm sure of her. It's hard enough for me to trust you. I don't think I could trust a stranger."

She shot him a smile that made his heart race. "You trust me?"

"I already said I do. I'll tell you if that changes."

"Then trust me in this. Alys would never betray us."

Hellfire! He should have stood his ground with Owain and refused to take her. Because with her standing so close, gazing up at him with those wide blue eyes, it was taking all his resolve to keep from pulling her to him and kissing her senseless. He had no strength left to deny her.

"Very well," he said. "We'll find Alys. But once we've introduced ourselves, I'll do the talking. I need to make up my own mind about her before deciding how much to reveal."

To get to the village, they had to walk through a mile of woodland after reaching the bottom of the hill. Where the trees ended, there were sheep and cattle grazing on common land, followed by strip fields. Many of them were newly ploughed; puddles of water glistened in the furrows.

By the time they had reached the first cottage, they were both wet and cold from the persistent rain.

"Now," said Huw, side-stepping to avoid tripping over a hen that was pecking in the dirt at his feet, "lead us to the tavern."

A cobbled lane wove past houses and stalls, leading to the castle that loomed over everything at the far side. Narrow paths led off from the track on both sides, giving access to huddled buildings that leaned in all directions. The smell of wood smoke and manure clung to everything. The street was full of people scurrying about their business. Most turned to stare as they passed.

"This way." Matilda pointed down what appeared to be the second widest lane. "I can't remember for sure, but it looks familiar."

As they walked down the lane, a stout woman approached them, carrying a brimming bucket of slops with both hands. Matilda glanced at her and then stopped, her face alight with a smile.

"Alys," she said, before he could stop her from speaking. "It is Alys, isn't it?"

Huw held his breath. All could be lost in a few brief heartbeats. He squeezed Matilda's arm, praying she would take the warning not to say more than necessary.

Alys paused and looked Matilda up and down. She

frowned. "You do look familiar, but I can't for the life of me say where I've seen you before."

"Oh Alys, don't you remember me? It's Matilda. I know it's years since you last saw me, but—"

"Bless my heart! It's my little Matilda! Look at you, all grown up." Alys eyed Matilda's clothes and frowned. "But why are you dressed like that? What's happened?"

Matilda opened her mouth again, but Huw cut in. "We shall explain all, mistress, but it needs to be told in private." Thankfully, the lane was deserted, but someone could walk by at any moment.

"Of course. Wait here while I deal with this"— Alys nodded toward the bucket—"then you may come with me. The tavern will be quiet for another hour or two. We can talk there in peace."

While Alys hurried to empty her bucket in a stinking ditch, Huw eyed the buildings farther up the lane. They were all low, thatched buildings. Most had open shutters, behind which tradesmen plied their wares, but the last house in the lane had a sign outside with a crude picture of a boar's head scratched upon it. The sign was hung with vine leaves. This must be the tavern.

Alys returned, wiping her hands on her apron. "Come with me. You can take your rest and tell me everything."

They followed Alys up the lane. Once in the Boar's Head, Alys poured them some wine, then she filled a brimming cup for herself, and they sat beside the hearth to dry themselves off. "Now tell me what brings you here." She turned her gaze upon Huw. "And with such a fine young man."

Thinking quickly, Huw said, "Matilda has escaped from her guardian." He was afraid that Matilda would reveal the truth of their mission if he didn't give a good reason for her being here and in such a state.

With a knowing smile, Alys said, "Ah, and she's run away with you?" She pinched his cheek. "I can't say I blame her. If I were twenty years younger, I'd be tempted myself."

Huw opened his mouth to correct her, then thought again. Safer to let her think they had eloped and were seeking shelter from a wrathful guardian. What she didn't know, she couldn't betray.

He put his arm around Matilda and pulled her close. Heaven knew it was no trial to pretend to be in love with her. As long as that was all it remained. A pretense.

The sneering voice fought to make itself heard again, reminding him why love was not an option. *You are nothing.*

He unwound his arm from Matilda and put some space between them. It was easier to think that way. "You won't give us away, will you? We're married now. Sir Reginald threatened to see me hanged if I lay a hand on Matilda, but I couldn't face life without her."

"Never you worry, my dears, you can stay here awhile, and no one will ask questions. I've been needing another hand to help me, ever since the last lad was carried off by the sweating sickness last summer."

"Oh, thank you, Alys!" Matilda flung her arms around Alys's waist. "I'm so glad we found you."

"As to that, what brought you to Coed Bedwen, if you were running from your guardian? He pays regular visits to the castle, you know. There'll be all hell to pay if he finds you here."

Huw exchanged a brief glance with Matilda. That was a good question.

"Is he here now?" Huw asked. He felt Matilda tense beside him.

"No, but he never gives much warning of a visit."

"Even if he was here, I doubt he would recognize me, dressed like this," Matilda said. "The truth is, Alys, I thought of you at once. I've missed you so much, and I wanted to see you again."

"Oh, you poor lamb," said Alys, enveloping Matilda in a hug. "I've missed you too."

There was no more talk of their reason for choosing Coed Bedwen. Huw breathed again. Matilda was coping well, despite her aversion to lies.

There was fresh discomfort when Alys led them, candle in hand, up a set of creaking stairs to a tiny room in a raised gallery at the back of the tavern. Its main function was as a storeroom for herbs. Great bunches of sage, hyssop, rosemary, and lavender hung from the rafters, filling the air with their fragrance. By the flickering candlelight, Huw could just make out shelves bowed with the weight of jars. Against one wall was the traditional Welsh bed, stuffed with rushes and covered with a coarse sheet and a blanket.

"I know it's not what you're used to," said Alys with an apologetic smile. "But it's warm and dry up here."

"It's perfect," Huw said, although he knew from experience that the bed would feel as though it was stuffed with rocks.

"Now you get some sleep. I can see you're worn out. I must go and serve in the tavern."

"One last thing," said Huw as a thought hit him. "It would be best if you didn't mention our presence to anyone. But if anyone asks, don't use Matilda's name. She's going by the name of Mallt." He repeated the story they had decided upon. "Fitzjohn's men are here and all would be lost if word got back to him of Matilda's whereabouts."

Alys nodded. "You can depend on me."

Huw prayed that was true. He still wasn't convinced of the wisdom of taking shelter with Alys, but it was too late to change things now.

She lit a few rush lights for them and then left. In the silence that fell, Huw could hear the stairs groan as Alys descended.

He turned his eyes back to the bed.

Chapter Nine

Matilda looked at the bed. Surely that couldn't be big enough for the two of them, yet where would the other sleep, if only one of them took the pallet? Despite herself, she yawned. It had been a tiring day, and she ached all over from the long journey. Whatever they decided, it would have to be soon. She couldn't stay awake for much longer.

"You take the bed," said Huw.

"Where will you sleep?" There wasn't room on the floor for a man of Huw's height to lie stretched out.

"I'll do well enough in the corner, rolled in one of the blankets. I've slept in far more uncomfortable situations, believe me."

She did believe him. Owain's spy could hardly expect a lavish welcome wherever his duty took him. She shivered, imagining the filthy alleys and chilly barns where he must have sought shelter.

She wished there was a way she could make up for the hardships he had endured as a result of her grandfather's actions. If only he would let her. She felt another twist of disappointment as she recalled how he had turned away when she had reached out to him, tried to apologize for her heritage. There was a gulf between them that she couldn't cross.

"We can share the bed. We're married, after all," she said. Her insides quivered; sharing the narrow bed would mean lying close together. Despite her first stirrings of desire, she couldn't push aside her deeply ingrained distrust. However, not only had he promised not to touch her, she also wanted to close the gulf between them, to make amends for her family's wrongs.

She couldn't put that jumble of thoughts into words, though. Instead she nodded to the entrance to their room, which only consisted of a sackcloth curtain. "Anyone could look in and see us. There would be awkward questions if we weren't seen to be sharing a bed. And we can't afford questions."

Huw glanced at the door and grimaced. "You're right." Then he smiled. "I'm glad to see you've been paying attention. I'll make a spy out of you yet, Mallt."

His smile transformed his face, making him appear younger, almost carefree. This was how he would have looked if he hadn't spent his life in the shadows, chasing secrets. Of course, if his life had been different, they would never have met. She wouldn't be here.

She rubbed her temples. So much had happened over the past few days she'd had no chance to take in the huge changes in her life. Now it was sinking in. She was in a strange land, married to a man she hardly knew. Dependent on him.

That brought back the sick, fluttery feelings she had no desire to examine, together with the words that always haunted her.

I'll always be there for you. Would she never be free of them?

Bending down, she tried to distract herself by removing her boots. She fumbled with the leather thong around her left ankle, only to find it too snarled to loosen.

Huw crouched beside her. "Sit down. I'll do that."

Once she was perched on the lumpy mattress, he supported her foot on his lap and worked at the knot. Every now and again, his fingers would brush against her calf, above the top of the boot, sending sizzling sparks up her leg. Oh, yes. She felt desire for him. However, it only served to frighten her. Desire led to love, and that could only end one way. Eventually he would let her down. She couldn't endure that desolation again.

She watched him as he worked, his brows drawn together in concentration. The lamplight lit his sharp cheekbones and strong jaw with a golden glow. She fought the urge to trace those angles with her fingertips. It was best to keep her distance. Stay safe.

If only she could get that message through to her body.

Finally, he managed to loosen the knot, and he eased the boot off her foot. His fingers caressed her instep. Heat pooled in her belly, between her legs. Merciful saints, what was happening? Aunt Gwenllian had never told her a touch to the foot could affect her *there*.

"Shall I do the other one for you?"

She could only nod. If she opened her mouth she would beg him to untie her garters as well. The thought of his hands touching the flesh above her knee made her face flame. Or there was always the tie at the neck of her gown. Or her girdle.

The moment the other boot was off, she shot to her feet. "I can do the rest, thank you." She had to put some distance between them before his nearness scorched her to a crisp.

She faced away from him and stripped off her tunic and hose, only leaving on her coarse shift. She bundled the clothes in her shawl to use as a pillow and, shivering as the chill air nipped at her ankles, slipped beneath the blankets.

Huw's footsteps approached. She squeezed her eyes shut and shifted closer to her edge of the mattress when she felt him get in beside her. The whole bed shifted as Huw made himself comfortable. His foot brushed against her calf, then he jerked it away as though it burned him.

Even with Huw's body next to hers, she couldn't get warm in this draughty attic, covered by only a thin blanket. She curled into a tight ball and hugged her arms to her chest but couldn't suppress her shivers.

Behind her, Huw cursed. "This is ridiculous." He wrapped his arms around her, pulling her close. "I'd be a very poor husband if I couldn't even keep my wife warm at night."

The heat of his body seeped through the thin linen that was all that separated their flesh. At first Matilda tensed, but gradually she relaxed into the embrace, felt his warmth spread through her muscles, soothing, easing the tension. She'd never realized what a comfort it could be to have a man's strong arms around her, never imagined she would feel so secure.

"Better?" The rumble of his voice vibrated against her back.

"A little." His arm rested against the underside of her breasts. If she moved just a little, his hand would brush a nipple. She shivered. This time not from the cold.

"You did well today," Huw murmured against her hair. "You know I didn't want you here, but if you hadn't, I'd probably be hiding out in a flea-infested barn tonight."

Matilda struggled to keep her senses. She mustn't allow herself to be fooled by the glowing heat radiating through her body. She might have promised to trust him for the time they were here, but as far as she was concerned, that only went as far as following his orders and being where he expected her to be. It didn't cover the deep-down trust he had no right to command. She doubted she could ever trust a man to such a degree.

"What should we do tomorrow?" She asked the first question that came into her head to block out thoughts of the unfamiliar tingling in the pit of her belly and between her legs.

"I'm going to talk to Alys," he said. "I know you trust her, but I need to be sure myself."

"And if you can?"

"Don't you see? This tavern must be the only place in the village that supplies wine. I'd be prepared to bet Alys regularly supplies wine to the castle. Ale too, if they don't brew their own."

"Why's that important?" Matilda felt a surge of resentment that she should be fighting these strange sensations, whereas Huw seemed unaffected by her nearness. Had he promised not to touch her, not to gain her trust but because he found her distasteful?

"We have to get into the castle somehow. What better way than to deliver their wine? They'll welcome us with open arms."

"I see. Do you want me to ask Alys tomorrow?"

"No. As I said, I need to be sure myself. I'll do the

talking."

He moved closer again and settled his cheek against Matilda's head. "Do you feel warmer now?"

Warmer? It felt like she was lying on a griddle.

"Much, thank you." She paused, then said, "Huw, don't you...?" Didn't he what? Want to kiss her? Couple with her? "Don't you want to sleep?" she asked finally. Her pride wouldn't let her ask the question she really wanted answering.

He sighed. "We ought to. We'll need clear heads tomorrow."

He shifted away slightly and lay still.

Matilda thought she would never be able to sleep, but the long journey had taken its toll and the heaviness of sleep soon tugged at her eyelids. The last thought that crossed her mind before sleep claimed her was curiosity over what coupling with Huw would be like. They were married. They would have to do so sooner or later. Suddenly it seemed cowardly to put it off.

A whisper in the back of her mind told her that she wouldn't think that way if she didn't enjoy being held in his arms, but she was asleep before she could explore that thought further.

****

"You should talk to Alys now."

Huw dropped his armful of logs onto the woodpile and wiped the sweat from his brow. The irritation he'd felt ever since waking up beside her bubbled over. "Why don't we just climb to the top of the church tower and announce our plans to the whole village?"

He felt a stab of remorse when Matilda paled and rubbed her temples. He'd noticed that gesture before. It was something she did when she was upset. He gave a stray log a kick, then winced at the sharp pain that shot through his toe. Hellfire! Now she had him feeling sorry for her.

"I'm sorry," he said in a more conciliatory tone. "Take no notice of my mood. I don't know what ails me today." He picked up another armful of logs from the load he had just been splitting. In truth, he knew exactly why he was in such a foul mood. Waking up this morning with a desirable woman in his arms had proved an unexpected hardship. It was ironic that now he had allowed himself to admit Matilda's innocence and his desire, they were in no position to act upon it. Besides, Matilda had practically told him to go to sleep last night. She obviously didn't feel ready to consummate their marriage. Some men might have taken what they wanted, but he would never do that.

His lips twisted in a wry smile. "Hardship" was an apt word, considering the state of arousal the heat of her flesh beneath her thin shift had provoked. He had leapt from bed before she could awaken and feel the evidence of his desire. Only pausing to pull on his clothes, he hurried outside, praying the sting of the chill dawn would cool his ardor. That, and the exertions of the task he had chosen, had had the desired effect, but not improved his temper.

He forced his mind back to the conversation. "There's a woman in there with Alys now, helping her clean the common room. I'll wait until she's gone."

Their opportunity came after the noon meal. Matilda was put to work sweeping up the stale rushes on the tavern floor and laying fresh ones, while Huw carried in the jugs of wine. Alys was also there, cleaning the tankards. No one else was present, for the woman who had been helping earlier had left.

"Your life must have changed a great deal, since you ceased taking care of Matilda," said Huw to Alys.

"Oh my Lord, yes," said Alys. "There's plenty as say it's a great step down for me to be working in a tavern after living with a rich family, but I'm content with my life here, although I do miss my husband."

"Matilda speaks very highly of your care for her after her father died."

"Poor lamb; that was such a dreadful shock. I couldn't have left her alone after such a thing."

Huw frowned. Was there more to the death than Matilda had let on? He was tempted to ask, but then again, it had nothing to do with what was happening at the castle, so he held his tongue.

Besides, Alys rattled on without any prompting. "I'd always thought Will Comyn was a weak man, but I'd never—"

"Alys." Matilda cut off her old nurse's flow of words with a sharp glare. "Where would you like me to put the old rushes?"

"Bless you, my dear. Just throw them on the midden."

Matilda hefted the basket of soiled rushes in her arms and headed for the door. As she passed Alys, she darted her a look that Huw interpreted as a warning. A warning about what? He had not missed the way Matilda had frozen at Alys's mention of her father. Nor had he overlooked how her knuckles had whitened as she gripped her broom. He wondered what she was trying to hide.

Even after Matilda was out of earshot, Alys remained silent. Clearly, she had taken Matilda's unspoken warning to heart. Huw tried to get her to open up again by steering the conversation back to the current occupier of the castle.

"I gather Sir Reginald is not a popular man in Coed Bedwen," he said.

With a grimace, Alys looked behind her, as though checking for eavesdroppers. "Hush, it's not safe to say such things."

Huw lifted some of the jugs onto a high shelf and waited. He had learnt that silence was often the best way to encourage a reluctant tongue to wag. Pressing for information often made informants seal their mouths.

They worked in silence for a while, then Alys murmured, as though to herself, "Coed Bedwen has become a fearful place ever since Fitzjohn took charge."

He raised his eyebrows to indicate he was listening, but maintained his cautious silence. Encouraging confidences was like coaxing a timid kitten to leave its hiding place. This time he was helped by Alys's garrulous nature.

"I'm not saying the Comyns were popular here; they were Norman, after all. For all that, they weren't cruel masters. Now, Sir Reginald, he's a different prospect. He's far too free with his fists, and he allows his men to terrorize the villagers. It's got so that no one dares to venture out alone."

"Can't you appeal to the commote court?" asked Hugh.

Alys made a contemptuous gesture. "They won't lift a finger to help. Not with Sir Reginald's men threatening anyone who dares defy him. Even if they weren't afraid, they wouldn't be able to do much. Sir Reginald has rebuilt the keep in stone. It would be more trouble than it was worth to try and take it. More's the pity."

The venom in her voice surprised Huw. Could it be that she had a more personal reason for her dislike? He took a guess. "What has he done to harm you?"

"Not me. My nephew." She pressed her lips together and turned her back on him. She fiddled with the tankards, but Huw caught her wiping her eyes with her apron.

He bided his time, knowing she would speak when ready. If she had a serious grudge against Fitzjohn, maybe Matilda was right. Maybe they could take Alys into their confidence. The saints knew they could use all the help they could get.

"Poor Cuthbert," Alys burst out, snatching a tankard and scrubbing at an invisible spot. "You ask anyone in the village. They'll all tell you he was a good lad, who wouldn't harm a fly. He was trying to help, that's all."

"What happened?"

"It was two years ago. Sir Reginald was riding through the village, returning from a hunt. The clasp of his cloak must have broken, for it fell off. Cuthbert picked it up and ran to return it, but he startled Sir Reginald's horse, and it shied. Sir Reginald fell and twisted his ankle. He ordered his men to thrash Cuthbert."

"To death?" Huw asked, his blood running cold.

"He might just as well have done. They beat him until his back was raw. That night he took a fever. Two days later he was dead." Alys buried her face in her apron, her shoulders shaking.

"I'm so sorry, Alys." Huw patted her shoulder awkwardly. He never knew how to behave when a woman was weeping.

At that point, Matilda came in. Huw breathed a sigh of relief when she put her arms around Alys, soothing her until she finished sobbing.

Matilda shot him an accusing look. "What have you been saying to her?"

Alys brushed her away, wiping her eyes. "Now don't go blaming your young man. I was just telling him about my nephew. Poor mite. And I worry about my younger brother—he works up at the castle. I hope to God he stays out of Fitzjohn's way."

"I'm sorry," said Matilda, looking lost. "Is there anything we can do to help?"

"Not unless you're offering to carve Sir Reginald up and feed him to the ravens."

Even knowing what he did, Huw was shocked at her vehemence. He held Matilda's eye and gave a significant nod. Her eyes widened in comprehension. Strange to think he hadn't wanted her company on this mission, yet here they were, reading each other as though they'd been married for years.

Matilda led Alys to a chair and handed her a cup of wine. "Alys, what would you say if I told you we might be able to get rid of Sir Reginald?"

"What, kill him, you mean?" Alys asked, darting uneasy glances at the doors and windows.

"Not necessarily. But get him out of Coed Bedwen. Put it back under Welsh control."

A slow smile tugged at Alys's lips, and color returned to her cheeks. "I'd do all I could to help," she said.

"Would you get me into the castle?" Huw asked.

"Get *us* into the castle," said Matilda, glaring at him.

"This is no game, Mallt," he started, but Matilda cut him off with an impatient gesture.

"And I'm no child to be coddled, so stop treating me like one. Owain ordered us to do this together, so either I'm coming with you, or neither of us goes. Which one of us is going to explain to the king why we failed in our mission?" Matilda faced him down, her hands on her hips, her cheeks flushed. It struck Huw that for the first time in his life, he had met a woman whose determination matched his own. Whether that boded well or ill for their task, he couldn't say. What he did know was that she meant every word.

Matilda turned back to Alys. "We're here for two reasons. First to scout out the castle's defenses, which is why *we*"—she glared at Huw—"need to get into the castle. But most importantly, I'm the rightful heiress of Coed Bedwen, and I intend to take it back. The king of Gwynedd has agreed to help. Will the villagers rally behind us?"

Alys's eyes shone. "There's no love for Fitzjohn here, and I guarantee there's not a single man or woman in the village who won't turn out to help. Even if it does mean we're to become Welsh subjects."

Huw bit back a smile. It seemed that to Alys the choice between allying with the Welsh or the devil was a narrow one.

He opened his mouth, but before he could speak Alys asked, "How do you plan to get inside the castle?"

"Do you supply wine or ale to the castle?"

"Both," replied Alys. "But why—?"

"Who delivers it?"

Alys's face lit up in comprehension. "I usually pay a couple of lads to take it up in my cart. You mean, you—?"

Huw nodded. "Your next delivery will be taken by me and Matilda. It's time we had our first look around the castle."

"When are they expecting the next delivery?" asked Matilda.

"Tomorrow morning," Alys replied.

Chapter Ten

Huw returned to his task of lifting the wine jugs onto shelves, aware of the familiar tightening between his shoulder blades he always felt when action was imminent. This time it was worse because he not only had himself to worry about, but Matilda as well. He still couldn't be sure Matilda wouldn't do something to give them away. Not that she would do it deliberately, but that her inexperience would lead her to make a mistake. He would leave her behind, only she wasn't one to sit back while others acted. The way she had flung herself into hatching her own escape plot from Redcliff was proof of that. If he left her here, he feared she would go alone.

"I won't let you down, Huw."

Huw set the jug he was holding upon the shelf with great care, to show Matilda he hadn't been startled by her sudden appearance behind him. Only then did he turn to face her. "And how do you know that's what I was thinking?"

"Partly by the black scowl on your face, but mostly from the way you've lined up those pitchers with a precision a master mason would envy."

A glance over his shoulder showed him a line of jugs, all the same distance apart, handles protruding at identical angles. His lips twitched and some of the tension drained from his shoulders. "You can read people well. That's encouraging."

"I wouldn't have insisted upon coming if I hadn't thought I could manage."

"I know that. It's not you I doubt, Mallt. I would feel the same about anyone I was expected to work with. I—"

"Work alone. Yes, you've made that clear."

The irritation in her voice startled him. She seemed to be working herself up to saying something.

Sure enough, he had only had time to place the last two jugs on the shelf when she squared her shoulders. "Huw, don't you—?"

She broke off, frowning, tilting her head toward the back room. Huw listened and heard it too—Alys's quiet sobs.

Matilda handed him a cup. "Pour her some wine. I'll go and talk to her."

She hurried out, leaving Huw wondering what she had wanted to say.

Matilda soon reappeared with Alys, her arm around her old nurse's shoulders. She steered Alys to a bench. "Sit by the fire awhile. I'm sorry we upset you."

"Oh, bless you! It's not you," said Alys between sobs. "But all the talk brought back memories of poor Cuthbert."

Huw handed Alys her wine and then stood back. This was something he would far rather leave to Matilda.

After a quick glance at Huw, Matilda sat on the bench next to Alys and put her arm round her. She didn't say anything at first, just hugged Alys, who cradled the rough pottery cup and gazed blankly into the flames.

Presently Alys stirred and took a gulp of wine. "I'm sorry," she said. "You must think me a foolish old woman."

"Of course not," Matilda said. "There's nothing foolish about mourning a loss. And what happened to your nephew…" She shook her head. "I can't imagine what that must have been like."

Alys nodded and squeezed Matilda's hand. "Thank you for understanding, dear."

As Huw watched, it struck him that Matilda was precisely the kind of woman he would choose to be his wife and the mother of his heirs. She was more than a mere beauty who would grace his household and warm his bed. Her blend of quick wits and courage called to him. He wasn't blind to her faults. He still feared her forthright speech and impulsiveness could get them into trouble, but her kindness and compassion more than made up for that.

A memory of his father flashed into his mind.

"The Comyns were sired by the devil himself." Huw's father stood looking down at Coed Bedwen, his hands clenched in fists at his side. "Never forget what they took from us; never forget that they are evil." Huw shuddered when his father turned, and he saw the desolation and loss in his face. "Promise me that if I fail, you will do your utmost to retake Coed Bedwen and rid the earth of the last of those devil-spawn."

Watching Matilda now, he couldn't imagine anyone less like devil-spawn. Would someone touched by evil take the time to comfort an old woman? He remembered what he had said to Owain when the king had ordered him to fetch her from Redcliff: *"I don't understand why you would want to bring a woman with tainted Comyn blood into your court."*

He shriveled with shame to think of those words now. She may be a Comyn by birth, but she couldn't help that. Her blood was no more tainted than his.

All the same, he had made a vow to his father, and he would never know peace until he had accomplished it. While he could no longer make Matilda suffer for it, he had to find a way to satisfy his oath, too. He was no closer to seeing how he could do that.

After a while, Alys dabbed her eyes with the corner of her apron. "I do feel better now, my dear. Thank you."

"Is there anything else I can do?" Matilda asked.

Alys gave a sad smile. "You've done everything you can. I just have to do my best to get on with my life and pray no one else meets the same fate."

"Huw and I will do all in our power to make sure that never happens," Matilda said. "We'll do whatever it takes to bring Coed Bedwen back into Welsh hands."

"But you're a Norman," said Alys.

Matilda shook her head, her eyes hard. "The Normans have done nothing but deny me my rights," she answered. "I'm done with England and the Normans. My mother was Welsh, and it's time I claimed that side of my heritage."

Her voice was firm, but Huw caught a flicker of doubt in her eyes. He frowned. She needed to be free of all doubt if they were going to be successful. The Welsh and English inhabitants of Coed Bedwen wouldn't support her if they suspected any lingering loyalty to the Normans.

"Don't forget you're married to a Welsh man and your uncle claims you as kin. You *are* Welsh, Mallt." If he used her Welsh name, he could forget her Norman heritage.

The grateful smile Matilda flashed at him sent a shard of guilt arrowing through his gut.

****

Matilda's heart lightened. If Huw could guess her doubts and take the trouble to reassure her, maybe it wouldn't be as difficult to work with him as she had feared. Everything he did was making her misgivings about handing him control on this mission melt away.

Alys gave Matilda a wan smile and then rose to her feet. "I must get on. There's work to be done. Would you two be dears and load the wine barrels into the cart? It won't be long before my first customers arrive, and there won't be time to do it tomorrow. They're expecting the delivery shortly after daybreak."

"Of course," Huw said. Before he left the room, he placed a hand on Alys's shoulder. "You have my word I'll do my utmost to ensure your brother's safety, as well as that of all the other innocent folk in the castle. No one else will suffer your nephew's fate."

Alys smiled and squeezed his hand in silence, then left to do her work.

Matilda swallowed to clear the lump in her throat as she followed Huw to the outhouse where the barrels were stored. The sincerity...the *tenderness*...behind Huw's promise to Alys lingered in her mind. He might be a master of deceit, but he had no reason to lie to Alys. She thought back on all his words and actions. Yes, he had been harsh at times, but then he had led a harsh life. However, so far, he had done everything he had said he would. He had said he'd get her away from Redcliff and he had. He'd promised to deliver her safely to King Owain and he had.

He was a decent man. A good man. He didn't deserve her mistrust.

"Huw, I owe you an apology," she said once they were in the outhouse.

Huw paused in the act of placing a plank of wood to form a ramp up to the cart. "What do you mean?" he asked, frowning.

"I never apologized for drugging you that night."

Huw leant back against the cart. "I can't blame you," he said. "I was angry enough at the time, but I understand why you did it."

She shook her head. She wanted to get her feelings out in the open so they could work together in mutual trust. "It's not just that. It's my whole manner to you since Owain said we were to marry. I blamed you, thought you had tricked me. But I see now that you were just as shocked as me. And even though I was angry you hadn't told me about your claim on Coed Bedwen, I understand why you held back."

Huw gave a crooked smile that set her pulse fluttering. "I dread to think what you'd have done to me if you'd known. The poppy syrup was bad enough. I've half a mind to appoint a food taster, to keep me safe whenever we quarrel."

Then his smile faded. "Why are you telling me this now?"

"Because there's been so much tension between us. You were right when you said we needed to depend on one another. I wanted to clear the air, make it easier for us to work together."

She hesitated, unsure if she should say what else was on her mind. But if she was serious in dispelling any lingering resentment, she had to be sure Huw had dealt with his side of it. Or at least was willing to try. "The tension's not just on my side, though." She drew a deep breath. "I know you must feel anger over the suffering my grandfather inflicted upon your family. You didn't say anything when I mentioned it before, but I have to know—do you hate me for being a Comyn?"

****

Huw schooled his features to hide his dismay. "I don't hate you, Mallt. What your grandfather did isn't your fault." He rolled a barrel up the ramp to give himself time to think. He was on dangerous ground. If he let slip about the blood oath, it would shatter the fragile trust she had formed for him. She mustn't find out until he had resolved on how to satisfy his oath. And only when Coed Bedwen was safely in his hands. Part of Wales.

Part of Wales. That reminded him of what she'd said earlier and showed him the way to deflect the conversation.

"Did you mean what you said about claiming your Welsh heritage?"

Matilda shoved another barrel up to the ramp, then straightened her back with a wince. "Of course. Until now, all the men in my life have been Norman. They all let me down."

"Even your father?" Come to think of it, he had sensed Matilda was concealing something about her father last time she had mentioned him.

"I know he loved me, but..." She rubbed her temples. "When it mattered, he wasn't there for me. He"—she indicated the barrels standing upon the beaten earth floor with a sharp, angry gesture—"he couldn't face life without my mother, so he escaped from his pain through drink." She gave a sound somewhere between a laugh and a sob. "One day he drank himself into a stupor and didn't wake."

Huw ached for the six-year-old girl who had needlessly lost her father so soon after her mother. He swayed toward her, yearning to take her in his arms, offer the comfort she'd been denied for so long, but her stony expression warned him to stay away.

She shoved at a barrel, sending it thudding into the ones already waiting to be rolled up the ramp. "So, I'm done with England, with the Normans. I want to forget about my Norman side and remember only my mother's side. My Welsh side."

Then her fierce expression softened. "I miss her. I wish she could be here now, to advise me. I'm only just beginning to realize how difficult she must have found it, adapting to life in a Norman household. Until I came to Wales, I didn't know how strange our customs must have seemed to her."

Huw frowned. "*Our* customs?"

Matilda gave him a blank stare. "What do you mean?"

"You said *our* customs, not *their* customs. If you want to be Welsh, you need to claim Welsh customs as your own, instead of Norman ones."

Matilda's shoulders slumped. "You're right." She gave a sharp laugh. "It's funny how my life is the reverse of my mother's. Looking back, I don't think my mother ever felt truly at home in a Norman household. All the stories she told...the songs she sang to me...they were always about Wales. Have I put myself in the same position—am I fated to always be an outsider here? Will I ever truly feel at home?"

She looked so forlorn that Huw's heart twisted. "It's not the same, Mallt. You have family here. Your mother was all alone in England. You've grown up with Welsh songs, Welsh tales, speaking our language."

He closed the distance between them and cupped her chin, forcing her to look him in the eyes, willing her to believe him. And now it wasn't simply so she could convince others of the rightness of her cause. For the moment he forgot she was a Comyn. All he saw was his wife, who needed reassurance. Comfort.

"You *are* Welsh, Mallt. It's in your blood and in your heart. You will always have a home here."

She blinked away the tears beading her eyelashes. "I...thank you," she said. "You're the last person I would expect to understand. I meant what I said back on the hill, you know. I hope regaining Coed Bedwen will help make up for what you've suffered."

She smiled up at him, a soft smile that lit up her face, transforming it from beautiful to breath-stealing. The blood roared in his ears. All thought of Coed Bedwen disappeared. All he knew was he desired her, and he couldn't resist any longer.

A stray lock had escaped from her veil and curled upon her cheek. Unable to stop himself, he reached out and brushed it with his thumb, then traced the curve of her cheek down to her lips. Then he stooped and pressed his lips to hers.

She gasped against his mouth. Her lips were soft and tasted of honeyed wine. When he ran his tongue along them, she opened her mouth with a soft sigh.

A dim warning chimed in the back of his mind,

only just reaching his lust-befuddled senses.

Remember your oath!

He pulled back, gasping for breath. It was one thing to decide Matilda was innocent of her family's blood guilt, quite another to willingly break his oath to the extent of kissing her. His blood oath would always be between them. He should remember that and not let her beauty beguile him.

Even so, it took all his strength to wrench his gaze from her still-parted, full lips and step away.

"Forgive me. I shouldn't have done that." He couldn't look at her, afraid he would lose his senses and give in to his body's yearning. Instead he hefted another barrel and shoved into the cart where it crashed into the others with a force that threatened to burst it open.

****

Matilda's senses swam, and she sagged back against the wall that was mercifully close enough to support her before her knees gave way. What had just happened? One moment his lips had been on hers, his touch sparking her flesh to life like a flint to steel. Yet now he couldn't even look at her.

She pressed trembling fingers to her lips. She had never been kissed before. Never imagined Huw's lightest touch would set her pulse thrumming, leave her aching for more.

"There's nothing to forgive." It was hard to force out the words when the air had been squeezed from her lungs. "If it's because you promised not to touch me until I'm ready..." She hesitated, but she'd always spoken her mind to Huw before, and she wasn't going to stop now. "Well, maybe I'm ready now."

She placed a hand on his arm, but he snatched it

away as though it burned. "This isn't the time or place, Matilda." He hefted another barrel. "Come on; we've got work to do."

His words were a slap in the face, jolting her from her daze. He didn't want her. For all his words of comfort, his protestations that she belonged here, she would always be a Comyn to him. A reminder of all he had lost.

Turning her face away so he couldn't see her hurt, she resumed her task. All she could do was concentrate on her task, remind herself she was here to win back Coed Bedwen, nothing more.

Ignore the ache in her heart. No man was to be trusted, not even Huw ap Goronwy.

****

The sun was only just peeping above the horizon, their shadows stretching far to the west, when they hitched Alys's gray mare to the loaded cart and made the jolting, creaking ride to the castle.

As uncomfortable as it was, Matilda was grateful to be here, away from the stifling closeness of their storeroom bedchamber. She had scarcely slept a wink, painfully aware of Huw's closeness, of his legs tangling with hers each time he shifted in his sleep. She'd ended up balanced at the edge of the mattress, reliving the kiss over and over in her mind. She prayed they would find a means to get into the castle for longer than this brief visit. Many more such nights and she would sicken from lack of sleep.

As they rounded a bend and saw the castle looming ahead, Huw said, "Don't forget we are just looking today. No asking questions, no raising suspicions or drawing attention to ourselves. Simply look, listen, and remember all you see and hear. You never know how useful a piece of information may prove, no matter how insignificant it may seem at first.

"Above all, any talking that needs doing, I'll do myself. You stay quiet."

She bit back a retort at Huw's peremptory tone. It was pointless arguing. Whatever she said or did, she would never make him forget her tainted Comyn blood.

"And one more thing," Huw said. "Try to look less Norman. Slouch. Hang your head. Don't meet anyone's gaze."

As he spoke he seemed to shrink. He lost his confident, almost arrogant, air and hunched upon his perch, his eyes darting to the left and right but never fixing upon a point. She did her best to copy his mannerisms. When Huw gave a slight nod and murmured his approval, she hated herself for the glow of pleasure it gave her.

The gates creaked open when the cart rattled up to them. As Alys had said, they were expected.

A guard approached and leaned against the cart. "You're not the same people who usually bring the wine," he said. "What's happened to them?"

Her heart broke into a gallop. Were they under suspicion already?

"I don't know about any others, sir."

Matilda remembered just in time not to turn and gape at Huw. His voice was hesitant, his Welsh accent so exaggerated it was difficult to understand.

"Alys at the Boar's Head paid us to bring this here. That's all I know."

The guard muttered something under his breath that sounded like, "Welsh scum." Then raising his voice and enunciating each word clearly, as though speaking to a backward child, he said, "Drive the cart up to that doorway over there." He pointed to a building at the far side of the bailey. "The steward will show you where to unload the barrels."

"Yes, sir. Thank you, sir." Huw urged the mare to move on and followed the guard's directions.

Matilda looked around as they crossed the bailey. The first thing that struck her was how much building had happened since she had last been here. It was clear that Fitzjohn had never had any intention of giving up Coed Bedwen. He would never have spent heavily on rebuilding the keep and outer wall in stone or extending the great hall if he had thought Matilda would be taking possession of it.

That meant he was not going to give it up without a fight.

She turned to Huw, about to comment on it, but the words died when she saw the expression on his face—mingled wonder and yearning.

"After all these years, I'm finally here." He seemed to be speaking more to himself than to her.

Matilda didn't know what to say. Suddenly she felt ashamed for having asked him why Coed Bedwen was important to him. It was in his blood as much as it was in hers.

The steward, a graying, thin man with a harassed air, came out to meet them, and Huw quickly regained his servile posture. If Matilda hadn't seen him just now, she would never have guessed what this place meant to him.

"All these barrels are to be stored down in the cellar," the steward said, pointing to the stone steps that led down from the door. "Then collect the empty barrels that have been placed by the steps." He sneered up at Matilda. "I see you Welsh are so lazy, you have to bring your women with you to do your work."

Matilda tensed and came close to snapping at him, but Huw clasped her hand under cover of his cape. He squeezed it, warning her to remain silent. "That's right, your lordship."

Huw's clasp lingered a fraction longer than necessary. Once again Matilda's thoughts flew to the heart-stopping kiss. Was it her imagination, or did his fingers tremble slightly? Then he released her, and the moment passed.

They jumped down off the cart and began the job of unloading the barrels. The steward disappeared into the cellar, leaving them to heft the barrels alone. It was heavy work, but Matilda was grateful for the way it took her mind off Huw's nearness. Now they were in the castle, any distraction could be fatal.

"Let them think we're imbeciles," Huw muttered in Welsh as they unloaded the barrels from the cart. "People are more likely to speak freely in front of someone they underestimate. You know that yourself. Remember the servant girl?"

Matilda nodded. The meeting with Owain seemed so long ago now. As they carried the first barrel toward the steps, she whispered, "Just promise me that when all this is over, we can have a kinder man as our steward."

It was heavy work getting all the barrels into the cellar. Matilda would have loved a drink of some of the wine they had sweated to carry, but the steward was holding a conversation with another man in the cellar and didn't even glance their way as they worked, let alone offer them refreshment.

Huw muttered something in Welsh she didn't understand, but from the tone she doubted it was complimentary.

Remembering Huw's instruction to listen, she did her best to overhear the steward's conversation. He was talking in French, making no attempt to lower his voice. Obviously, he thought she and Huw were too ignorant to understand. Servants moved about unseen, indeed.

"I don't care how long it takes you," he was saying, "I expect you to report the numbers by sundown."

"But I keep telling you, it's impossible," the other man replied, with an emphatic stabbing gesture. Matilda thought he looked familiar. He must have worked in the castle when she'd lived here. "We're working ourselves into an early grave in the stables as it is," he said. "You know Fitzjohn took away half my lads for his timber-felling scheme. Those left are the bare minimum to care for the horses and keep the stables clean. There's no one to spare to help me inspect the yearlings. I can give you an estimate in three days. Not before. Not unless you can supply me with more workers."

"You know as well as I that's not possible." The steward rubbed his forehead. "Very well. I'll give you until sunset tomorrow. And that's my final word."

Matilda picked up one of the empty barrels, hardly able to believe her first attempt at spying had produced such promising results. She climbed the steps, all the while struggling not to send Huw a triumphant smile.

"I know; I heard too," Huw said softly when they

reached the cart.

"If we could get work in the castle, it would make things so much easier," Matilda said.

"Maybe, but it wouldn't be so easy to leave."

"Would you have worried about that if I wasn't with you?" Matilda asked. Surely the Huw who had gone into Redcliff first as a beggar and then as a troubadour wouldn't have hesitated to take work as a servant.

Huw gazed at her for a moment, his mouth drawn in a grimace. Then he nodded. "But let me do the talking."

Chapter Eleven

"Aren't you going to talk to the steward now?" asked Matilda when Huw made no move.

"And let him know we were listening in to his conversation?"

Matilda's cheeks burned with mortification. If she wasn't careful, Huw would decide she was a danger to their mission and would find a way to keep her away from the castle. Part of her wished that she could go back to the Boar's Head and shelter with Alys while Huw worked in the castle. It was only just sinking in what dangers—and hard work—they would face in Coed Bedwen. Huw was used to it, whereas her stomach was tied up in knots at the mere thought of what they might encounter.

"Mallt?" Huw's voice roused Matilda from her thoughts. She looked up to see him watching her thoughtfully.

He put a hand on her shoulder. "Is something the matter?"

She glanced round to check no one was close enough to hear and then said, "It's just...I've not been any help so far. And it didn't even occur to me that going direct to the steward was a stupid thing to do."

"I'm the one who should be apologizing. Mallt, these things are obvious to me because I've been doing this for so long. You're doing much better than I was, my first time."

"Really?" Seeing Huw's grin made her spirits lighten. She couldn't imagine him ever making a careless mistake, but it was kind of him to console her.

The creaking of the cellar door made them both glance round. The steward and the other man walked out into the bailey. Not wanting to be seen loitering, Matilda made a show of tightening the ropes that held the barrels down in the cart to stop them rolling.

Huw joined her. "See? You instinctively know the right thing to do. You're doing well." He secured a loose end of rope. "And now I'll give you some advice. If you want someone to do something for you, make them believe it was their idea all along. It will make your task much easier."

Then, as the men drew closer he hissed, "Follow my lead. Pretend you're tired of travelling."

He climbed up into the cart. "Hurry up, Mallt!" He spoke in French. For a moment she wondered why, until she realized the men would be able to understand. "There's a long way to go today, and we've still got to unload the cart at the Boar's Head."

An inkling of what Huw was trying to achieve sprang into her mind. "Why do we have to leave at all?" she asked, remembering to copy the rough French of a servant, rather than the refined language of a noblewoman. "I like it here."

"You know why. Alys can only give us work for a few days. In a small village like this, we're unlikely to find more. We'll fare better in Shrewsbury." He shook the reins. "Come on, woman, we don't have all day."

Matilda hoisted herself into the cart, and Huw tapped the mare with his whip. With a lurch, the cart rolled forward. What was he doing? Why didn't he wait?

She clutched his arm. "Huw—"

"Patience."

The cart trundled to the gates, and the steward turned away. Matilda slumped in her seat. They had failed. The steward was going to let them leave, and their best chance of getting into Coed Bedwen was gone.

She caught a movement from the corner of her eye. She glanced back. The other man—she guessed he was the stable master—was speaking to the steward, punctuating each word with emphatic jabs of his forefinger. Then he pointed at Huw. Matilda held her breath when the steward looked their way. Finally, he gave a curt nod and broke into a run.

The cart was already rolling down the steady incline toward the gates when the steward caught up with them and took hold of the mare's harness, bringing them to a halt.

"Did you say you're looking for work?" he asked.

"That's right, sir," Huw replied. "We're heading for Shrewsbury."

"And why are you looking for work in the first place?"

"We lived on a farm a day's walk to the west, but it was struck by fever last summer. So many died that my lord had to abandon it. We've been seeking work ever since." Even though Huw could speak perfect French, he spoke haltingly and with a far more pronounced accent than usual. Yet again, Matilda was struck by how he seemed to become the person he was acting.

"As it happens, we need a hand to work in the

stables, if you're willing."

"I don't know." Huw picked up the reins again. "I think we'd do better in Shrewsbury."

Matilda felt a jolt of shock. What was he playing at?

"That's a long way to go without being certain of work."

Matilda breathed again. It seemed Huw was right. Now the steward thought this was his idea, he was determined to get his way.

"There's my wife to think of as well." Huw indicated Matilda.

"We could find work for her, too. The laundresses need help. The wages are a penny a day."

It was time to give Huw a helping hand. Matilda took his arm. "That sounds generous to me," she said, praying neither man sensed her horror of working as a laundress. "I'm sure we'll be better off here."

Huw gave a grudging nod. "If that's what you want." He turned to the steward. "I accept your offer."

The steward's harassed expression faded. "Good. Report to me tomorrow morning."

Huw nodded and set the mare to walk on.

Only when the gate closed behind them did Matilda grin at Huw. "You did it! And you were right—the steward was practically begging you by the end."

She went cold as a thought struck her. "Did you do that to me when I asked you to take me away from Redcliff?"

Huw shifted on his perch. "What do you mean?"

"You know what I mean. Did you manipulate me into accepting your help?"

Huw rubbed his forehead. "You have to understand I didn't know you then. I was just trying to find a way to persuade you to come."

"So you did manipulate me." Matilda didn't know what to think about that. After all, she had been desperate to leave and without his help, she might still be in Redcliff.

"Is that going to be a problem?" Huw asked.

"You haven't done it since?"

"No. I know how important trust is to you. I promised to be open with you, remember."

She relaxed. After all, he hadn't needed to admit to tricking her. She would have been none the wiser if he'd denied it.

I can trust him, she thought. *I must.* But she still couldn't silence the tiny voice of doubt.

"I hope you won't mind laundry work." Huw picked up one of her hands and brushed the palm with his thumb. "I'm afraid your hands will suffer." Matilda shivered. How could he not feel the crackle of lightning between their hands?

"I can't say I like the idea." She coughed to clear the tremble from her voice. His touch made her think of their kiss, how only the lightest brush of his fingers had scorched her flesh. Blessed saints, if only a simple touch could scatter her wits like this, what would happen if he kissed her again?

What were they talking about? Ah, yes. Laundry. "It's necessary. I'd do anything to reclaim Coed Bedwen."

Huw looked at where his thumb was circling her palm as though he'd only just noticed what he was doing. He dropped her hand in her lap, recalling her from her sensual memories with a jolt.

"Tell me what you noticed in the castle."

She folded her hands, studying them as she struggled to order her chaotic thoughts. She mustn't let Huw know how much his touch affected her. "The main thing I noticed was the changes that have been made in the buildings. My buildings!"

"Ours."

She gave him a crooked smile. "Very well, ours. Although as far as Sir Reginald is concerned, they are mine. The keep has been completely rebuilt. It was wood when I lived here."

"He obviously doesn't intend to give them back. And he's doing his best to ensure no one takes them from him." He paused then went on, "How many guards did you see?"

"I only saw the one on the gate, but I assume there were two, like at Redcliff."

"Never assume. Always check." His expression softened. "Although there were two, in fact. I did look."

"Then why ask me?"

"Because you need to know what to look out for. We don't know how often we'll be able to meet. You must be able to act independently. In fact..." He eyed her thoughtfully.

"What is it?"

"There's a task that needs doing, and you'll be better placed to do it than me. But I don't want to force you if you're not up to it."

She straightened her back. "Whatever it is, I can do it."

"Don't promise anything until you hear what I want you to do. It's risky."

"What is it?" She quailed at the thought of the danger, but she had to prove herself to him. Convince him she was necessary.

"If Fitzjohn has any sense, he'll have food and water supplies in the keep in case of trouble. At the first sign of attack, he'll retreat there, and we'll be forced to sit out a lengthy siege. We don't have the men or resources for that. However, if one of us can get into the keep and salt the supplies, he wouldn't be able to stay there."

"And that's what you want me to do?" It took all her effort to keep her voice steady.

"As a laundress you'll have access to all the living areas of the castle and the kitchens. I would be questioned if I was seen there, but—as you pointed out to Owain—you would be able to pass unnoticed."

She gave Huw a shaky smile. "I might have known you would get your revenge for that sooner or later." She drew a deep breath. "Very well, I can do it."

"Are you sure?"

"Very."

"You're a brave woman, Mallt."

Mallt. She liked it when he called her that. It helped her forget her Norman side. Forget her life as Matilda and the men who had let her down.

After a short pause, Matilda said, "What did you spot at the castle? You never did say."

"To be honest, I didn't notice much more than you in the bailey, except to confirm the number of guards at the gate." Matilda felt a fleeting satisfaction. "But there was one thing that needs further investigation."

"What was that?"

"Didn't you notice how draughty the cellar was?"

"Yes, but what of it? It's a large space."

"But there was only one door. And no windows. Yet there was a distinct current of air."

"Maybe there was another door we didn't see."

"Maybe. But it's worth investigation."

****

All thoughts of draughty cellars were far from Matilda's mind when she approached the laundry yard at the rear of the great hall. Just before walking up to the castle, Huw had grabbed Matilda's hands and scrubbed them with a handful of soil.

"Ow! What's that for?" she had cried, cradling her sore, filthy hands to her chest.

"If you turn up for work with soft, white hands that have obviously never done anything more strenuous than embroidering a hem, you'll rouse suspicion."

Well, there was no chance her hands would pass as a fine lady's now. The nails were rough and blackened, and although her palms were free of calluses, they were reddened and scratched.

Yet despite his treatment of her hands, the thought topmost in her mind was how much she would miss him. They would be apart most of the day. It was odd how she had got used to his company in the short time she had known him. She felt safer with him.

She stopped dead, in the middle of the bailey. *She felt safer with Huw.* Protected. When had that happened? It was years since she'd felt safer with a man than alone.

"You, girl! What are you doing?"

The hail jolted her back to awareness, and she saw the steward looming over her, hands on hips. "You're not being paid to stare at the sky like a moonstruck

157

maid. Get to the laundry yard this instant."

Her cheeks scorching, she stammered an apology and hurried away. That would teach her to think about Huw when there were more important matters requiring her concentration.

The laundry yard was behind the great hall, next to the kitchens. It was out of sight of the bailey, at the edge of a steep cliff that overlooked the river. There was no wall here; the cliff was defense enough. From here she could see the whole of the bend in the river that cradled Coed Bedwen. The ford was visible and beyond it the long road that wound south and east through low hills to Shrewsbury. She could almost forget she was in a castle, if it weren't for the two women bending over huge wooden tubs in the lee of the great hall, scrubbing sheets and chattering like starlings.

"How dreadful," said one of the women, the older of the two, tall and lean with a streak of gray hair peeping out from below her head covering. "Isn't there anyone he can appeal to?"

"Who would he go to?" said the younger woman, a mouse-like girl in comparison to her companion. "It's all Normans in charge here now. He'd never get a fair hearing."

She straightened up then and saw Matilda hovering beside the wooden frame where several dripping sheets were already draped. "Hello," she said. "Are you the new girl? We were told to expect you."

"That's right. I'm Mat—Mallt," she said, cursing herself for nearly stumbling at the start.

"We're glad to have you here, Mallt," said the older woman. "I'm Nesta, and this here is Elen. And this"—she pointed to a tub next to hers—"is where you'll be working. We've a lot to get through today, thanks to the steward, in his wisdom, deciding all these linens are to be washed."

Matilda wasted no time but rolled up her sleeves and picked the first of the coarse sheets from the pile. Then with surreptitious glances at the two women, she copied their actions, plunging the sheets into the tub. It wasn't long before her knuckles were raw from rubbing the coarse linens. The mixture of water, wood ash and lye stung, inflaming the cuts. She was grateful for the warmth of the sunshine on her back. The thought of doing this job in the winter made her shudder.

"I couldn't help overhearing what you were saying earlier," she said to Elen. "Is something wrong?"

"It's my brother," Elen said. "My family has always held a farm a few miles from here. When my parents died, my brother took it over, only for the bailiff to tell him the farm is on Coed Bedwen's demesne. Suddenly, from being a free Welshman, he's become an English serf."

Matilda was too shocked to speak for a moment. "I'm new to this area," she said after a moment. "Has this sort of thing been going on for long?"

"Ever since the Normans first arrived," Nesta said. "And it's only got worse since William Comyn died."

Matilda's heart clenched. She hadn't been prepared to hear of her father, especially in terms of Norman injustices. It was all she could do to bite back assurances that when she took over at Coed Bedwen she would make sure Elen's brother was reinstated. She missed Huw's steadying presence. If he were here, she'd be more confident of avoiding careless mistakes.

For a strange reason, the thought of him helped

focus her mind. Gathering her courage, she encouraged the women to tell her what they thought of Coed Bedwen. By noon, she had learned more than she ever wanted to know about the habits of the folk who inhabited the castle. But at least the women had proved entertaining, which had kept her mind off the discomforts of her task.

Her back ached, her knuckles were bleeding, and the arms and front of her gown were soaked, intensifying the chill from the breeze. She would never look down on a laundress again. She plunged her hands into the cloudy water and muttered a particularly ripe oath as it stung her raw hands. Then she laughed at herself. Matilda would never use such language; Mallt clearly did.

She had never been so glad to hear the noon bell ring, calling everyone to dinner. She was about to follow Nesta and Elen when she saw Huw, leaning against the corner of the hall.

"You go on ahead. I want to talk to my husband," she called.

"Take your time," Nesta replied, looking Huw up and down. "I'd want to do more than talk if I was married to him."

The two women ran off, giggling, leaving Matilda to curse her fair complexion, for she could feel her face burning.

"How has your morning been?" Huw asked as soon as the women were out of earshot.

"Tiring," she said with a grimace. "But I've already found out more about Fitzjohn's treatment of the villagers." She told him what she had learned about Elen's brother. "First Alys's nephew and now this. We shouldn't have trouble persuading people to revolt if that's how Fitzjohn treats everyone."

"Good work. Anything else?"

"I've found out where the salt is stored—in one of the outhouses next to the kitchen. As soon as I have a valid excuse to get into the keep, I'll see to the supplies."

"Take your time; don't take any unnecessary risks."

"I won't. How has your morning been?"

"Uneventful. I've been exercising the horses under the stable master's watchful eye. I'd hoped to get him to talk, but he's proving close-mouthed. If I can get away this afternoon, I intend to investigate the cellar."

****

By the time Huw returned to the stables after the noonday meal, he was feeling more confident about Matilda's abilities. The gossip she had learnt from the laundry women could prove vital, and she had already tracked down the salt store. Maybe working with her wouldn't be so bad after all.

"Here," said the stable master when he got in, "you can shovel out the muck in the stalls now the horses are out for their exercise."

The stable master left, leaving Huw alone. Yes, Matilda was far better placed for learning the castle gossip.

He had just returned from wheeling the last cartload of manure to the dung heap when the stable master approached him, a leather strap in his hand. "Take this to the blacksmith and get him to mend the buckle. You've earned yourself a break. There's no need to come back until it's done."

This was the opportunity Huw had been waiting for. The blacksmith was on the far side of the bailey, not far from the gate. Once he left the strap with the blacksmith, he sauntered up to the keep, his thumbs in his belt, doing his best to look as though he was simply stretching his legs. However, when he reached the cellar door, his hopes were dashed. It was locked. Of course it would be, with the amount of wine stored in it. He would have to pick the lock if he was going to investigate the source of the draught, and he couldn't do that in daylight.

The blacksmith wouldn't have finished with the buckle yet, so Huw strolled around the other bothies nearby. His mind wandered to his oath, trying to find a way to reconcile his denial that Matilda was a fair target for revenge with his need to fulfil his promise to his father.

Maybe he should do as Owain suggested and accept a blood price. Matilda might be innocent, but his heart cried out for restitution. The Comyns should be made to pay for their crime.

The problem was, there was only one payment he would accept—Coed Bedwen. Could he take Coed Bedwen and force Matilda to leave, live with her uncle? But Owain had made it clear that Gwynedd depended on this alliance with Powys. And Matilda was key to that. The alliance would be unlikely to survive if he cast aside the king of Powys's cousin.

No. There seemed no way he could fulfil his oath.

Unbidden, memories that had been clamoring for attention since he had met Matilda surfaced. *His great-uncle, grasping him by the arm after his father's funeral, breathing wine fumes into his face as he spoke.*

"Why should I keep you here any longer? You own nothing, you bring me nothing. You are *nothing!"*

He shuddered, shaking off the memories. He had fought long and hard to become someone other than the frightened, lonely boy his great-uncle had cast out. And the feeling that in pursuing the blood oath he was restoring his family's honor had gone a long way to achieving that end. But now, where he had once found purpose, there was only emptiness. Maybe his great-uncle was right after all.

There was a flurry of action at the gates when he made his way back to the blacksmith, but he ignored it. The bailey was always full of comings and goings. But when he was on the point of entering the bothy, the stable master ran up, his two grooms in tow. When he saw Huw, he grabbed his arm.

"Quick, man! There are visitors' horses to tend to."

So that was the commotion at the gate. He followed the stable master to where four horsemen were dismounting and handing over their horses to the waiting grooms. Huw hurried to take the horse of a man at the back of the group. It was only as he passed the stable master that he glanced up to see who the leader was.

An icy chill ran down his spine. It was Fitzjohn. He dipped his head to avoid Fitzjohn's gaze. All the way to the stables he could think of only one thing: he must warn Matilda.

Chapter Twelve

All Huw wanted to do was abandon the horse and race to the laundry yard.

As soon as he had led the horse into the stable yard, he tried to leave, only to run into the stable master.

"Where do you think you're off to?" the man asked, scowling.

"I still haven't collected the strap from the blacksmith," Huw replied, thankful he had a genuine reason. His nerves were jangling to such an extent that he doubted he could have come up with a convincing excuse otherwise.

"That can wait. These horses have been ridden hard. No one's leaving until they've been cared for."

Now the stable master's attention was on him, there was no way he could make his escape. Gritting his teeth, he walked the horse around the yard to cool him down, all the while his heart thundering in his ears. It was only when a glance across the bailey showed him Fitzjohn striding through the doorway of the great hall that he allowed himself to relax somewhat. Matilda was safely in the laundry yard, out of sight, and even if Sir Reginald did leave the hall before Huw could warn her, he wouldn't go there.

"That's it, steady boy." He led the horse in a slow circle. He was talking to himself as much as to the stallion. It was a sign of how much Matilda had beguiled him that he had allowed himself to become so anxious about this setback. Even at times when his own life had been at risk, he had never got into such a fret. It was bad for his judgement and ultimately dangerous for Matilda and himself if he couldn't keep calm.

By the time he closed the stall door on the stallion, the sun had disappeared behind the hills.

"Fetch me that strap now," the stable master said to him, "and then you're done for the day."

"Thank you, sir," said Huw and dashed out. When he finally strode into the laundry yard, he blew out a breath when he saw Matilda pacing at the edge of the cliff.

"Where are the other women?" He glanced around the muddy yard. The huge tubs were now empty, and the drying racks were bare.

"They've gone to the hall. I told them I was feeling faint and wanted some air."

Good. They could talk freely.

"You're leaving," he said. "Come on. I'll take you back to Alys. If necessary, I'll tell the guards at the gate that you're down with a fever. They won't be able to get you out of here fast enough."

She stepped back, folding her arms. "Why? We've already been through this. I'm staying here."

"Fitzjohn is here. In the hall."

Matilda paled. "What's he doing here?"

"It doesn't matter. All you need to be concerned with is the fact that he's here. If he sees you, he'll cart you back to England, and you won't step beyond the gates of Redcliff until you're his wife."

"But he can't do that. I'm your wife now."

"Once he finds out, he'll do his best to ensure you're my widow."

Her eyes narrowed. "Don't try to manipulate me, Huw. I know your tricks, remember. You think I'll beg you to take me to safety if I think your life's in danger. Well, you're wrong. Sir Reginald is looking for Matilda Comyn, a Norman lady. He won't look twice at Mallt ferch Gwilym, the laundress."

Huw cursed. It hadn't occurred to him to trick Matilda into leaving. If it had, he would have been far subtler. "I wasn't trying to trick you, Mallt. I just want you to be safe. What caused you to mistrust men so? You can't judge us all by Fitzjohn's actions."

Then he remembered the warning glance she had directed at Alys when Alys had mentioned her father. "Or is it your father?"

She flinched.

"It *is* your father, isn't it? What did he do?"

"Nothing." She folded her arms across her stomach as though it ached. "Oh please, Huw, I'm tired and cold. Can't you leave it? I just want to lie down and go to sleep."

He saw then the dark smudges under her eyes and the soaking wet sleeves that were rolled up to her elbows. Of course she must be exhausted. He bet she had never done such a hard day's work in her life, and she was facing the prospect of doing it all over again the next day. And the next. He wouldn't push her any more tonight. But it didn't mean he would let the matter drop entirely.

"Very well." He took her arm. "We'll be bedding down in the hall. Stay in the shadows and keep your head down, in case Fitzjohn is near."

As they rounded the corner and approached the hall, Huw's eyes fell on the cellar door at the foot of the keep. In the rush of anxiety that had accompanied Fitzjohn's arrival, he had forgotten all about the locked door. With the situation looking ever more dangerous, he must investigate the cellar that night. The sooner Matilda was out of here, the better.

For a moment he considered waiting until Matilda was asleep and going without her. Then he pictured her expression when she found out. No more secrets. Not if he wanted to gain her trust.

In the twilight, he could see people from all over the castle, hurrying toward the hall. He pulled Matilda off the path, far enough to avoid being overheard.

"I tried to get into the cellar earlier, but it was locked," he said. "As soon as everyone is asleep, I'm going to pick the lock."

"Then you'll need a lookout." Matilda put her hands on her hips and looked at him with eyebrows slightly raised. It was clear there was only one way this argument would end.

He sighed. "I'll wake you when it's time."

To his surprise her face lit in a glowing smile. "Thank you."

"What for? Putting you in even more danger?"

"No. For telling me what you planned. You could have crept out leaving me none the wiser." She took his hand and pressed it. "I'm starting to believe I can trust you after all."

****

Bedding down in the hall was a new experience for Matilda. When she had lived in Coed Bedwen with her parents, they had slept in a curtained off room behind the dais. In Redcliff, Fitzjohn had living quarters in the keep. Curling up on a pallet with everyone else in the household was uncomfortable, not just because the straw in the thin mattress was lumpy, but also because she was unused to sleeping among such a mass of people.

In contrast to the physical discomforts, however, her growing ease with Huw both surprised and warmed her. Until now, no man had confided in her or deigned to discuss anything besides domestic concerns with her. Yet despite Huw's initial objections to her company, he had respected all her contributions to their venture, even going so far as to allow her to join him in the risky exploration of the cellar. Yes, she was nervous of discovery, but her fears of Huw were subsiding.

"At least Fitzjohn doesn't seem to be here," Huw murmured as he dragged a couple of pallets against the wall, the flickering firelight turning his shadow into a stooping giant on the plastered walls. Matilda wished they could go closer to the fire, but she could see the wisdom of remaining here, where there was no light save the occasional amber pool cast by rush lights.

It was too cold to consider removing their clothes. Besides, they would wake everyone up if they stumbled around getting dressed when they got up in a couple of hours. She just curled up on the hard pallet. This time she was so tired that when Huw climbed in beside her, she made no effort to move away.

She sniffed. "Uurgh! Did you roll in manure as well as shovel it?"

She felt Huw's chuckle vibrate against her back. "Count yourself lucky I didn't get work cleaning out the cesspits."

Then more softly, he said, "Go to sleep, Mallt. I know you're tired. I'll wake you when it's time."

She closed her eyes, but she couldn't clear Huw's words from her mind.

"It is *your father, isn't it? What did he do?"*

They nagged at her. Brought back memories she had tried so long to bury. A butterfly and the words: *I'll always be there for you.*

No! She clamped her hands over her eyes. She mustn't think about it. It was too painful. And she was tired. Too tired to face up to the grief, the abandonment that always accompanied those memories.

Gradually the murmur of voices in the hall quietened down. The fire crackled and spat. Huw stirred, pressing closer, and it struck her how comfortable she felt with him beside her. His presence calmed her, banishing the bad memories. Instead her mind wandered to those breathless moments in the Boar's Head outhouse, when Huw had kissed her.

Was it possible? Had she really found a man different from all the others? He hadn't needed to tell her of his plan to break into the cellar, yet he had. He had praised her when she had earned it, and he had shown compassion to Alys. Everything he had done since arriving here had revealed him to be honorable. Trustworthy.

And the way her insides fluttered when Huw stirred again, brushing her thigh with his, told her that her feelings might have gone further than just trust.

The warmth of his body comforted her, made her feel safe. Her tired muscles eased, and soon she drifted toward sleep.

Steady pressure below her ear awoke her, and she

was instantly alert. Aside from the odd grunt or snore and the waves of sonorous breathing, all was quiet in the hall. Huw was kneeling beside her, his face just visible in the firelight. He put his finger to his lips and then pointed to the door. She nodded and rose to her feet, allowing him to take her hand to help her up. Then, still clutching his hand, she allowed him to guide her around the perimeter of the hall toward the door. Huw must have the eyes of a cat, because he managed to get them there without stumbling over any of the sleepers stretched out on the floor.

She held her breath as Huw reached out for the latch and lifted it. Did the hinges creak? She couldn't remember. She just had to hope that anyone who saw them creep out would think they were seeking out a quiet spot to enjoy a tumble together.

Fortunately, the huge double doors had a smaller wicket gate set in it. This was the one Huw opened, and Matilda released a shaky breath when it swung open with only a whisper of a creak. Huw put his hand to the small of her back and guided her through, then he followed. Just the press of his hand sent flickers of desire through her blood. She could almost believe they truly were sneaking out to find somewhere to couple. Her heart gave an uneven thud at the thought.

Out in the bailey, the chill air cleared her senses. She chided herself for her lack of concentration. Huw had trusted her enough to bring her, and she would not let him down by allowing her attention to stray.

She studied the view carefully. The bulk of the keep loomed ahead of them, blotting out the stars. Straining her eyes, she could just make out the figures of watchmen at the gates and upon the walls. The saints be praised, they were gazing out across the village so wouldn't notice them creeping across the bailey.

His hand still on her back, Huw steered her against the long wall of the hall. He pressed his lips to her ear.

"Keep in the shadows. Crouch down; it will break up your shape. Make you look more like a shadow than a person."

She nodded, trying to shake off the erotic images caused by Huw's lips against her ear, and stooped. They followed the wall toward the keep.

They had just reached the point where the straight wall of the hall met the curve of the keep when the noise of creaking hinges made them shrink into the corner. A shaft of yellow light streamed out into the bailey from a point higher up, a short distance around the circumference of the keep.

Then, silhouetted against the light, two figures appeared. They must be standing at the top of the steps that led into the keep. Blood roared in her ears when she recognized the bulky outline of Sir Reginald.

The other man spoke first, and Matilda recognized the voice of Fitzjohn's constable. "I'm sorry I was unprepared, my lord. Perhaps if you'd sent us warning ahead of your arrival, I—"

"Cease your babbling. I'm not interested in excuses."

The sound of Fitzjohn's voice made Matilda cling to Huw. He took her hand and gave it a reassuring squeeze.

Fitzjohn continued, "I'm here in search of Matilda Comyn."

It was all Matilda could do not to squeak. She clung onto Huw all the tighter. It was only his comforting presence that prevented her from running away and gave her the strength to continue listening to the man she most feared.

"She ran away from Redcliff at Easter. I've had my men searching for her. I even appealed to King Stephen, but so far there's been no sign of her."

"She's not here, my lord, I'm sure of that."

Despite her ice-cold fear, or maybe because of it, Matilda was overcome by an insane desire to laugh. She pressed her hand to her mouth, fighting the attack, struggling not to imagine the look on Sir Reginald's face if he found out she was standing a mere stone's throw from him.

"Well, make sure your men are on the alert for her," Sir Reginald said. "I want the guard doubled. I wouldn't put it past her to appeal to her family in Wales for help. If they take it into their heads to get involved, there'll be all hell to pay. You know what they're like when that *galanas* business of theirs is involved, and I'm sure I've brought enough of them down on my head by now."

Galanas. She was sure she'd heard that word before, but she couldn't think clearly enough just now to remember. She would have to ask Huw later.

The conversation ended, the constable strode down the steps and toward the hall doors. He passed so close that his cloak fanned Matilda's face.

Sir Reginald muttered to himself for a moment, then the door slammed shut, snuffing out the light.

Matilda released a shuddering breath.

"That was close," Huw murmured. Then he pulled her nearer. "You're shaking!"

She fought to keep her voice low. "What do you

expect? You'd be shaking too if you knew you were being hunted."

"It's not too late to change your mind. You *should* change your mind. They wouldn't find you at the Boar's Head."

"No. And I've already given you my reasons for staying. I won't waste my breath repeating them. We knew Sir Reginald would be looking for me, so nothing's changed. It was just disturbing to hear it from his mouth, that's all."

"Come on, then." Huw took her arm. "Everyone's out of sight again. Let's find that door."

They crept around the foot of the keep, passing the stairs where a pair of torches set in sconces marked the main entrance to the keep. Not far beyond that, they came to the dark recess where the cellar door stood. Huw fumbled in his pouch and brought out a narrow bundle of cloth, about the length of his hand. When he unwrapped it, she heard the clink of metal. Peering around his arm, she saw he was holding a set of long, needle-like pieces of metal, twisted into various hooks.

Huw grinned up at her. "The tools of the spy's trade."

He was going to pick the lock with them. She stepped forward to watch, but Huw shook his head. "I need you to stand lookout. If we're caught breaking in…"

There was no need for him to finish. Matilda could imagine the outcome only too well.

She stationed herself at the edge of the shadows, straining her eyes and ears for the slightest movement. A slight movement up on the wall made her catch her breath. It was a watchman, but she relaxed when she saw he was standing with his back to the courtyard, gazing out into the darkness beyond the castle. Behind her, through the pounding of blood in her ears, she could just discern a faint metallic scratching. Then came a tiny but distinct click. Huw opened the door a fraction, then gestured to her to wait.

"We'll need this." He pulled something out from the breast of his tunic. He darted back to the foot of the keep's staircase and then returned, shielding something that glowed with his hand: a candle. He must have lifted it from the hall.

He walked to the open door. "Are you coming?"

Chapter Thirteen

Huw ducked through the door.

"Wait!" he said to Matilda who moved to follow him. He groped along the wall until his hand plunged into a niche. Here was one of the cresset lamps he remembered from their last visit. He lit the three wicks with his candle, cursing under his breath at the hot wax that spilled over his fingers, then he located the lamp on the opposite wall and lit that as well.

He ushered Matilda inside. "I didn't want you falling down the stairs." He pointed to the shaft that opened near his feet, now illuminated by the pale glow from the lamps.

"Now let's find the source of that draught." Pausing only to wedge the cellar door ajar to ensure a through draught, he descended the staircase, holding the candle aloft. The familiar thrill of chasing secrets flooded his body, mingling with the sense of danger, shortening his breath.

He reached out for Matilda's hand and found it clenched and chilled.

"You don't have to come," he said. "You could stand watch if you'd prefer."

"I'd rather be in here," she replied. Despite the slight shake, her voice was resolute. "I feel safer with you."

An unexpected warmth flooded his heart. He'd

never imagined he could feel such a surge of possessive pride or take such joy in being Matilda's protector. He squeezed her hand and felt her fingers relax and then entwine with his.

Not that what he was doing now could be described as protecting her. His stomach twisted into a knot of guilt. He would have to take especial care with her, because he'd never forgive himself if she came to harm.

"Stand there," he said to her when his feet reached level ground. "I'll light some more lamps. We don't want to be tripping over things at every move."

It didn't take long to light just enough lamps to see by. He had taken careful note of their whereabouts when they delivered the wine. The wavering light set the shadows dancing on the whitewashed walls and showed him barrels, clay jars, and bales of wool stacked around the room.

"Now," he said, "can you feel the draught?"

They both walked around the chamber. Huw prayed he was right about the existence of another opening in the cellar, or they would have wasted a much-needed night's sleep. In the back of his mind was the hope they would find a hidden way out of the castle. It would mean a speedy end to their time in the castle and right now he wanted to get Matilda away from here to a place of safety as soon as possible.

"Here!" said Matilda suddenly. "I can feel air on my cheek."

Huw stood beside her and held his candle up, passing it back and forth in front of him. At one point the flame flattened, coming close to blowing out.

He allowed himself a satisfied smile. "The air is coming in through the door, so it must be moving toward that wall." He pointed to a towering stack of barrels. "It would be barrels. Why couldn't it be wool?" After a day of shoveling manure, his muscles protested at the prospect of more lifting.

He blew out the candle and set it down, then moved over to the closest barrel and heaved it on its rim, half rolling, half dragging it aside. The draught was definitely stronger here.

Matilda joined him, and they lifted the barrel together.

"Huw, what does *galanas* mean?" she asked.

He nearly dropped his end of the barrel. "Why do you ask?"

"Sir Reginald mentioned it just now. I think I've heard the word before, but I can't remember where."

Praying that she would never link it with him, Huw said, "It's the law relating to a blood feud. Have you heard of the English *wergild*?"

They finished moving the barrel, and Matilda straightened up. "Wergild? Isn't that a fine paid for injuring or killing someone?"

"That's right. It's to prevent blood feuds from spiraling down the generations." Should he demand a blood price from Matilda when they were safely in charge of Coed Bedwen? Would that satisfy his vow to his father? His father had wanted blood, but Huw knew he could never harm her. Yet how else could he satisfy the oath that was all the more binding now his father was in his grave?

It was a problem that needed to be resolved soon. And alone. It wouldn't do for Matilda to learn the true nature of his vow, not when her trust in him was still wavering.

Matilda moved to the next barrel. "In that case I wouldn't be surprised if Sir Reginald owed a fortune to many families around here. We've only been here for a day, and already we've found out about Alys's nephew. And, of course, what happened to Elen's brother was terrible, even though no one was hurt or killed. I should think there were plenty of people who would be glad to see Sir Reginald out of Coed Bedwen. I doubt we'll have trouble persuading folk to join a revolt."

"You may be right," he said, relieved she hadn't linked the idea of *galanas* to their own families. "But that means we'll have to be on our guard even more."

"Why?"

"There are huge risks. Think about it. If Fitzjohn is even suspicious of such a plot, he might have planted his own agents to pose as rebels. And even if he hasn't, there are still risks. Never forget what a man might do if he fears for his loved ones—he might be compelled to give up his co-conspirators. Or he might turn traitor in return for a reward. Every man has his price. The more people we bring into a plot, the greater the risk."

"I know, I know. And you trust no one."

He gave her a sharp glance and the words came out of his mouth before he could stop them. "At least I have a good reason for my distrust, Mallt."

If he could have cut his words out of the air before they reached Matilda's ears he would have. He had tried to put the incident with the poppy syrup behind them. Dragging it up again would hardly improve the fragile trust they'd built between them. He braced himself for Matilda's snapped response.

Much to his surprise, instead of flaring with anger, she touched his arm. "You're right. Forgive me."

He sighed and covered her hand with his, ignoring the voice in his head that urged him to get on with the task at hand. "I'm the one who should be sorry. It's no wonder you have difficulty trusting me after being in Fitzjohn's dubious care." And what of her father? But he bit back the question. She hadn't exactly taken it well last time he'd pressed her, and they both needed their full attention on the task at hand.

Easier said than done when every inch of his flesh ached to be near her. Lying by her side in the great hall had been pure torture. He had held her as she dozed, guarding her sleep, yearning to roll her beneath him, explore her every curve, not stopping after a single kiss this time but lose himself in the passion he'd sensed the first time their lips had met.

Hellfire! Now he was the one putting them in danger. He dropped her hand and put more space between them. "Come on. We need to find the source of this draught before the night grows old."

The moment he put his hand on the next barrel, it shifted, making him stagger.

"That's strange; it must be empty."

He tapped at the next one, resulting in a hollow thunk. All the other barrels in the same group were likewise empty.

"This must be it," Huw said. His pulse raced. "These barrels can all be easily shifted by one person. There has to be something behind."

He pushed them aside and found a board against the wall behind, rising to about chest height. It wasn't fastened to anything; Huw could lift it aside with one hand.

The moment the board shifted, a strong breeze

ruffled his hair. He found himself gazing into the mouth of a roughly hewn tunnel.

Matilda crouched down beside him and peered into the darkness. "There *is* another way out." Despite her long day in the laundry yard, the scent of honeysuckle lingered on her skin, made no less alluring by astringent overtones of lye.

"We don't know if it leads outside." Huw struggled to maintain concentration. "It might be a path to a well or spring. I know of other castles that have those, to prevent their water supply being cut off in case of a siege."

He went to fetch his candle and relit it from one of the lamps, then returned to the tunnel and used it to light the entrance. The pool of light illuminated the beginnings of a stairway, carved out of the rock. It fell too steeply to see far.

"There's only one way to find out where this leads."

He stooped and entered the tunnel. Matilda followed, her hand on his arm, her touch burning through the woolen sleeve. He was about to put his foot on the first step when a noise that sounded like a faint knock echoed through the passage. He froze, wincing when Matilda's grip on his arm tightened.

"What was that?" Matilda hissed.

The sound of distant footsteps growing nearer saved Huw from answering.

He shoved Matilda back into the cellar, flinging himself after her. His heart beating painfully against his ribs, he pushed her toward the door. "Get out!"

She resisted him. "What about you?"

He pointed to the lamps and displaced barrels. "I'll

follow as soon as I've dealt with those."

To his dismay, Matilda tore herself free and ran back to the tunnel mouth. She tugged the board back in place and heaved at the barrels. "It's quicker if I help."

He was tempted to fling her over his shoulder and carry her out, but then there wouldn't be time to snuff the lamps and replace the barrels. They would both have to take their chances here.

He tore around the cellar, blowing out the lamps, leaving just his candle lit, and closing the door. There wasn't time to move the full barrel he had shifted first, but he didn't think it looked obviously out of place.

The footsteps paused just behind the board. It was too late to escape. He set the candle down on the floor beside a large wooden chest and then shoved Matilda behind the bales of wool, hissing, "Whatever happens, stay there." The last thing he did before diving behind the chest was grab a flask from its top. He prayed it held wine.

He snuffed out the candle and prayed some more.

Without the candle light, the cellar was plunged into a darkness that was a physical weight against his eyes. Wood scraped upon the floor. Then came the hollow knock of the empty barrels being pushed away.

A pool of light appeared on the vaulted ceiling. Huw crouched lower, clutching the flask to his chest. Pray God Matilda had the sense to keep her head down.

There were further grating noises. Whoever it was must be replacing the board and barrels. Huw yanked the stopper from the flask, knowing the slight noise would be masked by the louder scrapes and thuds.

The noises stopped. Huw held his breath. Soft footsteps approached. Then the figure of a man passed his hiding place. He was holding a lantern which cast a golden glow onto a familiar face. It was the stable master. What in Heaven's name was he doing here?

Not that the reason was important right now. All that mattered was for the stable master to leave without noticing their presence. Huw strained his ears for any giveaway movement from the wool bales, but there was nothing. Thank God Matilda was doing what she was told for once.

The moment the stable master reached the steps, he paused. He lifted his head, looking like a hound seeking a scent.

Hellfire! An icy hand squeezed Huw's heart. That was exactly what the man was doing—he could smell the acrid scent from Huw's snuffed candle. He tucked it into his tunic, praying to all the saints he could remember. There was nothing else he could do but pour the wine down his tunic and then place the flask by his foot.

"Show yourself!" The stable master's voice wavered a little.

Good. That might mean he wasn't supposed to be here either. If so, there was hope.

Huw gave a grunt and kicked the flask, sending it skittering across the floor.

The stable master walked back toward him. "Who's there?" he said. "Show yourself."

There was a definite edge of fear in his voice. Huw tucked the knowledge away.

He shifted and groaned. "Go 'way," he mumbled. "Lemme shleep."

A light shone on his face and he made a show of shading his eyes and squinting.

The stable master crouched down and took hold of the front of his tunic. He started to tug Huw to his feet but then let him fall back, his nose wrinkling. "You're drunk," he said. "How did you get in?"

Huw pointed to the door and then let his arm flop to his side. "Door's open. Seems rude t'turn gift down." He was taking a risk, but the stable master was about to discover the door was unlocked, and he didn't want to be revealed as a lock-picker.

Speaking as though to himself, the stable master said, "I must have forgotten to lock it behind me." Huw sent up a silent prayer of thanks that his gamble had paid off.

The stable master tugged his tunic again. "Come on, man; get up. If you're caught here, there'll be all hell to pay."

This wasn't part of Huw's plan. If he went with the stable master, he would be left with the choice of leaving Matilda here, or revealing her presence. "Gerroff. Leave me alone." He tried to bat the man's hands away, but he found himself being heaved to his feet.

"Come along. You'll thank me for this in the morning. I'm saving you a spell in the stocks at the very least."

Wonderful. The man clearly had a conscience. Huw had no choice but to stagger out, leaning heavily on his savior. He hated the thought of leaving Matilda alone in the dark. He just prayed she would trust him to come back for her.

He stumbled on the steps and came to a halt, swaying. "Here, what're you doin' here, anyway?"

"Just some business for the steward, never you

mind what. Best you don't mention it to anyone, and I'll keep it quiet that you were here."

Interesting! He wasn't here legitimately, either. This had the marks of a conspiracy. Was it possible he and Matilda weren't the only ones plotting a revolt?

He allowed himself to be led again. Once through the door, he leaned all his weight on the stable master, making it impossible for the man to hold him. He slumped to the ground.

He felt a hand shake his shoulder, but he didn't stir. The stable master wouldn't want to cause a commotion so would be bound to leave him.

"Don't say I didn't try," the man muttered. "You're on your own now."

Huw heard the grate of a key turning in the lock, then footsteps. He counted to a sufficiently high number to ensure the stable master was out of sight, then he scrambled to his feet. He had only one thought now, and that was to get back to Matilda. She was alone and in the dark and must be terrified he wouldn't return.

It struck him then, a visceral jolt. He would always be there for her, put her safety above all else. Much as he'd tried to deny it, he cared for her.

He had to hold back a laugh, remembering the reason he'd given for his single state when she'd drugged him. It still held true. He had nothing to offer her but danger, lies, and secrets.

Unless he won Coed Bedwen. Yes, he would fight for his birthright and lay this cursed blood feud to rest. Only then would he be a worthy husband for Matilda.

As for his great-uncle's words, he would ignore them. Surely with Matilda in his heart, he could overcome his self-doubt.

****

The darkness pressed in on Matilda, clawing at her eyes, constricting her chest. When she heard the key turning in the lock, she had to press her hands to her mouth to prevent herself from crying out. With Huw here it had been bearable, but to be alone...locked in...

She could try to feel her way to the tunnel. She shuddered. No. It had been bad enough with Huw and the candle to light their way.

Whatever happens, stay there.

Huw's hissed command came back to her. But had he expected to be marched out of here? Had he been captured? She pushed aside one of the wool bales and then sank back. No. She had said she would try to trust him. And after all, if she had done as he'd asked and left when they'd first heard the footsteps, she wouldn't be here alone now. She would wait and trust him to return.

But trusting someone by daylight was one thing, quite another when it meant being smothered by thick darkness, while her mind dreamt up images of Huw, locked in the keep, being beaten. She strained her ears for signs he was coming back, but the blood pulsed in her ears, so she couldn't tell if she was hearing noises from inside her head or out.

With her arms hugged to her chest, she huddled into the soft fleeces, praying Huw wouldn't let her down.

A soft scratching made her sit bolt upright. It came again. A click. The lock turning. Then came a tread on the stone steps. She pressed a hand to her chest to ease the painful beat of her heart. Should she call out? But what if it wasn't Huw?

Then the ceiling reflected a faint glow.

"Mallt?"

She gave a sob and flung aside the bales. "Huw!" She scrambled to her feet and found herself swept into a secure embrace. "I was afraid you weren't coming back."

"I'd never leave you alone, Mallt. You have to believe that."

"I know that now." And she did. Her doubts faded to nothing. In her moment of fear, he hadn't let her down. In all the time she'd known him, he had proved trustworthy. She had just been too foolish, too wrapped up in past fears, to see it.

Still trembling from the terror of the dark, she needed his comfort. Craved the reassurance that only his body could give her. She pulled his head down and captured his mouth in a searing kiss.

He groaned and walked her backward until the back of her knees caught on a bale and they tumbled down on top of it, Huw's weight pressing her deep into the fleece. She ran her hands across his shoulders and down his back, relishing the feel of firm flesh. At the same time, Huw's roving hand trailed fire across her body. When he brushed the side of her breast, she shamelessly shifted molding her breast to his palm.

With a groan, Huw tugged the neck of her gown open and freed a breast from the confines of her shift. Then he lowered his mouth, taking her nipple between his lips, flicking the sensitive tip with his tongue.

Matilda moaned, arching up as sparks of intense pleasure coursed through her, leaving every inch of her flesh sensitized, longing for his touch.

Huw lifted his mouth and cursed. "Heaven help

me, Mallt. If you want me to stop, say so now."

"Don't stop. I need you. I—"

But she was cut off by another demanding kiss.

With so little light, her other senses were heightened. When Huw stripped off her tunic and shift, she lay back on the fleece, relishing its caress on her back and thighs. Just the sound of Huw's clothes falling to the floor inflamed her, as she imagined the hard, muscular body that was being revealed. Then the bale shifted, and a hot tongue trailed down her stomach to swirl around her navel. She whimpered, muscles deep within clenching with longing as the tongue trailed lower.

Soon she was intoxicated by the slide of flesh upon flesh, the rasp of his stubble, his long fingers stroking and teasing her to the peak of pleasure. Then she gasped when he wedged himself between her thighs. Her desire for him overcame her fear of the pain to come; she arched toward him, sliding her hands down his back, pulling him closer.

Then he was inside her, stretching and filling.

She bit back a cry at the discomfort, but he must have sensed her pain for he eased back.

"Should I stop, Mallt?"

"No, oh no!" She tilted her hips, desperate for more. Desperate to show how much she trusted him. Needed him. She wrapped her legs around his waist, urging him deeper.

He eased in until he was fully inside her. She felt impossibly stretched, yet along with the discomfort came a deep joy at knowing she was now joined with Huw in more than just name.

She whispered the one thought that overpowered

all the rest. "Huw!"

As though he had been waiting for it, he withdrew and thrust in again. With each thrust the discomfort eased and the pleasure intensified until she lost all thought of where they were. All she knew was this moment. Flesh on flesh. Huw.

The coil of pleasure in her belly tightened until she thought she couldn't bear any more of this exquisite torture.

Then she arched up against him as she shattered into a thousand pieces, sobbing his name over and over like a litany as she tumbled into rapture. Huw gasped her name in her ear, and she felt him tense in her arms then lie still.

She didn't know how long they lay there, his weight on hers, heartbeats thundering, while their breathing slowed. Gradually she became aware of her surroundings—the scent of candle wax, the tickle of the wool, the chill draught on her damp flesh.

Huw stirred and eased himself off her. "Did I hurt you, Mallt?"

"No." She shifted and winced. "Well, maybe I'm a little sore."

"I'm sorry. I should have waited."

"Don't you dare apologize. I wanted it…needed you. I was so frightened all on my own in the dark. I thought you'd been captured. And then you came back." A half sob caught in her throat. "I never thought I could need you so much. It overwhelmed me."

"I wouldn't have left you there. Even if I'd been caught, I'd have found a way to escape and come back for you. I'll always be there for you."

I'll always be there for you.

Again, those words sounding a dim warning in the back of her mind, but she ignored it. Huw had been there when she had needed him. He had proven he could be trusted. Hope swelled in her chest, and she leaned over him and kissed him, pouring all her gratitude and tenderness into the act.

"What was that for?" Huw asked with a soft laugh when she pulled away.

"To thank you. For being there for me and allowing me to finally believe we might have a happy future together."

For the first time she allowed herself to imagine living in Coed Bedwen with Huw, not in a state of permanent mistrust and fear, but as a couple, meeting the challenges of running the castle together, sharing the frustrations and joys. A couple like her uncle and aunt, who were besotted with each other after years of marriage.

She caught her breath. Was she in love with Huw?

She didn't know. She had no idea what love felt like. But after years of being afraid of love, of fearing the weakness and dependence it brought, she wasn't afraid any more.

****

Huw felt a burst of warmth in his chest. Their lovemaking had silenced his malicious inner voice. Making love to Matilda, hearing her soft gasps of pleasure, feeling her body tighten around him in ecstasy, had made him believe that his oath had lost its grip on him.

"Thank you," he said. "For taking a risk in me. For trusting me when I know you have every reason to mistrust me."

He kissed her again, then sat up with a regretful sigh. "As much as I want to stay here, we mustn't risk being caught. We have to investigate this tunnel and get back to the great hall before it gets light."

He pulled on his clothes, invigorated by a new purpose. Now he wasn't fighting for himself, but for their shared future.

And maybe…just maybe…giving his heart to Matilda would silence that nagging inner voice for good.

Chapter Fourteen

When they reached the steps, Huw took Matilda's hand. "Hold tight. These are steep."

He still wasn't happy to have Matilda here in Coed Bedwen, but now it was nothing to do with anger at her Comyn blood. It was all to do with fearing for her safety. He couldn't bear the thought of anything happening to her. He didn't want to let her out of his sight for one moment, but of course it wasn't possible for them to stay together at all times. It made him more determined to finish their mission in the shortest possible time.

In the meantime, he had to admit it felt good to hold Matilda's hand. His skin still felt sensitized after their lovemaking. His entire body was achingly aware of her. The air crackled between them like sparks of lightning.

"You're very quiet, Huw." Matilda's voice echoed down the rocky passage. "You don't regret what we've done, do you?"

"No. Do you?"

"No." She stumbled on an uneven step. Huw tightened his grip on her hand and steadied her. She gave a soft laugh. "Although perhaps it's affected my concentration."

It came as an unpleasant jolt to Huw to realize he had been so focused on Matilda that he had no idea how far they had walked. "You're not the only one." He drew a deep breath. "We must make more of an effort to concentrate, before we make a slip that could give us away."

"I can't believe I didn't know about a tunnel when I lived here," said Matilda, making a visible effort to study the rough stone walls. It was gratifying that she should take his orders to heart.

"You were very young. Maybe your parents didn't want you to know in case you took it into your head to explore."

"Possibly."

There was another pause while they negotiated a particularly steep section, then she said, "What do you think that man was doing here?"

"The stable master? I hope to find out in a moment. I suspect it was clandestine. He wanted me to keep his presence secret in return for him not reporting me."

"But what—?"

"Hush! We're nearly at the bottom. I can see stars."

The steps finally ended, and the tunnel opened upon a blackthorn thicket. When Huw leaned out, he caught the sound of running water. His pulse quickened. It looked like they had stumbled upon an alternative route into the castle. This could be the key to winning back the castle.

"Are we down by the river?" Matilda asked.

"It looks like it." Huw pushed aside the bushes and stepped out. "Yes. We're still a little way above it, but the cliff isn't so steep here. It would be a scramble, but not impossible to get down to the river. We can't be far from the ford, either. Wait here. I'm going to find out exactly where this leads."

He scrambled down the cliff, finding plenty of footholds to make it down to the river bank with ease. He glanced up to the top of the cliff and saw that whether by chance or design, this section of the bank was out of sight from the keep and the walls. Lower down, the bank was lined with trees, which would provide cover and allow someone to reach the village without being seen.

That was all he wanted to know. He was about to climb back up to Matilda, when he noticed footprints and trampled grass a few paces from where he was standing. He crouched to examine them briefly, then he returned to Matilda where he reported what he had found.

"Can we bring Owain's men into the castle this way?" she asked, her eyes shining.

"We couldn't get a whole army in unseen, but a handful, certainly. One more thing. I saw a mass of footprints down there. At least three men were there recently. I rather think our stable master was meeting some men from the village. Or possibly farther afield. Men he didn't want to be seen with."

"What does that mean?"

"I can't be sure, but maybe our job has just been made easier."

"In what way?"

"It's possible there's already a group of disaffected men waiting for the right time to act."

"And you think you can persuade them now is the right time?"

Huw grinned. "We can try."

****

As Huw staggered into the stable yard the next

morning, he pulled his hood farther over his eyes to shade them and groaned, clapping his palms to his temples. Getting the information he needed required him to play a convincing hang-over sufferer. He did his best to throw off the memory of last night's lovemaking, no matter how much it still clung to him. He needed to look pale and haggard, not glowing with remembered pleasure.

A hand slapped him on the shoulder. "Regretting last night?" He turned and blinked up at the stable master, whose jovial smile failed to conceal a certain tension in his jaw.

"If only I knew what I was supposed to regret," he said.

He studied the stable master carefully. There was a secret here, and he and Matilda had decided last night that finding it out was a necessary next step.

The lines around the stable master's mouth and eyes eased. "Don't you remember anything about last night?"

"The last thing I remember is playing dice with some fellows and sharing a jug of ale. The next thing, I'm lying outside the keep and the stars are fading."

"The keep? It's a good thing you woke up before anyone found you." The stable master pulled him through the door. "It's no use setting you to exercising the horses this morning. You'd better stay inside and clean the tack."

Huw doubted this was for his benefit so much as to let the stable master keep an eye on him in case he recovered his lost memory. It was what he had hoped for. It gave him a chance to draw him out and see if his suspicions were correct.

The stable master pointed him to the far wall, where all the tack hung from hooks. "Start with that. And stay in here until your head clears. You wouldn't want Fitzjohn to catch sight of you in this state."

"Why?" asked Huw, "Is he likely to punish me? I'd have thought I was beneath his notice."

"There's no knowing what he'd do. He's got a violent temper, so I'd avoid him, if I were you."

"Thanks," said Huw. "I'll bear that in mind. I come from farther west, so I'd not heard of him till I arrived here."

Huw scrubbed at a bridle in silence for a while, while the stable master examined the hoof of a gelding in one of the stalls. Presently he came out and leaned against a post.

"You say you come from farther west?"

Huw nodded, buffing a buckle with a soft rag until it gleamed.

"What brings you to Coed Bedwen?"

Huw repeated the tale he and Matilda had agreed. He finished by saying, "My wife and I thought it would be easier to find work in the Marches. Norman households employ more people than Welsh ones."

"Maybe, but the Marcher lords can be cruel masters, Fitzjohn in particular."

Huw's interest pricked. This was where he had been hoping the conversation would lead. However, he had to move carefully. The stable master might have a genuine grievance with Fitzjohn; on the other hand, it might be a trap, a test of Huw's loyalty.

"I'm surprised to hear you say that," he said. "Cruel or not, Fitzjohn is the man who pays, feeds, and shelters you."

"Of course, of course. It would be wrong to speak against him. I'm not doing that, you understand."

Huw scrubbed at a spot of rust, pretending to be engrossed in his task, but he shot a sideways glance at the stable master. The man had a sheen of sweat on his upper lip, and a flush highlighted his cheekbones. However good an actor he might be, those symptoms were impossible to fake. Huw was as sure as he could be that he was not laying a snare. Which meant whatever activity he was engaged in, it was without the knowledge of his superiors and very likely working against them.

Interesting. Yet the stable master had the air of a man out of his depth. If that was the case, Huw needed to find out what was going on so their activities didn't clash. And if there was a group of rebels lacking a strong leader, Huw intended to fill that gap.

"I didn't think you were speaking against them," Huw said to reassure the man. "After all, you are English."

"English, yes. Not Norman." The stable master's face twisted as though he were about to spit. He lacked experience, or he wouldn't have allowed himself to be goaded like that.

"What's the difference? It's all the same to the Welsh."

"I'm a Saxon. We were here long before the Normans took our land. I'm not saying all the Normans are bad, mind you. Most of them are just trying to live a decent life, same as we all are. I was a groom here in William Comyn's time."

"Was he the lord here before Fitzjohn?"

"Yes. He was a fair lord," the stable master replied,

"I'll grant him that, even though it did break my heart, the way he ended things. And he with a young daughter."

"Why? How did he end things?" Huw's grip on the buckle tightened, causing the sharp iron to dig a painful groove in his palm.

"He lost all interest in life after his wife died, even in his daughter—sweet little thing she was, too. He died not long after. Folk say he drank himself to death, but I know the truth."

"What's that?" Could this be what Alys had nearly let slip? Whatever it was, Matilda hadn't wanted him to know. This could be the key to her mistrust of men. Even though things were improving between them, if he learnt the truth about her father, he might be able to help her.

"It was my sister that found him, see, along with his poor daughter, although I pray she was too young to understand. He'd got hold of a flask of belladonna and downed the lot. God have mercy on his soul."

Huw crossed himself, his heart wrung with pity. No one, let alone a child, should have to make such a discovery. No wonder she bore scars. Now his overriding impulse was to dash to the laundry yard, take Matilda in his arms, and promise he would never abandon her as her father had done.

That would have to wait, though. There was a job to be done, and all his instincts told him the stable master would play a large part in it.

"Did Comyn's daughter marry Fitzjohn, then? Is that why he's lord here now?"

"No, poor lass. She's been spared that, for now, at any rate. Fitzjohn already has a wife. Or, rather, had. I gather the poor woman has died. But getting back to William Comyn's daughter, she was made Fitzjohn's ward. It was a black day for her and Coed Bedwen when King Stephen made that decision. By all accounts, Fitzjohn's kept the girl caged away and denied her a marriage. Ever since he's had the management of Coed Bedwen, he's been felling good timber and draining the land dry to fill his own coffers. There are those of us who—"

The lame gelding chose that moment to whinny and stamp his foot. The noise seemed to recall the stable master to himself. He pushed himself upright and muttered, "Never mind. Get on with your work." He retreated into the gelding's stall.

Huw knew better than to press further. The man was frightened, and so he should be if he was scheming against a man like Fitzjohn. He had probably felt able to confide in Huw because as a Welshman, he would be unlikely to hold any love for the Normans. But Huw's mind buzzed, wondering what he had been about to say.

Even more than the stable master's possible conspiracy, however, the matter of Matilda's father occupied his thoughts. He needed to see her as soon as possible.

Accordingly, as soon as the stable master released him for the noonday meal, he dashed round to the laundry yard. Various garments and undergarments were stretched upon the drying racks, but the women had gone, probably to the meal. There was nothing for it but to go and eat and hope to speak to her before the afternoon's work began.

Matilda was with the laundresses and some other women at a trestle table near the door. There was no room for him, so he snatched a quick meal at another table and then left, catching her eye with a meaningful nod as he passed her table. The other women giggled and nudged her, obviously teasing Matilda, suspecting they were arranging a tryst.

Heat pooled in his groin as he remembered their urgent, passionate coupling of last night. He thought back to his objections to bringing her on this mission with a wry grin. Would he have been so against it if he had known then how exciting a hasty tryst in a forbidden room could be? On the other hand, it was so much harder to concentrate on the mission when one's mind was filled with lustful thoughts of ripe curves and a hot mouth.

He paced along the edge of the cliff. Bloody hellfire, he'd better cool his thoughts down before he combusted.

"Do you have news?"

His heart leapt when Matilda appeared. Even in her stained, shapeless gown, she was a beautiful sight. The sunshine gave her skin a lustrous glow, and the guarded wariness that had previously haunted her expression was gone, replaced by an air of confidence.

He brushed away a golden curl that peeped from beneath her coif, his fingers lingering on her jaw. Her eyes darkened, and he knew her thoughts had strayed to last night's lovemaking.

There was no reason why he couldn't make the most of their meeting. He sat on the bank, at a point just before it steepened into the cliff edge and patted the patch of grass next to him. "Come and sit with me, Mallt. Seeing as we're trysting lovers, we might as well act the part."

His pulse sped up when, with a smile, Matilda sat beside him and snuggled against his side.

"I spoke with the stable master this morning," he said. "He told me he used to work here in your father's time."

Her muscles tensed beneath his arm. "Oh? Did he say anything about my father?" Her voice was light. Brittle. It was clear she didn't want him probing her wounds, but now he had allowed himself to acknowledge his deepening feelings he wanted to do everything he could to help her. Heal her.

"He told me he was a fair lord to work for. But..." there was no easy way to put this, so he plunged straight in. "He also said your father took his own life."

She twisted out of his hold. "You wormed it out of him, didn't you? That's what you do—make people tell you things that should remain hidden."

She scrambled to her feet and glared down at him, her arms spear-straight at her sides, fists clenched. "You knew I didn't want to talk about him, so you went behind my back and found out anyway." She choked on a sob and turned her back to him.

Huw closed his eyes for a moment. So much for helping. What had he expected—Matilda to thank him for digging into her past, fling herself into his arms and say all was well? He gave a harsh laugh. He might be expert at worming out secrets, as Matilda put it, but he was a fool when it came to understanding women.

Matilda turned. His gut twisted when he took in her red-rimmed eyes. "Are you laughing at me?"

He climbed to his feet, shaking his head. "I'm laughing at myself, for being such a clumsy oaf." When he put an arm around her rigid shoulders, she didn't pull away. He let out a breath.

"Forgive me, Mallt. Sometimes I get so embroiled in hunting out secrets that I don't know when to stop. Just because you're my wife, it doesn't give me the right to force something from you that you don't want to share. But I wanted to know about your father because it's clear your father's death scarred you deeply, and I can't bear to see you hurting."

Matilda studied him, frowning, then her shoulders relaxed fractionally. "I forgive you. Now, tell me what you've discovered about the stable master, before we have to return to work."

She would have been more convincing had she not glared at him, fists clenched. Still, there was no time to pursue the matter of her father if she was determined to bury the truth. Not that he intended to give up, but there were more important concerns. He sat next to her and related the conversation with the stable master and his suspicions.

"I don't think I can get any further with him unless I can gain his trust," he concluded. "He's clearly nervous. And inexperienced."

"So how do you plan to do that?"

"If we had more time, I could afford to act more cautiously. But with Fitzjohn here—looking for you— we must move fast. I want to take the stable master into my confidence."

"Tell him why you're really here?"

Huw nodded. "But this involves you, too. He knows we're married. If I tell him who I am, I'll have to tell him about you, also. Are you prepared to take that risk?"

She plucked a blade of grass and studied it, her

brow furrowed. "If you're wrong, he'll go straight to Fitzjohn."

"I'm not wrong."

She gave a grim smile. "This is where you're asking me to trust you, isn't it?"

He nodded.

She dropped the grass and wiped her hands. "In that case, when do we approach him?"

Warmth flared in his chest. Just a week ago, she would never have trusted him so readily. With every passing day, her guard was lowering. He had to believe he would eventually gain her complete trust. "We?" he said. "It would be safer if I spoke to him alone."

"If we're both at risk, we both talk to him. And anyway," she looked down, blinking. Huw's heart clenched when he saw tears beading on her lashes. "I want to see if he remembers me. With my father."

She drew up her knees and hugged them to her chest.

Huw hesitated, then said, "I'm sorry about what happened. That was a terrible thing for a six-year-old to face."

There was a long silence. From Matilda's shuddering breaths, she was trying to control her tears.

At length she said, "I didn't understand what I'd seen at first. I saw the flask but didn't know what it had contained. I think Alys must have destroyed it, probably to make sure my father received a Christian burial. For a long time, I believed the story that was put about, that he'd died after drinking himself into a stupor."

Huw hardly dared breathe. He wanted to take her in his arms, give her the comfort she'd never had at the time, but to do that might break the spell and close her off from him again.

"It was only some time later, when Alys was teaching me about remedies, that I remembered the smell. Funny…the things you remember that seem so insignificant at the time. The first time she showed me belladonna, that ghastly smell took me straight back to the morning I walked into that chamber and found him. There was a litter of wine skins all around him, but I remembered the smell that clung to the flask by his side."

She wiped her face and when she spoke again, her voice was controlled, matter-of-fact. "I knew then what he'd done. He'd followed my mother. He loved her too much and me not enough."

Huw put his arm around her then, and she leaned against him but didn't break down as he had expected.

He couldn't shake off the feeling that there was still more to discover. To find out her father hadn't cared enough for her was a terrible thing, but did it really explain her mistrust? He dismissed the notion. First her father then Fitzjohn had let her down. They had hardly provided her with a good example of what a caring man should be like. But his instinct niggled at him that there was more.

After her last outburst, however, he knew better than to pry where he wasn't wanted.

****

"Thank you," Matilda said eventually, enjoying the comfort of Huw's strong arm around her. "It's difficult for me even to think about my father, but it has helped to talk about him."

She leaned her head against his chest. At every step, Huw had understood her, gone out of his way to show he cared. Maybe things between them really would be well when they were settled in their new lives, without having to plot or look over their shoulders at every step.

And last night…last night had opened her eyes to whole new possibilities. Their physical closeness made her long for an emotional closeness, too. It had never occurred to her before that confiding her hopes and fears to Huw could ease her mind. Instead of feeling as though she had handed him more power over her, unburdening her heart had left her more carefree than she had been since her father's death.

Although she still hesitated to depend on him completely, she dared to imagine life with Huw as a joy not a trial to be endured.

With her new-found confidence, she poured out more thoughts as they occurred to her. "It's funny, isn't it, how memories work," she said. "I'd forgotten all about discovering my father until Alys showed me belladonna a few years later. But most of the time around then—between my mother's death and my father's—is a complete blank."

Huw stirred and looked down at her, frowning. "Well, you were very young. I don't have clear memories from that age, either. Smells do recall memories, though. Only this morning, the smell of saddle soap took me right back to the day I tried to ride my great-uncle's stallion, when I was five. Thankfully, his stable master found me and stopped me before I could do myself any harm."

"The stable master," said Matilda, sitting up as a thought struck her. "Huw, how did he know my father had taken his own life? It was such a big secret."

"He said his sister told him. Apparently, she was there when you discovered your father."

"His sister? I was with Alys." She gasped. "Of course! Her brother was a groom here. I never made the connection."

"You mean the stable master is Alys's brother? She did mention she had a brother in the castle, now I come to think of it."

"I'm sure we can trust him, Huw. He taught me to ride. He was always kind to me."

Huw nodded. "We'll speak to him tonight."

No question, no prompting her if he was sure she was right. She glowed at the respect and trust Huw demonstrated. Telling him about her father had been the right thing to do. It had deepened the trust between them. The trust she felt in him.

****

They found the stable master alone in the stables, tending to the lame horse. The light was fading fast so all the lanterns hanging on the beams were lit.

The stable master frowned when he saw them. "You should be resting," he said. "There's another hard day's work for you tomorrow."

"I need to talk to you," Huw said. "I wasn't entirely honest with you earlier."

"What do you mean?"

"When I said I didn't remember anything about last night, I was lying. I wasn't drunk. I saw you come through the tunnel."

The stable master attempted to smile, but it looked like a grimace. "Tunnel? What tunnel? I think that wine must have addled your brain."

"I went through the tunnel after you'd gone. I

know you had a meeting down by the river."

The stable master paled. In a hoarse voice he asked, "Have you reported me to Fitzjohn?" Perspiration beaded his brow, and he mopped it with a hand that trembled.

Matilda's heart twisted with pity. "That's enough, Huw. Can't you see you've frightened him half to death?"

She took a deep breath. If they wanted his trust, they must trust him in return. Taking a step closer to the stable master, she said, "Don't you remember me, Godric? It is Godric, isn't it? Alys's brother?"

"That's right. How did you—?"

"Don't you know me?" she repeated.

Godric picked up his lantern and held it up to her face, frowning. "You do look familiar, now I come to look at you properly, but I can't think—"

"It's me, Godric. Matilda Comyn. You were kind to me when I was younger, taught me to ride."

"Lord bless me, so it is! You've got the look of your mother about you, I can see that now. But what are you doing here, my lady, all…" He made a gesture that took in her splotched, rough gown and reddened hands. "And you're married to a stable hand?"

Huw shook his head. "Not a stable hand normally. We're here on other business. After our…encounter last night and our chat today, I thought you might be able to help us."

The man gaped at them. "How?"

"We're trusting you with our lives," Matilda said. "We have reason to believe that you, like us, want to oust Sir Reginald and his Normans from Coed Bedwen." She studied his face, her heart pounding.

Huw had trusted her judgement without question. She prayed she wasn't mistaken, because if she was, she had just handed Godric the rope to hang them with.

"Who were you meeting last night?" Huw asked.

Godric swallowed, looking from Matilda to Huw. Then he seemed to make up his mind and nodded. "I was meeting with the folk who want to see Fitzjohn driven from Coed Bedwen."

Chapter Fifteen

A knot of anticipation squeezed Matilda's stomach. Godric's information had brought them a step closer to their goal.

Godric blotted more perspiration from his face. "Now I've placed my life in your hands, tell me who you're working for."

"The king of Gwynedd," Huw answered. "Coed Bedwen will become a fief of Gwynedd once more. Can you accept that condition?"

Thinking it might be a stumbling block, Matilda spoke up. "I'm fully in agreement, Godric. I haven't been coerced into this."

Matilda bunched her hands in the folds of her gown. If Godric couldn't agree, what would happen then?

Godric smiled and relief blossomed. "Bless you, my lady. Anyone can see you're happy with your man, here. It would never have crossed my mind that you were forced into it. You two belong together." He looked at Huw. "And I have no problem turning to the Welsh. As I see it, the king of England has done precious little to protect anyone's rights, bar his own. If the king of Gwynedd wants Coed Bedwen, then as long as he will protect the folk living within its bounds—even the English—then I'm happy."

Matilda had hardly taken in the last of this speech;

she was too busy pondering Godric's assessment of their marriage. Happy with Huw? It struck her then that if there was any man she could hope to find happiness with, it was Huw. He had treated her with respect, with tenderness. And time and again he had proved himself trustworthy.

A leaden weight lifted from her heart. Hope blossomed. She had found the one thing she'd thought impossible: a man who made her feel secure and safe. Maybe when all this was over, she would indeed face a happy future with him.

"Matilda?"

She jumped, seeing Huw looking at her, eyebrows raised.

"I'm sorry. I didn't hear what you said."

Huw frowned. "I assured Godric that as long as we oversaw Coed Bedwen, we would protect all its folk, whether Welsh, English, or even Norman, just so long as they accepted Welsh rule."

"Yes, of course." She smiled at Godric, forcing herself to concentrate. The only way she could seize her chance of happiness with Huw was by retaking Coed Bedwen. "I am half Norman, half Welsh, remember. King Owain chose me to rule Coed Bedwen with Huw because as well as being the rightful heiress through my father, I have links to Welsh royalty through my mother. And though I may not have English blood, Alys is dear to me, and I promise to treat the English as fairly as I will the Welsh and any Normans that choose to remain."

Godric smiled. "Then I'm content, and the others will follow my lead."

"Very well," said Huw. "Now to business. Tell me

what your plans are. And who knows about the tunnel?"

No matter that she should be paying attention to Godric, Matilda was unable to drag her eyes from Huw, the animated spark in his eyes at the prospect of action. Exactly how *he* made *her* feel.

"The tunnel is the key, my lord. Fitzjohn doesn't know it exists."

Huw's head snapped up at that. "How did you manage to keep it secret? Surely the steward would have noticed the empty barrels?"

Godric shook his head. "Oh no, he's too high and mighty to move barrels himself. It's the cook and the kitchen staff who look after that, and the cook is one of the key members of our group." He settled himself upon a bundle of hay near a window. One of the shutters was open. "Best sit here, my lord and lady. We can see out into the bailey. Make sure no one's in earshot. There seem to be more watchmen out tonight."

Huw and Matilda joined him. Peering out of the window, Matilda saw no one would be able to approach the stables without passing within view. As Godric had said, there were more watchmen patrolling the walls. Fitzjohn's order to double the guard had clearly been obeyed.

"The tunnel was first built in your father's time, my lady. It didn't go all the way down to the river then. He wanted to dig a well but died before it could be finished. When it became clear Fitzjohn was going to bring the place into ruin, those of us who were against him decided to dig the tunnel you found. We intended to use it to bring armed men into the castle."

"Who do you mean by 'we'?" Huw was leaning forward. Matilda could tell he was already running through various plans of action in his mind.

"In the castle itself, so far just myself, the cook, and the blacksmith. Although there's a lot of ill feeling against Fitzjohn, so we hope most of the servants would at the very least not prevent an uprising if not actually join us in a fight. But we haven't dared spread the word for fear of it reaching Fitzjohn's men. Most of the men in the village are also involved."

"I see you've made a good start," said Huw. "This should make things much easier for us." Then he frowned. "What stopped you from taking action?"

"There were so few of us. We might have been able to take the guards by surprise and hold the castle for a day or two, but as soon as reinforcements arrived, we wouldn't have stood a chance."

Huw nodded. "Then that's where we come in. With the forces of both Gwynedd and Powys behind us, there won't be a problem holding the castle. Besides, King Stephen is unlikely to have the resources to divert his attention to Coed Bedwen when he's defending himself against Maude."

Godric's eyes were shining. "After all this time, it's hard to believe this is finally going to happen. When do we act?"

"First, we have to salt any food and drink stored in the keep. The last thing we want is for Fitzjohn to shut himself and his men up in the keep for weeks."

"That's my task," Matilda said.

Huw frowned. "We should rethink that. It's too dangerous. Perhaps Godric or one of the laundresses—"

"It has to be me. Nothing's changed since we last discussed this. I'm the only one to be trusted who can enter the keep without suspicion." Something had changed, though. Last night had changed everything. It gave Matilda a thrill to know Huw cared for her enough to try shielding her from danger. It seemed there was a man she could trust after all.

Her realization made her even more determined to win Coed Bedwen. For Huw's sake as well as her own. "I have to do this, Huw. I'm the best person for the job."

The lines between Huw's brows deepened, but he gave a curt nod. "Very well. If you're sure."

"I'll do it tomorrow morning. The sheets from the keep are to be washed tomorrow, and I offered to fetch them immediately after chapel."

"Just don't take any risks." Huw's concern kindled a glow in her chest that eased the knot of dread. "As to when we act, it needs to be as soon as we can get a message to Owain. Fitzjohn is already looking for Matilda and suspects she might come here. That's why the guard has been doubled. They seem to be concentrating on people entering the castle, but the longer we stay, the greater the risk of Fitzjohn seeing her."

He glanced out of the window. Matilda wondered what he was doing until she realized he was taking note of the number of guards. "I'm going to ask Owain to send us twenty armed men to get into the castle through the tunnel. That will be more than enough to take control, even without the help of more servants. Owain's main force can wait outside the village, ready to cut off any attack from that side and to get into the castle once the gates have been opened."

"I'm sure most of the villagers and servants will be willing to help," Matilda said, remembering the ill feeling for the Normans from Nesta and Elen. She doubted Elen's case was isolated.

"But we can't count on it," said Huw. "And most of them will have only had the most basic training." He frowned. "Still, they would be useful to keep guard on any prisoners." He looked at Godric. "Spread the word to those we can trust."

Then another thought occurred to Matilda. "How will you get to the tunnel entrance without being seen from the walls?"

"We've already done several trial runs," said Godric. "That's what I was doing last night. The men can get to the river from the village without being seen from the castle. There's a low alder scrub which will provide cover until they draw level with the entrance."

"And that section of the bank is out of sight of both the keep and the walls," said Huw with a pleased nod.

"The men in the village will guide the soldiers to the right path," Godric said.

"Then we'll need to get word to the villagers as well as Owain," Huw said. "We—"

He broke off, putting a finger to his lips. Matilda heard footsteps approaching. She shrank back, out of sight of the window, her pulse racing.

Huw seemed unconcerned. He slipped into the stall that contained the lame horse. In front of Matilda's eyes, he shrank, became an insignificant servant. He made a show of picking up the horse's leg and examining the hoof. "There you go, my beauty," he said. "We'll have you galloping with the others in no time."

Matilda wondered if she could ever remain so calm in the face of danger. Her first instinct would have been for them all to hide, but when she thought about it, she saw that would have made the guard suspicious. The lanterns were all lit, and he might have heard their voices. Huw's quick thought had provided the guard with a reasonable explanation.

Godric quickly recovered himself and joined Huw. Matilda kept out of sight, knowing her presence would not be so easily explained.

After a few moments while the men fussed over their patient, Huw relaxed. "He's gone."

Matilda wiped clammy hands on her gown and sat back on the hay.

"One other thought occurs to me," said Huw, as though the interruption hadn't happened. "Matilda and I will leave through the cellar tomorrow, once she's dealt with the food and water. It's time we made our report to Owain and have him bring his forces here. How did you get in last night? Do you have a key?"

"Yes, I managed to steal the steward's key and make a copy."

"Then make an excuse to miss chapel tomorrow morning and unlock the door for us."

"Easily done. I'll just say this gelding still needs my attention," Godric declared.

"Good," Huw said. "Then next time you see me, it will be to take Coed Bedwen. Matilda will be safe away from here during the fighting, of course."

Matilda opened her mouth to protest, then thought better of it. Common sense told her that as she had no experience with weapons she would only endanger anyone who felt duty bound to protect her. "I'll wait at the Boar's Head. It will be the best place to use as a meeting place for the villagers."

Now Huw looked like he was going to object, but then he gave a grudging nod. "Agreed. But promise you'll stay inside until it's safe."

"As long as you promise to come as soon as Coed Bedwen is ours." She wanted Huw to come for her, not Owain or her uncle. It might make sense for her to avoid any fighting, but the thought of waiting at the Boar's Head, not knowing if Huw was alive or dead, made her feel sick.

"I promise. Don't worry about me, Matilda. I'll always be there for you."

I'll always be there for you. An icy cold dread shot through her gut.

Huw took her hand. "Are you unwell? What's the matter?"

"I…no…it's nothing. I'm quite well."

She took a few deep breaths, and the feeling eased. She attempted a smile. "It's just the excitement of all the planning, that's all."

But a deep uneasiness remained that was nothing to do with the prospect of action. It was a memory that she struggled to keep buried. And along with it came the deep conviction that eventually, all men would let her down.

****

Huw looked at Matilda a moment longer, sure that her sudden pallor was due to more than the anticipation of action. He hoped she wasn't going to be ill, but if she was, it was high time to get her safely away.

"We'll leave in the morning," he said. He had been reluctant to leave, not wanting the main action to fall to others. Untrained others at that. However, his worry for Matilda pushed that from his mind. Now he couldn't get her away soon enough.

After that there was little more to say. Once they'd checked none of the watchmen were looking their way, Huw and Matilda slipped from the stable.

Huw slipped his arm around Matilda's waist and nuzzled her ear, relishing the shiver and gasp of pleasure this elicited. "With so many watchmen about, we're bound to be seen before we reach the hall," he murmured. "They'll ignore us if they think we're returning from a tryst." Mainly, however, he had to admit he relished the opportunity to hold her close.

Matilda leaned into his embrace. "I can't bear to think they're looking for me," she said. "I'm glad we're leaving tomorrow." There was a slight tremor in her voice. She obviously hadn't recovered from her turn.

"Tell me what's really wrong," he said. "Do you feel ill? You went as white as a ghost back there."

"I'm not ill. I don't know what it was. I felt…oh, I don't know." She gave a half laugh. "You must think I'm mad."

"I don't. Something clearly affected you." He tugged her closer, enjoying the way her slender waist felt so right in the crook of his arm.

"It was…oh, this must sound foolish, but have you ever had that feeling when something really terrible has happened, and you wake up in the morning and just for a moment you think everything is well, then the memory of the awful thing hits you?"

He nodded. It had happened to him several times after his parents had died. The blissful forgetfulness, followed by the sickening lurch of reality. And again, after his great-uncle's brutal words.

"Well that's how I felt just now, only…" She

shook her head. "No. Ignore me. It's just a foolish fear. It'll pass."

She didn't sound convinced, but by this time they were only a few strides from the doors to the great hall. There was too great a danger of being overheard, so Huw couldn't press her further.

The wicket gate was flung open with such force that it rattled on its hinges. Acting faster than thought, Huw pulled Matilda aside.

"Send him to me in the morning," a voice snapped. Fitzjohn.

Huw heard Matilda gasp with fear. They had only the barest instant before Fitzjohn would be through the door. Large torches blazed on either side of the archway, providing more than enough light for Fitzjohn to see their faces. There was only one thing to do. Making sure his back was to the door, he seized Matilda in a devouring kiss. He wrapped both his arms around her, ensuring that she was completely hidden from view.

Half of his attention was on the sounds in the doorway, but that was fighting with the urge to lose himself in Matilda's kiss, the way she opened to him, parting her lips to allow him to taste her deeply, tangle their tongues in a heated caress. By the heavens, the sooner they were safely established in Coed Bedwen, with a chamber, and, more importantly, a bed to themselves, the better.

Fitzjohn's footsteps had faded, but he didn't release Matilda just yet. Better to be on the safe side. He molded his body to hers. She trembled in his embrace and wound her arms around his neck.

Finally, he pulled away, fighting for breath. The

nearby torch illuminated her face, showed him her swollen lips, flushed cheekbones, and eyes glazed with passion. He knew she was his. Her body responded to his like iron to a lodestone. But he wanted more than her body. He wanted her heart. And that still eluded him.

"Are you sure he's gone?" Matilda peered over his shoulder.

"Quite sure. But that was close. And if you ran into him without me to protect you…it doesn't bear thinking about."

"We're leaving tomorrow. As long as we take extra care, we'll be safe."

"I know. But I…"

She smiled. "You hate leaving when the action is about to start."

He grimaced. "You know me too well. It feels…cowardly."

"You risked your life coming here. How is that cowardly? Besides, you'll be leading the soldiers through the tunnel. You're not leaving the action. You're starting it." Her mouth pulled down. "Admit it, it's the thrill of danger, of near-discovery that drives you. I was watching you tonight. You came alive when we were discussing plans, and when the watchman drew near, the air around you crackled, you were so…impassioned. That's why you don't want to leave, not because it feels cowardly, but because danger is your bread and water. You thrive on it. And, admit it, you don't know if you can survive without it."

It was unpleasant, to be on the receiving end of such an outright challenge. He was the one who was supposed to expose buried truths, not Matilda.

"Go on," she said. "Be honest with me. You promised. Be honest with *yourself*. Would you ever truly be satisfied with a life devoid of all danger?" The unspoken words were clear: could he be happy with her?

Maybe this wasn't the right time or place, but he could no longer hold back from pouring out the truth.

"Once I would have agreed with you. You're right—I did need danger like I need to breathe. But now…the one thing I want most in the world is you. And I want to protect you, make sure no one hurts you ever again. You've filled a…a void in my life that I thought would remain forever empty." The power his blood oath had held over him was gone forever, replaced by his desire to take care of Matilda. Not that he would ever reveal that side of himself. There was no need for her to know.

He took a deep breath. "I love you, Matilda. Never doubt that. I love you more than life itself. If you believe nothing else, believe that."

Matilda looked up at him, a sweet smile transforming her face that caused Huw to catch his breath, hope blossoming in his heart. Then she nestled her head against his chest.

"I do believe you," she said. Those four words set the blood pounding in Huw's ears. "You know how hard I find it to trust men, to trust you, but now…after last night I saw how foolish, how unreasonable my mistrust of you has been. You've never let me down, and I'm starting to believe you never will. I—"

But Huw couldn't wait for any more. He pressed her back against the wall and kissed her again, pouring all his love into the act. Finally, he had broken down the barriers in her heart. Soon he was yearning for more than mere kisses. He wanted to make love to her, demonstrate with his whole body just how much he loved her. Judging from the way Matilda clutched at his shoulders and pulled him tightly against her, she felt the same.

He broke the kiss breathing heavily. "We'd best go in before I do something foolish." Like take her right here against the wall.

At Matilda's disappointed sigh, he gave a soft laugh. "It won't be long before we have a bedchamber all to ourselves where we can spend every night in each other's arms, but it's not seemly for the lord and lady of Coed Bedwen to be caught coupling in the shadows of the hall." No matter how much he wanted to.

He gave her one final swift kiss. "Soon nothing and no one will keep us apart ever again."

****

"I overheard Fitzjohn saying he was riding out this morning," Matilda murmured as they filed out of the chapel after morning prayers. "I'll deal with the supplies in the keep right away, before he comes back."

"Take care," Huw replied. "Go on to the laundry yard and wait for me there when you've finished. I'll come and get you when our way's clear."

If only there was another way, someone else prepared to take the risk. But Matilda was right. She was the best person for the task, and he had to let her go. He watched her until she disappeared, then went to the stables.

Godric stopped him just outside. "Fitzjohn's given orders for his horse to be saddled," he said. "You should go before he gets here. The cellar door is open."

Huw nodded and hurried away, head down. He was so busy wondering where he should wait while Matilda was in the keep that he didn't watch where he was going and nearly ran into a man striding toward the stables.

A voice that made his blood run cold snarled, "Watch where you're going, fool." A quick glance up showed him Fitzjohn, his fist raised as though he was about to strike.

Huw hastily bowed his head. "Beg your pardon, my lord," he said in his thickest Welsh accent. Anything to avoid Fitzjohn associating him with the troubadour.

He moved to walk on, but Fitzjohn grasped his shoulder. "I haven't given you permission to go yet." Then his eyes narrowed. "You look familiar. I've seen you before, somewhere else."

Huw shook his head. "I've only just started here, my lord. I came from Aberffraw." He named the location of Owain's *llys* on Anglesey, knowing Fitzjohn had never been there.

Fitzjohn gave him one last, long look, then said, "Get on with your work then, man. And watch where you're going in future."

Huw walked away, fighting the urge to run. Just when he thought he was clear, he blew out a shaky breath. He glanced back to see Fitzjohn looking his way, frowning.

He walked on.

Then a voice rang out. "I remember him. That's the troubadour. Seize him!"

Huw ran, thinking fast. Behind the stable yard, the outer wall was lower than elsewhere, and a mounting block had been set beside the lowest portion. Beyond the wall, with a long jump, an escapee might just leap into the branches of the oak tree beyond and get away. Not that he had any intention of leaving Matilda, but if he could make it look like that's what he'd done...

He sprinted for the yard, knowing he had a good head start on his pursuers, who had started from the gates. He scuffed the manure heap on the way into the yard and laid a noisome trail onto the mounting block and up onto the wall beyond. A swift glance along the wall showed him that no guards were in sight. He jumped down and dashed back across the yard, breathing a prayer of thanks no one was using it this morning. If Godric saw him, he wouldn't give him away. A trough of water stood against the wall. From it, he was able to leap up and scrabble in the thatch, pulling himself up onto the stable roof. He climbed until he was almost at the apex. Anyone looking up would see him. He just prayed the guards would presume he had leapt from the wall and seek him outside without thinking of looking up at the roof.

Calming his breathing, he waited.

Chapter Sixteen

Huw clung on to the thatch, the straw cutting into his hands. He tried to shift around so he could look across the bailey, desperate for any sign of Matilda. However, before he could move, three men charged into the yard below him, followed by Fitzjohn.

"He came in here. I'm sure of it," Fitzjohn said, breathing heavily.

The men spread out through the yard, searching every corner, tipping over feed barrels; one even ran his sword into the manure heap.

"He's got to be here somewhere," said Fitzjohn.

Huw inched one hand down to rest on the hilt of his knife. He could kill Fitzjohn here. It would rid Matilda—and Coed Bedwen—of his menace for good. His hand itched with the longing to pull out the knife and throw it at the spot between Fitzjohn's shoulder blades. He would have done, had not the angle been too steep. The knife would most likely glance off Fitzjohn's shoulder, causing no more than a graze. He would be discovered and so would Matilda.

He held his breath, his heart pounding in his ears. Though his fear was for Matilda, not himself. If he could get her safely away from Fitzjohn, nothing else mattered.

"Look at the manure heap," said the man who was standing there, sword drawn. "The top's all scuffed."

The others moved toward him and spread out, eyes to the ground.

"Here!" said another. "The trail leads to the wall."

The group looked out to the oak tree beyond, then Fitzjohn turned, his face purple.

"I want men out with hounds, searching the whole area," he said.

The men dashed out of the yard. Huw breathed again.

If he had been alone, it would have been a simple matter to escape. He could have scrambled down from his perch and made a dash for the cellar and the tunnel while Fitzjohn's attention was elsewhere. However, Matilda's involvement was a complication. He wasn't leaving without her. If she came to any harm, he would never forgive himself.

He couldn't stay here. He thought fast. Matilda would be in the keep by now, and he couldn't risk going inside to find her in case he was seen and led Fitzjohn to her.

Then he remembered Godric saying the blacksmith was part of the conspiracy. The blacksmith's bothy was close to the keep. If he waited there, the blacksmith wouldn't give him up, and he would be able to watch for Matilda without drawing attention to himself.

After a quick glance around to check no one was looking, he slid down from the roof and, heart hammering against his ribs, walked out across the bailey. He fought the urge to run. That would only draw attention to himself. If he looked like he had every business to be there, no one would give him a second glance. Or so he hoped. It didn't stop him breaking out in a sweat, expecting at any moment to hear a shout that he'd been seen.

Only when he stepped into the shadows of the blacksmith's bothy did he let out a shaky breath of relief.

"Don't give me away," he murmured to the smith, who was stoking his fire and had paused to look at him.

"Never fear," the blacksmith replied. "Godric's already told me about you."

Relieved, Huw peered out from the shadows to watch for Matilda. He had only just reached cover in time. Fitzjohn was even now striding across the bailey, his face set in grim lines.

Huw's blood went cold when Fitzjohn mounted the steps to the keep. He didn't go inside but stationed himself at the top, looking back across the bailey. If Huw left the bothy, he would be seen. However, that wasn't what made his skin clammy with horror.

The moment Matilda left the keep, Fitzjohn would see her.

****

Matilda struggled to control her breathing as she paused beside the steps inside the keep. If only Huw had come with her, she wouldn't be so frightened. But, of course, Huw had no business in the keep and would have raised suspicion. She checked the folded sheets on her arm for what felt like the thousandth time, to ensure they covered the large clay pot containing the salt.

Strange to think she wished Huw were with her, when only a few days ago she had feared to be alone with him. Now even the thought of Huw comforted her, calmed her breathing. It was as though she could hear him, talking her through it.

Fitzjohn is going out for a ride. You'll be finished

here and out of the castle long before he gets back. Just take a deep breath and start moving. Even if anyone sees you, they'll ignore you. You're just a servant to them, remember—you said so yourself.

Her breathing slowed, and warmth returned to her frozen limbs.

Upstairs or down? Downstairs, she decided. The storage barrels would be heavy. She was far more likely to find them down here.

The keep was a new building, therefore unfamiliar to her. Where she stood, three doors lined a narrow passageway. She had no idea where any of them led. There was no alternative but to try each in turn.

A quick glance around the first door revealed racks of spears and arrows, and a bench covered in feathers for fletching. No food stores in there. She was just leaving when the clatter of booted feet upon the stairs sent her scurrying inside the second room upon trembling legs. She huddled against the wall behind the door, clutching the sheets to her chest. On the other side of the door came the sound of footsteps and shouting. Then all was quiet.

She released a shuddering breath. Her admiration for Huw was rising by the moment. How he had survived for years doing this kind of work without dropping dead from fright, she would never know.

Only then did she take in her surroundings and her heart leapt. The room was bare save for several large barrels and pottery storage jars stacked against the wall. She prized the lid off a barrel. Water! A quick check of the others revealed more water barrels, grain, and what smelled like pickled herring. She snorted. When she was mistress of Coed Bedwen, she would keep far better supplies. But Fitzjohn's negligence served them well. If she salted the water, no one would be able to survive on just the grain and herrings for long. With trembling hands, she poured out the salt into the water barrels. All she could do now was pray that no one tasted it before Huw and Owain started their attack.

Muttering a prayer of thankfulness that she'd completed her task, she dropped the sheets and hurried out of the door. Too late she noticed the man standing at the top of the steps. Fitzjohn.

She gasped and backed away, thinking to hide in the storeroom again. However, he heard her indrawn breath and turned, frowning.

"What are you doing here, girl?"

Terrified, she answered without thinking. "Taking fresh linen to your chamber, my lord." As soon as the words were out of her mouth, she knew she'd made a fatal error. She had spoken in flawless Norman French, not the heavily accented French a Welsh woman would have spoken.

Fitzjohn's eyes opened wide. Then before she could react he charged at her and seized her arm. "By God's blood—Matilda Comyn. You've led me a merry dance." He pulled her roughly toward the keep. "No chance of that troubadour of yours getting you out this time. We're scouring the castle for him. I'll have his head decorating the gate before sundown."

****

When Huw saw Fitzjohn seize Matilda, he thought his heart would stop. With a strangled cry, he braced himself to sprint up to the keep, with no thought other than to save Matilda. However, before he could take more than one step, he found himself grappled to a halt from behind.

"Don't be a fool," the blacksmith hissed in his ear. You'll just get yourself caught along with her, and there'll be no saving you."

If it had been anyone else, he would have listened to reason. What could one man hope to do against Fitzjohn and all his men? But this wasn't anyone. This was Matilda. He had promised she could trust him and he wasn't about to let her down.

He wrenched himself free and ran out into the open. By this time Fitzjohn had nearly dragged Matilda into the keep. He had to stop them before Matilda was inside.

Much to his frustration, no one was looking his way. He needed to create a stir. His eyes fell on a trestle table set up in the next bothy. Upon it was stacked an array of clay pots. With no time to think of anything else, he charged into it, knocking the pots to the ground with a clatter that drew the gaze of everyone in the castle.

Fitzjohn stopped dead and pointed at him with his free hand. "That's him! Seize that man!"

Two men-at-arms drew their swords and converged upon him. He made a show of trying to run away, but allowed them to catch him at the foot of the keep. They hustled him up the steps until he was face to face with Fitzjohn.

Matilda was still struggling in his grip, her eyes wide with terror. "No, Huw. Please run."

Fitzjohn turned a malevolent gaze from Matilda to Huw. "It's Huw now, is it? I seem to remember you going by a different name at Redcliff."

Huw pulled himself free from the men's clutches

and gave him an insolent bow. His whole aim now was to enrage Fitzjohn. He had to give Matilda a chance to escape. "Huw ap Goronwy at your service," he said.

"What do you think you're doing here?" Fitzjohn hissed.

"I could ask you the same question," Huw replied. "After all, Coed Bedwen belongs to me now." Behind him he was aware of Fitzjohn's men taking positions nearby, ready to move if he should try to escape. Well, he had no intention of doing that until Matilda was safe.

"What? Don't be ridiculous. I hold it as Matilda Comyn's guardian. And as soon as she becomes my wife, it will be mine."

"That's not possible, I'm afraid."

"Why not?" Fitzjohn pulled Matilda closer when she made another bid to free herself. He wrapped an arm around her waist.

It made Huw's blood seethe to see how his fingers dug cruelly into her side. When the time came, he would take great pleasure in killing him.

"Because she's *my* wife. Take your filthy hands off her this instant, cur."

"What?" Fitzjohn's face contorted with rage. Huw thought fast. There had to be a way to make Fitzjohn lose control and forget to watch Matilda. But it wasn't just Fitzjohn he was aiming his words at now. He had to make Matilda take her first chance to flee. If she was worried about Huw, she might try to help him. Huw couldn't risk that.

He had to make Matilda hate him.

"You heard," he said. "She's my wife. I watched you in Redcliff, saw you were planning to marry her to get Coed Bedwen. But I wanted Coed Bedwen for myself, so I persuaded her to come with me. It wasn't difficult. After all, why would she want to marry a goat's arse like you?"

"You—" Fitzjohn's face turned purple. He drew his sword and took a wild swing at Huw.

Huw sidestepped with ease and drew his knife. "Such an honorable man," he mocked. "Attacking me when I'm as good as unarmed. There again, I should have expected such behavior from a coward like you."

"Insult me at your peril, whoreson. Remember I have your wife at my mercy."

Huw licked dry lips, careful not to look at Matilda. If he did, his heart would break, and he would be unable to force out the words he knew he had to say. The only way he could persuade her to run.

He shrugged. "Do with her as you please. Coed Bedwen is mine now. That's all I wanted from her. It's the only reason I'd marry a Norman whore like her. That, and to get close enough to fulfil my blood oath against her family."

Matilda's shocked gasp pierced his heart. It took all his strength not to look her in the eye and beg her forgiveness.

"Of course," he continued, keeping his voice even, "you should know all about whores. By all accounts, your mother was one."

With an incoherent bellow of rage, Fitzjohn shoved Matilda aside and flung himself at Huw. From the corner of his eye he saw Matilda stumble down the steps and hurl herself through the cellar door. No one was watching her; all eyes were upon him.

There was no way he could escape now. He had known that from the start. The only thing that mattered to him was that Matilda was free. They could kill him now. He didn't care.

He doubted Matilda would ever look at him again after his cruel words.

He had saved her but destroyed the trust that he had worked so hard to earn. Destroyed their marriage.

Fitzjohn's men grabbed him, prized his knife from his fingers, and wrenched his arms behind his back.

"Lock him up," Fitzjohn said. "I want to question him further before I kill him."

****

Matilda's hands shook so violently she could hardly press the latch on the cellar door. It didn't help that the world shimmered through a haze of tears, but as fast as she swiped them away, more appeared. Her throat ached from the effort of choking back the sobs that threatened to draw attention to her escape. So far everyone's eyes were fixed on Huw's struggle against his would-be captors, but she paid the commotion little heed. Just one thought hammered at her head as she finally managed to release the lock: Huw despised her.

She slipped into the cellar and slammed the door shut behind her. Gasping, she snatched the lantern from its niche and stumbled down the steps. If she could force her trembling legs to carry her to the Boar's Head, Alys could provide her with an escort to Owain and safety.

A sob forced its way up her throat at the thought of what she would have to report; another followed when her eyes fell on the wool bales in the corner. Where Huw had made love to her with a tender passion that must have been as false as his black heart.

No. She mustn't think of that, or she wouldn't have

the strength to carry on. She shoved aside the barrels to reveal the board that concealed the tunnel mouth. Her resolve carried her into the tunnel and down the steps until she reached the first bend. Then her legs finally folded beneath her, and she hunched down upon the cold, damp stone, her arms hugging her knees. She couldn't hold back the sobs any longer. They echoed off the rough walls, mocking her.

The words he had spoken about her resonated through her mind. *Norman whore…fulfill my blood oath.*

How could she have been such a fool? Men weren't to be trusted. Hadn't she already learnt that the hard way? They only had their own interests at heart and didn't care who they hurt to get what they wanted. Huw had lied to her all along. He hadn't told her about his claim to Coed Bedwen until Owain had revealed it. Then he'd toyed with her, winding her in his web of lies until he had no more use for her. And then what? She shivered. *Fulfill my blood oath…* Had he been planning to kill her?

Bitter bile flooded her mouth.

To think she had come to depend on him, had taken comfort in him…

Had fallen in love with him.

She pressed the heels of her hands to her temples, as though she could erase that thought. It couldn't be. She had fallen prey to a master manipulator. Any feelings she had developed had been for a man who had never existed. She had experienced the callous truth of Huw's nature today, and it had cured her of those mistaken feelings for good.

Gradually the shock coursing through Matilda's

body faded as it was replaced by cold anger. She would do everything in her power to make sure he suffered for what he had done.

It crossed her mind to ask her uncle to take her in and refuse to assist Owain in retaking Coed Bedwen, but then she remembered all the people depending on her to deliver them from Fitzjohn's rule. Whatever else happened, she wouldn't let them down.

She bunched her hands into fists. She would do what Owain had sent her to do. But when it was all over and Coed Bedwen was in Welsh hands, she would make sure she was left in sole control. And her uncle and the king of Powys would know that Huw ap Goronwy was a treacherous whoreson. He could rot in Hell for all she cared.

Her renewed purpose gave her strength, and she scrambled to her feet. Although she hadn't heard any sounds of pursuit, she couldn't be sure Fitzjohn or his men weren't coming after her. The thought of Fitzjohn catching her in this dark tunnel sent her flying down the uneven steps. She wouldn't feel safe until she was with Alys in the Boar's Head.

By the time she arrived at the tavern, she was cold and weary. Her arms and legs were scratched and bleeding from brambles in the thicket, and her feet were soaked from trudging along the muddy river bank.

She found Alys setting a pot of water to boil over the fire.

"Oh, my poor lamb!" Alys cried when she stumbled through the door. "What happened to you?"

Bundled in a blanket and sat by the fire, hunched over a steaming infusion of chamomile flowers, she poured out her tale.

Alys clutched a hand to her chest when Matilda, fighting to keep her tone matter-of-fact, repeated Huw's words. "Huw said that? I can hardly believe it."

"Do you think I'm making it up?"

"No, of course not, dear. But I've always prided myself on being a good judge of character. You must be in my business. It never crossed my mind that Huw was harboring such loathing toward you. Did he give you any hint of it before?"

Matilda closed her eyes as the humiliation and rejection washed over her again. She relived the moment when his cruel words had crushed her heart. A harsh contrast to the tenderness and love he'd shown her only the evening before. "No. He took me in completely. I thought he was different from all the other men I knew, but it turns out he was just the same. He used me, Alys."

She drew a deep breath and opened her eyes, fixing them on the flickering flames. Now was not the time to give in to tears. When she spoke again her voice was hard. "Huw played me for a fool, but I won't let him get away with it."

"What are you going to do?"

"Stick with the plan. Originally Huw and I were going to report to Owain once we'd planned our strategy and organized a rebellion. I'll just have to do that alone. And if by some miracle Huw manages to escape from Fitzjohn, I'll do everything in my power to ensure he doesn't get Coed Bedwen."

Alys patted her hand. "If you feel able to travel, I think that's the right thing to do."

Matilda sat up straighter. "Alys, do you know which villagers would be willing to take part in an uprising?"

Alys's eyes shone. "All of them. They hold nothing but hate for Fitzjohn."

"Would they follow me?"

"Without a doubt. The Saxons are eager to oust the Normans, but they have fond memories of you, and the Welsh will rally behind the plan when they hear of your connection to the king of Powys."

"Then spread the word that I'm bringing King Owain to free them, and we need their help. As soon as I can, I'll return here with Owain's instructions."

"I'll start the moment you're safe away."

Some of the crushing pain eased. Now she had a purpose. A plan. She would do her utmost to convince Owain to leave her in sole charge of Coed Bedwen. Huw might be Owain's man, but she knew she could convince Owain that Coed Bedwen's continued stability would depend upon her presence. And not even all the gold in the world could induce her to share Coed Bedwen with Huw.

She twisted her lips into a smile. "Good. In that case, I need a horse." Then her courage faltered. "Although I don't know the way."

She had been depending on Huw to guide them. Just as she had come to depend upon Huw for so many things.

The realization pricked her anger. He had manipulated that dependence. Made her trust him while he bided his time, like a spider in its web. Well, she had learnt her lesson. She would never let a man get that close again. It was time to reclaim her independence.

She rose to her feet and turned to Alys. "I'll need an escort. You must know someone in the village who will serve." She might have learnt not to trust men, but to travel alone and unarmed through the Welsh hills would be foolishness in the extreme, even if she knew the way.

"Rhys the blacksmith will guide you. He's a Gwynedd man; he knows the country well." Alys took the empty cup from Matilda's hand and placed it beside the hearth. "Wait here while I go and fetch him. His forge is on the castle side of the village, so best you're not seen there."

Matilda couldn't remain still once Alys had left. She paced the room, hugging her arms to her chest until finally the heat and smoke from the fire became too oppressive and she flung open the shutters, gulping in the clean air.

Leaning out of the window, she could see the stone keep towering above the higgledy piggledy thatched roofs of the village. Somewhere up there was Huw. Was he in Fitzjohn's custody, or had he escaped and even now striding through the tunnel, intent upon fulfilling his blood oath? She shuddered and glanced at the sky. The sun was approaching its zenith. She had been in the tavern longer than she'd thought. Plenty of time for Huw to make his own escape. The sooner she was away from Coed Bedwen, the better.

As if in answer to her wish, the clatter of horses' hooves sounded upon the cobbled lane and Alys came into view. She was accompanied by a tall, dark-haired man, leading two horses, both saddled and bridled.

She hurried outside.

"This is Rhys the blacksmith," said Alys. "He knows the way to the royal *llys*."

"Good," said Matilda. "There's no time to lose."

She turned an appraising eye upon the horses, whose quality surely put them way above the means of a village blacksmith.

"They're a gift from Fitzjohn," said Rhys, his musical voice reminding her of Huw, making her heart lurch. "Now get up on the gray here. No time to lose."

He helped her to mount.

"But why would Fitzjohn give us horses?" she asked, once she was settled in the saddle.

"Ah, well, he doesn't know he has. That's why we need to hurry." Rhys mounted the other horse, a fine bay mare. "Godric brought them down first thing this morning, saying you would need them."

"Wait!" Alys grasped the gray's bridle to prevent Matilda from leaving. "What should we do with Huw if he comes through the village?" She lowered her voice. "Just say the word and we can make sure he never has the opportunity to harm you."

"No!" Matilda's vehemence surprised even herself. "He's Owain's man. I won't risk bringing the king's fury on Coed Bedwen. Have the villagers keep watch for him. If he's seen, I want him caught and held here for Owain to deal with. You'll have to bind him. He excels at picking locks."

Alys nodded and stepped back, releasing the gray. Matilda clapped her heels against its flanks, urging it into a trot. Tears welled in her eyes at the reminder of what her relationship with Huw had come to. The journey passed in a blur. All she was aware of was Huw's voice repeating the same words over and over. *Norman whore...blood oath.*

Chapter Seventeen

Huw sat on the floor of the bare room, nursing sore ribs. The last of the light had faded some time ago, and the patch of sky he could see through the tiny window slit was black and studded with stars. He wondered how Matilda was faring. If she had any sense, she would be safe in Owain's care by now. He prayed it was so.

The sounds of movement in the keep had died down. All but the watchmen must be asleep by now. It was high time he made his move.

He shifted and reached inside his shirt, wincing at the throbbing of a multitude of bruises. When Fitzjohn had finally noticed Matilda's disappearance, he had taken his rage out on Huw. His men had stolen his possessions and beaten him, but things could have been much worse. Fitzjohn lacked imagination when it came to persuading a prisoner to talk. After a beating had failed to force him to reveal Matilda's possible whereabouts, Fitzjohn had ordered for him to be left here with no food or water to see how long he could survive without them.

That was something he had no intention of finding out. He grinned as his fingers found the two pieces of sturdy wire sewn into a seam. He ripped them free. It was always useful to carry two sets of tools. They weren't as good as the picklocks that had been taken from him along with his knife, but they would do in an emergency.

There wasn't even enough light to see the wall, so he rose to his feet and shuffled across the room, arms outstretched. At first his fingers encountered cold, plastered wall, but he didn't have to follow it far before he felt the rough grain of the oak door. Finally, his questing fingers dipped into the keyhole, and he set to work.

As he probed the lock, his mind wandered back to Matilda. Would she ever forgive him for what he had said?

He twisted the hooked wire and felt one of the catches slot into place. Now for the next one.

Surely she would understand that he had done it for her own sake. He'd had to make sure she would leave the castle, not risk recapture by trying to rescue him. Soon he would have both her and Coed Bedwen. All would be well.

A moment later he heard the click of the lock releasing. He pushed the door open a crack and peered out. The fool Fitzjohn hadn't bothered to set a guard at the door, and lamps burned in cressets, guiding Huw down to the main doors. Like the great hall, there was a smaller wicket gate set into the door, and it swung open when Huw pressed the latch.

Holding his breath, he slipped down the steps and into the courtyard. Only to run into another man when he stepped into the shadows by the cellar door. He raised an arm to strike.

"Who's that?" A voice hissed.

He lowered his fist, releasing a shaky breath. It was Godric.

He pulled Godric into the doorway and keeping his

voice low, replied, "It's Huw. What are you doing out here?"

"Huw? Praise the saints! I was coming to rescue you."

Huw gave a soft laugh. "As you can see, you're a little late."

"Are you hurt?"

"Nothing that will slow me down. What about Matilda? I saw her go into the cellar. Have you had word from the village about her?"

"I haven't heard. No one's been allowed in or out of the castle since you were caught, and I didn't want to risk using the tunnel in case I was seen."

"I'll have to go that way myself. I need to find out if she reached Alys safely and where she is now."

"She should be well on her way to Owain. I took horses to the blacksmith this morning, then sent word of your capture before the castle gates were closed. If Matilda got out safely, she'll have known not to wait for you."

"I have to know for sure that she's safe," said Huw. "Be ready for the attack. Unless you hear otherwise, we'll make our move tomorrow night."

His concern for Matilda drove him to ignore his hurts and rush through the dank tunnel with all haste. Once through, his first thought was to go to the Boar's Head to ask Alys for news. However, he no sooner put his foot on the path to the village than he stopped dead. If Matilda had gone there, she would have told Alys what he had said about the blood oath. It wouldn't surprise him if the villagers were watching for him, waiting to strike him down and defend their Lady. As much as he felt he deserved whatever punishment they might mete out, he couldn't afford to risk it. Not when Matilda might need his help.

He left the lantern in the tunnel. Its light was more likely to give him away than aid him. Besides, it was a clear night, and the moon and stars provided enough light to guide him. With the roar of the river drowning his footfalls, he crept down the bank and picked up the wooded path to the village.

Once the path turned away from the river, the scent of wood smoke grew stronger, telling him he was nearing the village. He slowed down, straining his ears for sounds of pursuit. Save for the occasional rustlings in the trees and the screech of an owl, all was quiet.

The first thing he needed was a horse. He'd hoped Alys would have helped him with that, but now he would have to manage alone. Still, thanks to his time spent at the Boar's Head, he knew where he could find a mount. Alys kept one, and it was housed in a ramshackle stable a child could break into.

It wasn't long before he reached the end of the path. The woods ended, and he could make out the dark outlines of the huddled dwellings, defined by chinks of light seeping through shutters and around the edges of doors.

If the villagers had been watching for him, they had obviously given up some time ago and retired to their beds. The only movement Huw spied as he slunk through the shadows was a cat that turned to regard him with lantern eyes before darting into the shadows of a wood pile. Even the Boar's Head was silent, it being long past the hour when the last of the patrons would have been turned out.

Huw stepped lightly upon the cobbles of the yard

behind the tavern, careful to make no noise that would alert Alys. He grinned when his groping fingers met the stable door. This really was too easy. He had no difficulty forcing the lock. The door swung open, and he stepped inside.

The instant he pulled to door shut behind him, strong hands seized his arms on either side. He cursed and struggled to slip free, but he was hampered by his wish not to hurt anyone.

"Hold him still," cried a woman's voice.

"Alys!" Huw said. "You can let me go. You have my word not to escape."

A beam of light struck his eyes, making him blink. When his eyes cleared, he saw Alys standing before him in a pool of golden light, a lantern in her raised hand. She must have kept it covered until now.

"As if I'd trust your word, cur."

He gave a twisted smile. "I take it Matilda got to you safely, then. Has she gone to the king?"

Alys snorted. "Do you really think I'd give you any news of her, after what you said?"

"It was all a lie," he said. "I needed to frighten her, so she'd leave without me. Do you truly think I could harm her? I love her more than life." He cursed his foolishness at walking into the trap. Matilda could be in danger. He would never forgive himself if she came to harm.

Conflicting thoughts flickered in Alys's eyes. Pressing his point home, he said, "If I truly wanted to hurt her, I could have done so easily at any time. I was protecting her. I'd give my life for her."

Alys shook her head. "I'm not saying I don't believe you, but Matilda told me not to let you go, and I won't disobey her."

"Then take me to her and Owain. As your prisoner. Let them decide." It would be shameful to be led in front of Owain, bound as a prisoner, but he would endure the humiliation if it meant he could see Matilda with his own eyes and ensure she was unharmed.

"I must confess, we've no place to keep you here." She dropped her gaze, appearing to ponder the issue for a moment. Then she gave him a grim smile. "Very well. We'll go after Matilda and Rhys at first light." Addressing the burly men who held him, she said, "Bind him. I don't think he'll give us trouble, but we can't be too careful."

Huw prepared himself to pass what remained of the night in great discomfort. Not that he cared. The only thing that mattered was Matilda's safety. Alys's answer had at least assured him that Matilda had gone to Owain and she wasn't alone.

And maybe if he could persuade Matilda of the truth, she wouldn't be lost to him after all.

****

By the time Matilda arrived at the royal *llys*, her thigh muscles were burning. The sun was long down, but the sky was clear, and a half-moon hung above the tree tops, providing enough light to guide them.

Sleepy stable hands staggered out to take their horses, and she was ushered into the hall.

"The king says to wait for him here, my lady. He will be with you soon," said a servant-girl, placing a cup of spiced wine into her hands.

Matilda stood by the fire, feeling the warmth creep through her, easing her sore muscles. She understood why the king would want to talk to her now. He would be as anxious as she was to secure Coed Bedwen. But she was tired and heart-sore. All she really wanted to do was curl up in a warm bed and forget Huw's betrayal.

Although thoughts of bed made her feel worse. After their passionate loving in the cellar, she had yearned for the time when she would spend whole nights spent entangled with Huw in a large, soft bed. Her body betrayed her, going heavy with longing, but she fought to tame her thoughts. They could never be together again.

If Owain wouldn't banish Huw from Coed Bedwen, she would go to her uncle. Maybe he could enlist the help of his cousin, the king of Powys, although it rankled that she still needed a man's intervention. Her experience of Fitzjohn had taught her that men were not to be depended on. And as for her father…

She shoved the thought aside. She didn't want to think of that now. She never thought of his abandonment if she could help it, so why was the memory so strong now? The scent of spiced wine teased her nostrils, that particular blend of honey and spices transporting her to a day of sunshine and butterflies.

No! She slammed the cup on a nearby table, wine sloshing over the rim, forming a crimson pool.

"Lady Matilda!"

Owain's voice slashed across the unwelcome memory. She looked up to see the king striding toward her, his tunic hanging askew as though thrown on in a hurry.

"Forgive my delay. I wasn't expecting any arrivals this late." Then Owain looked about the hall. "Where is

Huw? The servant told me a man was with you. I assumed it was him."

She shook her head. "That was Rhys, the man who escorted me here. Huw was…was captured."

Owain guided her to a seat. "When did this happen?"

The hurt, the fright, and the anger were still too raw to be able to hold anything back. She poured out her tale, even mentioning Huw's blood oath.

"Ah, the blood oath," Owain said. "I'd hoped you'd have resolved that between you by now."

"You knew about it?" Matilda's voice was sharp. "Yet you ordered us to marry?"

Owain held up a placating hand. "I would never have done so if I'd believed you to be in danger from Huw. I watched you together from the start, and I could see he'd never harm you."

"Yet he told Fitzjohn—"

"Yes, I imagine he told Fitzjohn all sorts of things, none of them true."

"You think he was lying?"

Owain raised an eyebrow. "You think he would stroll up to his enemy and pour out all his secrets?"

"He didn't 'stroll up,' he was—"

The word "captured" died on her lips. In her mind's eye, she saw the moment Huw had stumbled into the potter's table, creating the disturbance that had led to his capture. At the time she had been too numb with despair to think it strange, but now it hit her how unlike Huw that had been. He had a catlike grace, always aware of his surroundings. Would he really have committed such a careless blunder? It was almost as if he had wanted to be taken.

But that meant… No. Surely not. She shivered, recalling the disdain in his eyes as he had said the words "Norman whore." It had been too horribly real to be an act.

There again, she had already seen Huw play a convincing beggar and minstrel.

Owain rose from his seat, recalling her to the present. He poured a cup of wine with frustrating slowness, his lips curved in a half-smile, then sat and took a sip before speaking. "I can see you have much to think about. Rest assured that when I see him again I'll expect a full accounting. However, I have no doubt he'll give me good reasons for what he said."

"But… Wait. When you see him again? Then you're going to try to help him?" Several emotions hit her at once. Relief. Anger. Hope. Fear.

Owain gave a bark of a laugh. "I have every confidence that he's in no need of our help. However, we'll waste no time. We leave for Coed Bedwen in the morning." Owain looked at her over the rim of his cup, his face softening. "You look tired. Go and get some rest."

He stood, signaling the end of the audience.

Tired as she was, Matilda's brain was racing too much for sleep. She tossed and turned until her blankets were as tangled as her thoughts. Huw's hatred of her…the blood feud…just remembering his cold eyes made her shiver. She had believed him without question. Yet the doubt Owain had planted in her mind refused to be silenced.

Huw had many opportunities to harm or kill her in the time since they had met. If the blood oath was all that drove him, he could have killed her the night they escaped from Redcliff. Now she wasn't fleeing or in fear of pursuit, she was able to take a calmer view on what had happened. Over their days together, she had come to trust him. Depend on him. Love him. Which Huw was more likely to be the true one? The careless one who had blundered into the grasp of Fitzjohn's men, or the one who had shown her over and again that he would protect her?

Protect her. Realization punched her in the gut, jolting her off the pillows with a gasp. She stared, wide-eyed, across the darkened chamber, her heartbeat thundering in her ears. It was so obvious, she couldn't think why she hadn't known it from the start. Huw had allowed himself to be captured, goaded Fitzjohn into a fight, all because he was protecting her. He had created a diversion to allow her to escape. And she had been too blinded by fear to see it.

She lowered her head to her knees with a moan. Until now she hadn't considered what Huw might be going through at Fitzjohn's hands, but now images of torture, of beatings, haunted her.

Then she saw him the first time they had met, the moment she had unmasked him.

"Don't give me away... Sir Reginald would see me hanged."

Hanging. That's what they did to spies. And Fitzjohn was doubly likely to carry out a death penalty, considering he wanted Matilda for himself. Maybe at this very moment, his men were erecting a scaffold in the bailey.

And it was all her fault. Huw wouldn't be in Fitzjohn's hands if she had just looked outside before blundering out of the keep.

How could she ever have doubted him? She curled onto her side and hugged the blankets to her chest. Owain, Alys, even Godric had seen Huw's care for her. Only she had been too blinded by her cursed lack of trust to see it.

I'll always be there for you. That's what he'd said to her only last night. And now because of her foolishness, she might never see him again.

I'll always be there for you... The words seeped into her dreams as exhaustion finally won and she drifted into an uneasy sleep.

She was back in Coed Bedwen. It was a hot summer's day, and she was chasing butterflies through the bailey, stretching her arms as far as they would go, wishing she was taller. A Robert-the-devil fluttered past, and she chased it, giggling as she swerved around people who called after her to take care. The speckled brown butterfly was caught by a breeze as it reached the hall and tugged around the corner. She followed, only to run smack into a man coming the other way. She craned her neck and saw her father looking down at her, his face drawn and haggard.

"Be careful, Matilda. Mind where you're going." *His breath smelled of honey and spiced wine.*

"I'm sorry, Papa." She reached up to take his hand. "Did I hurt you?"

"Oh, no. It would take more than a little butterfly like you to hurt me."

"But you don't look very well. Are you ill?" This wasn't the first time she had asked him this. It was a fear that had weighed her down ever since her mother's death. "Are you going to get ill like Mama?"

Her father made a choking noise, and he put his

hand to his eyes briefly, then he ruffled her hair and gave her the same answer he always did. "Of course not, Matilda; don't worry about me. I'll always be there for you."

Matilda jerked awake, feeling sick. She curled into a ball, hugging her knees to her chest. No matter how she tried to push the memory away, it wouldn't go. Everything was so vivid. The butterfly, the mingled scents of honey, spices, and wine. Her father's strained smile as he had ruffled her hair.

I'll always be there for you.

Empty words.

Only an hour or so later, he had taken his own life, leaving her alone and heartbroken. As a result of that day, she had erected a shield around her heart, never allowing herself to depend on a man again.

And yet Huw had broken through that barrier. She had overcome her deep mistrust and learned to depend on him. Love him.

Yet now it looked like her heart was going to be torn from her all over again.

Knowing that sleep would elude her for the rest of the night, she crawled out of bed and knelt upon the rushes.

"Blessed mother Mary, help Huw…help me," she whispered, her hands clasped in front of her. "It's happening again, and I don't think I can bear it."

****

When the first glimmer of dawn peeked through gaps in the shutters, she forced her stiff limbs to move. She rose and summoned a maid to help her dress, then fretted while the girl chattered on, admiring her green riding gown with its crimson embroidery at the neck and sleeves. She didn't care how she looked. All she wanted was to get back to Coed Bedwen as soon as possible, learn what had happened to Huw. The moment the maid had fixed the embroidered band that held her veil in place, she dashed out to find Owain's men mustering in the courtyard.

When Owain saw her, he walked over, frowning. "There was no need for you to see us off," he said. "You must be exhausted after your long ride yesterday."

Matilda couldn't get his words to sink in. "See you off?" she said. "But I'm coming with you!"

"Nonsense! I sent messengers to your uncle last night. He's riding to meet us today, and your aunt will come here. She'll await the news with you. This is man's business."

In other words, she'd served her purpose and was no longer needed. King or no king, she would not allow Owain to cast her off until he found use for her again.

"Coed Bedwen is *my* business, my lord. You made it so when you decided I was to be the figurehead for the uprising. What kind of figurehead would I be if I remained miles away in comfort, while others fought for my inheritance?"

Owain's brows shot up. "I won't have you near the fighting. You'd be a danger to yourself and those forced to protect you."

"Of course not. But the tavern in the village has become a gathering place for the uprising. I should be there." It would also be close to Huw, wherever he was. If he was still alive.

Pain tore through her chest, and she thrust the thought aside. She had to believe he was well. She didn't know if she could keep her sanity if harm had come to him because of her carelessness.

"Your uncle won't be pleased," Owain said.

She raised her chin. "It's not my uncle's concern. I'm married to Huw now, and in his absence, I make the decisions on how I manage my life."

Owain's lips twitched. "In that case, I wouldn't dare prevent you from coming." He ordered a servant to fetch another horse and muttered something under his breath. It sounded like: "Huw doesn't stand a chance."

It rankled that her desire to grasp what little control was possible in this world of men could be seen as a joke. However, she held her tongue and allowed Owain to help her into the saddle.

After a brisk ride, they met Gruffyth at the same place he had separated from her and Huw before. He hastened to her side.

"Are you well?" he asked. "I've been so worried."

She nodded. "I'm quite well, Uncle." Unless you counted the pain in her heart.

"I wish I could have persuaded you to stay with me instead of dashing off on this mad escapade. I hope it wasn't too hard for you."

"Actually," she spoke as it occurred to her, "it was fun in a way."

"Fun?"

"Maybe 'fun' isn't the right word. I admit I was frightened much of the time, but after being caged up in Redcliff with little choice on how I spent my time, it was good to feel useful." Although she would never launder so much as a kerchief ever again.

She didn't say any more for a while but reflected on her time in Coed Bedwen. She had discovered the joy of being active, of making decisions more important than what gown to wear that day. Yes. Being mistress of Coed Bedwen would be fulfilling. If only…

If only there was some way to shield her heart from the pain of either loving or losing Huw.

A commotion at the front of the party roused her from her musings.

"Riders approach!" someone shouted.

The men drew their swords and forced Matilda into the center of the group. Surrounded by horses and their armed riders, she was unable to see who was coming. The group advanced, and she followed blindly, her eyes fixed on the back of the man ahead of her. Then she heard an exclamation. The group halted, and there came the sound of low voices speaking rapidly. What was happening? Was it messengers from Coed Bedwen? Her mouth went dry. Maybe they brought news of Huw. Just when her curiosity reached an unbearable height, the men in front of her moved aside.

She found herself face to face with a man mounted on a sway-backed nag, his hands resting awkwardly on the pommel of his saddle. His face was bruised, and his lips were swollen and had obviously been bleeding.

"Well met, Mallt. I'm glad to see you're safe."

Just for an instant, her complex, conflicted emotions resolved themselves into simple relief.

"Huw!" she cried. She swung down from the saddle and dashed toward him, then stopped when she took in the rest of the scene. The reason his hands were on the pommel was because they were tied. His horse was haltered, and the lead rope tied to another equally rough workhorse, ridden by a burly man who looked familiar. Next to him was Alys. On seeing her, Matilda recognized the other man as a frequent visitor to the Boar's Head.

"Alys, what are you doing here?"

"We caught this one"—Alys jerked her chin toward Huw—"breaking into my stable. We tied him up as you ordered and thought it best to bring him to you."

Her heart thumped so hard it was difficult to think. She turned to Huw, drinking in the face she'd feared lost to her forever.

"You're alive." They were the only words she could force past the lump in her throat.

Huw's bruised lips curved into a smile. "Mallt." He sounded like a parched man on seeing water for the first time in days. "You're safe."

In that moment the last of her doubt fell away. Huw had said what he had to protect her. Had suffered for her sake.

"Thanks to you." Her voice was little more than a whisper. She reached toward him but couldn't bring herself to touch him. She didn't want to cause him more pain. "I'm so sorry, Huw. This is all my fault."

"Don't blame yourself, Mallt. Your capture was just foul luck. You're not responsible for what happened to me. Besides, what kind of man would I be if I couldn't protect my own wife? But..." He made a move as though to take her hand, cursed when his bindings pulled taut. "What I said... I'm sorry. You have to believe me—"

She shook her head and placed her hands over his. "Don't be sorry. I understand. You were protecting me."

"None of it's true. You have to believe me."

"None of it?" Her voice came out sharper than intended.

A shadow passed over Huw's face. "You're talking about the blood oath."

She nodded.

He leaned forward, his voice urgent. "Matilda, you have to believe me. The oath means nothing to me now. Your safety is all that concerns me."

There was no lie in his eyes. He meant what he said. She should feel relieved. Instead the knot of anxiety tightened in her chest.

She opened her mouth, but her uncle cleared his throat, bringing back her awareness of their audience.

She gave Huw a tight smile. "We'll talk about this later." Then, turning to the man guarding Huw, she said, "Untie him."

Alys stepped forward. "But you said—"

"Untie him. He won't harm me."

With an apologetic glance at Alys, the burly man dismounted and made a move toward Huw's bindings, but with a twist of the hands, Huw flung off the cord himself. All the while his eyes remained fixed on hers.

Huw gave a crooked smile that Matilda felt in the pit of her belly. "I wanted them to feel safe."

Her fragile hold on her emotions snapped. How dare he look so pleased with himself when she had suffered agonies over him all night? "This might have been a game to you, Huw, but I thought you were going to die. I thought—"

Her voice cracked, and tears pricked at her eyelids. She had to get away from him, or she would lose all control. She couldn't afford to give any reason for the king to have her escorted back to the *llys*, and he might well do that if he thought she was becoming hysterical.

She turned her back on Huw and stumbled back to her horse. When she had rebuilt the barrier around her heart, then she would talk to him.

When she was strong enough to resist the urge to fling herself into his arms.

She gripped the saddle, only to find that without a mounting block, she was unable to pull herself up into the saddle.

Strong hands seized her around the waist and lifted her. Even before she looked, she knew it was Huw and longed to lean into him, take comfort from his strength. The hands lingered, brushing the underside of her breasts. Heat flooded through her. How she yearned for him.

And that was precisely why she needed to protect herself. Love meant pain. That must be the reason for last night's dream—to remind her to guard her heart. Knowing Huw was safe, she must ensure she never again suffered the same pain she suffered upon her father's death.

Or repeated the agony of last night, when she feared Huw was dead.

She gathered the reins and gave him a cool nod. "I can manage from here."

Huw opened his mouth, but Owain snapped out an order to move on. With one last glance at her, Huw returned to his mount.

It took all of Matilda's strength not to call him back, but she must avoid him until she could be certain she had control of her emotions. However, when the party set off again, whether by accident or design, she found him by her side.

"Are you sure you're quite well, Mallt? Did you reach Owain with no incident?"

"I'm perfectly well." She should ask about his injuries, but the thought of what he had endured for her sake made her throat squeeze shut.

"I know you must be angry with me. I never intended for you to find out about the blood oath that way."

She drew a shuddering breath. Yes, anger. She could use that to drown out this other, more terrifying emotion. Gripping her reins so tightly her nails cut crescent moon grooves into her palms, she said, "And what would have been a *good* way to tell me you'd vowed to claim a debt with my blood?"

"It was never about you. My vow was against the Comyns, and I absolved you of all responsibility almost from the start."

Matilda frowned. "*Almost* from the start? Then you admit you did plan to harm me at first?"

Huw bowed his head. "Before I met you, the oath was my only purpose in life. When Owain sent me to fetch you, when you were just a faceless Comyn, yes, I'll admit I thought it was my opportunity at last to avenge my family. But the moment I first saw you, my heart cried out for you, even though I tried to ignore it. I could never do anything to hurt you. I'd sooner gouge out my eyes than harm a hair on your head. I'd have realized that from the start if I'd listened to my heart. I could never harm you—the woman I'll love with all my heart until my dying day."

It was too much. His impassioned declaration threatened to shatter what little self-control she had mustered. She had to end this. Now.

She held up her hand, shocked to see it trembling. "Stop, please. I…I do believe you. I know you could never hurt me. But I…"

Huw scowled. "But what, Matilda? What else could possibly keep us apart?" He gave a bitter laugh. "Or is it just my misfortune to love a woman who has never known a decent man until now? The men in your life have damaged you, but not all men are like that. We're not all like Fitzjohn or your father. Although what he—"

"Stop!" Her heart hammered her ribs like a battering ram. Giddy nausea overtook her. She clung to the pommel of her saddle to steady herself. She could not…*would not* revisit that memory. She wished she hadn't told Huw what she had about him, because she wanted to lock the door on the desolate girl she had been and forget the pain of a broken heart.

The curious glances from the other riders gave her the excuse she needed. "I know we need to talk," she said in a calmer voice, "but this is neither the time nor the place."

"Very well," said Huw. "But this isn't over. I haven't given up on you, Mallt." He swept her with his gaze, sending sparks up and down her body, as though it were his fingers that caressed her.

Heat rushed to her cheeks. She couldn't keep her composure in his presence, so she urged her horse into a canter and drew alongside her uncle. Even so, she felt Huw's gaze burning her back for the rest of the ride.

The sun was low on the horizon when Owain called a halt beside a farmhouse at the foot of a hill. "We're as close as we can get without drawing attention to ourselves," he said. "Huw and Matilda, you go on to the Boar's Head with your companions and contact the villagers. I'll send a messenger when it's time to move on the castle."

Thankfully it wasn't a long ride to the village, and Matilda managed to keep Alys between her and Huw. By the time they had settled the horses and gathered the fighting men in the tavern, night had fallen. Looking around, Matilda thought all the men of the village, bar the very old or sick, must be gathered here. Alys had clearly been right about the level of hatred Fitzjohn had inspired. Once Huw had explained the battle plan, everyone settled around the fire in the dim, smoky room to pass the time until Owain's signal came. Some of the men started to sing.

When one man broke into a mournful song of lost love, Matilda shot an involuntary glance at Huw. He was staring at her, an intense gaze that stripped her bare. She wished the man would sing something else. She had just begun to get her emotions under control, but now the song made her think of the passion Huw had awoken in her. The memory of their lovemaking twisted her heart. Tears filled her eyes.

Huw leaned forward. "Are you well, Mallt?" The concern in his eyes made the tears flow faster.

She stumbled to her feet. "I…yes. I'm just tired. Perhaps I should retire."

"No." Huw grasped her shoulders. "We need to talk. Now. Before I go off to fight."

She couldn't refuse him. Not when there was a chance he might never come back. She owed him that much. "Very well, but not here."

Knowing he would follow, she walked to the door and slipped outside into the starlit courtyard, which was, thankfully, deserted.

Huw reached out an arm as though to touch her but let it drop to his side.

She swayed toward him, her body aching to feel his arms around her. It was all she could do to keep her feet rooted to the spot. "What is it you have to say?"

Whatever it was, she doubted it could quell the fear in her heart.

Chapter Eighteen

Matilda gazed upward. The moonlight bathed her face in a silver glow, and Huw saw she was blinking. Most likely fighting tears. But what could he say to make things right?

All he could do was repeat what he'd already said. "I'm sorry you had to learn about the blood oath like that, but you have to believe me—I would never hurt you."

She put her hand on his arm. Her touch seared through the woolen sleeve. "I do believe you. I trust you."

Her words should have reassured him, but the glimmer of tears in her eyes cast a chill around his heart. "Then I don't understand. What's the problem? I'd never allow any harm to come to you. I'd protect you with my life. Everything I have is yours. Including my heart. What more could you want?"

Her face softened, and his heart leapt, thinking he'd won. He stepped closer so their bodies were nearly touching. Her honeysuckle scent fogged his senses. Her hand was still on his sleeve, and the heat from her touch rippled across his flesh and set the blood roaring in his ears. He raised a hand to brush the tears that had spilled down her cheek, but she halted him. She placed a hand on his chest. A hand that trembled.

"What about the blood oath?"

"What about it? It means nothing to me, Mallt."

"How can you be sure? Nothing can take back what my grandfather did to your family. It will always be there…unspoken perhaps, but always between us." She released his arm, and the chill at the loss of her touch was instantaneous.

He cursed the day he had ever been persuaded to make such a ruinous vow. "If God punishes me for reneging, then so be it, but I can't believe he would want an innocent woman to suffer for her grandfather's sins. You must believe me. I don't hold you responsible. I don't need Comyn blood or a blood price. You freed me from my need for revenge. All I need is you."

"I wish it was that simple, Huw. Truly I do. But…oh, holy Mother, I didn't know how difficult this was going to be." She broke off with a sob and turned away, wiping her eyes.

Icy cold dread squeezed his heart. He had been against the marriage at the start, but the thought of losing Matilda made him feel as though he were being torn in two. It was impossible to imagine.

His heart pounded. Surely there was a way he could persuade her. To force her to believe in his love. But any form of trickery, of deceit was no longer an option and without that, what was left of him?

You are nothing!

The memory of his great-uncle's words made his mouth go dry. All he had to offer her was the truth of who he really was deep inside. If that was the only way to win her back—to tell her the absolute truth—then he would do it. He would strip his soul bare for her.

And if she still rejected him then he truly was

nothing.

He drew a deep breath. "I haven't finished, Mallt. Hear me out."

She turned her head, revealing tear-filled eyes that glittered in the moonlight. He gripped her shoulders, turning her, holding her gaze, compelling her to read the truth in his eyes as he spoke. "For years the blood oath held me. It was the only thing I had left. But you brought me to my senses. As I got to know you, I saw you as a woman in your own right, not merely a Comyn. You shattered my beliefs. I couldn't hold on to the oath any more, but all the time, something my great-uncle said to me made me afraid to let it go."

Matilda's brow furrowed. "What do you mean?"

"I told you that when my father died, my great-uncle made it clear I had to leave."

Matilda nodded. "Yes, but I don't see—"

"That was true, but it wasn't the whole truth." He clenched his fists as he forced himself to repeat the words that had gouged deep wounds into his soul. "We had only just laid my father in his tomb when my great-uncle took me aside. He told me…" Huw struggled to keep his voice steady. "He told me he had only supported me for my father's sake, but now he was gone it was time I knew I meant nothing to him. That's what he said: 'You own nothing, you have nothing to offer me. You *are* nothing'."

He was glad it was too dark to see the pity in Matilda's eyes, but he could hear it in her voice when she spoke. "What a vicious thing to say. What did you do?"

"I left. I couldn't bear to stay, knowing my great-uncle despised me. Eventually I made my way to the royal court, and that's when Owain took me into his service. But that's not the important thing. I need you to understand this: for the longest time I believed him. I thought I was worthless. The only thing I had left to cling to was the blood oath. I thought if I fulfilled it, then I would regain my worth. Even when Owain spotted my talents and gave me a place as his spy, nothing I achieved had any value to me. It helped me forget, but nothing more. I thought I needed to take my revenge on the Comyns...on you...before I could start living.

"And then I met you. I struggled against my feelings, because it meant letting go of the only thing that gave my life meaning. But you changed me."

He took Matilda's shoulders, turning her toward the moonlight so he could search her face for a sign she believed him. He could see the battle in her eyes, but he couldn't tell if he was winning her over. The only thing he could do was keep going.

"You've freed me, Mallt. The oath has no power over me. You can silence my great-uncle's voice if you'll love me. And I'll never stop loving you."

He cupped her chin in his hand and tilted her face toward his. "I'll always be there for you, Mallt."

To his shock, her eyes filled with tears. She twisted out of his grip. "Don't say that," she said. "Don't promise me one thing when all along you know—"

"Know what?" A black was crushing his chest. He had bared his scars. If that wasn't enough, he had nothing else to give.

"My father. What you just said... 'I'll always be there for you.' My father said that to me. He..." She turned her face away and pressed her fingers to her quivering lips.

A surge of impatience swept through him. "Speak plainly, Matilda. What did your father do that was so terrible that you can't accept my love?"

She straightened up and looked him in the eye, both hands clenched into fists at her sides. "One afternoon, my father made that promise to me. He told me he'd always be there for me. I was so happy. I thought that after all his grief over my mother, he'd finally come back to me." Her voice hitched, and she drew a shuddering breath before continuing. "Then he told me he'd see me later and returned to his chamber. That was when he…"

A sob choked her next words, but he didn't need to hear them. His irritation ebbed, leaving only deep sorrow for what Matilda had carried in her heart all these years. "I'm so sorry, Mallt. I—"

She cut him off with a chopping gesture and shook her head. "I need to say it. To make sure you understand." Her voice wavered, but she managed to carry on. "Within the hour, he had taken the dose that killed him. He loved me, I know that. He knew I loved him, depended on him. He held my future happiness in his hands. But in the end, none of that was enough for him. His grief was too strong. He abandoned me and ripped out my heart."

Huw didn't wait to hear more. He gripped both her hands, willing her to believe his next words. "I would never do that to you. Never abandon you."

"How can you be sure? Oh, I don't mean that I don't trust you. Our time together has taught me that even if I can never trust any other man, I can trust you. But in the end, my father's grief overwhelmed his love for me. And now I'm afraid...so afraid that in the end your blood oath will eat away at you...overcome your love for me. Not that I fear you would hurt me, but that after a time you wouldn't be able to look at me without remembering the suffering my grandfather caused. It would tear us apart. And to lose yet another person I loved...that would finish me, Huw. I couldn't endure that pain again."

An iron hand gripped Huw's heart and squeezed tight. His throat was raw, every word a jagged spike of pain. "Tell me what I can do. What will ease your fear?"

"I don't know. Maybe you don't think the blood oath matters any more, but to me...now I know...it weighs heavily on me. Even without the fear of it separating us, I'd feel forever indebted to you. I... Give me time, please, Huw. I'm just not ready to place my future happiness into another man's hands. Especially not with the chasm of an unpayable debt between us." She looked away. "I've come to a decision, and I need you to accept it. When my uncle returns to his home, I'm going with him. I need to be apart from you...to think."

Gently but firmly she withdrew her hands from his. Tears flowing down her cheeks, she turned and walked away.

Huw made no attempt to follow her. She had said she needed time, but he knew she was trying to soften the blow. She wouldn't tell him she was leaving him for good right before he had to go into battle. But he had no doubt that afterward, she would tell him she couldn't be with him.

He had held nothing back, revealed everything, and

she had rejected him.

He truly was nothing.

****

Without looking back, Matilda stumbled inside, her vision blurred by a veil of tears. She blundered past Alys, ignoring her anxious inquiries and climbed up to the store room, where she lay down on the pallet. Her throat ached, and she felt hollow inside. Part of her was desperate to run back outside and fling herself into Huw's arms, say she'd changed her mind. But each time she tried to imagine risking the pain, she would remember the devastation of her father's death. The sick dread when Huw had been in Fitzjohn's hands.

I'll always be there for you. The words haunted her. Sometimes it was Huw who spoke, sometimes her father, but the warning was the same. Letting Huw into her heart would be risking her peace of mind. Whatever he might say, he would never truly be able to dissociate her from her family. From the blood oath. And when he finally gave up the struggle…

No. She could never endure another abandonment. Best to retire to her uncle's household and wait until she had her treacherous heart under control. Surely, given time, she would find a way to rein in this powerful yearning she felt for Huw. Then she could return to Coed Bedwen, and they could enjoy separate lives in the same place, an arrangement common in many Norman marriages.

Her heart wrenched. What was worse? Being apart from Huw, or forced to see him every day, knowing he could never love her?

She buried her head beneath the blanket and sought to block her misery with sleep, but it was futile. Lying on a bed she had shared with Huw only a short time ago forced images of her with Huw into her mind, a cruel reminder of what she had lost.

Much later, her eyes burning with weariness, she heard a knock on the door and then voices and the clatter of armor and weapons being fastened. Owain's messenger must have arrived. She kept her eyes closed and held her breath. She wanted to wish them safe but didn't know how she could face Huw.

The door opened and closed again, and she let out a breath, thinking everyone had gone.

Then the stairs creaked. Huw's voice made her jump. "We're leaving now, Mallt. Owain's waiting."

It was no good. She'd never forgive herself if something happened to him. She raised herself up on one elbow and looked across the room. Huw was standing by the door, just visible by the glow of the rush lights. He was wearing a hauberk—Owain's messenger must have brought it for him—and a sword at his belt.

"Take care, Huw. I know things are...difficult between us, but I'd hate it if you were hurt."

He made a move as though to go to her, but stopped. After one last, lingering look, he strode to the door, the chain mail of his hauberk clinking with every move. Then he was gone. Perhaps forever.

At that moment she knew it was already too late. Huw was going into battle, and if he was killed, she would never recover. She loved him. She couldn't bear to live without him.

If he returned safely, she would do all in her power to overcome the power of the blood debt that threatened to tear them apart.

Chapter Nineteen

Huw pushed aside the brambles concealing the tunnel entrance. Freshly lit lanterns revealed the stone steps winding up into the shadows. He blessed whoever had thought to leave them there—Godric, he guessed—and turned to the band of men he had led to this spot. A select group whose aim was to enter the castle through the tunnel and open the gates to let in Owain's main force.

"Is everyone ready?" he asked.

There were nods all around.

"You know what to do. Let's move. And remember, silence from now on." He led the way into the dim passageway.

The trouble with silence was it gave too much space for thought. As he climbed through the tunnel, the echoes of the men's footsteps and the soft chink of chain mail did nothing to block his thoughts.

Over and again he saw Matilda bathed in moonlight, her lips quivering with suppressed tears.

I need to be apart from you.

He had taken the biggest risk of his life. He had confessed his deepest thoughts and fears, told her of his rejection by his last surviving relative. He had stripped his soul bare and in return… He swallowed to ease the ache in his throat. In return, Matilda had made it clear she couldn't bear to be with him. He should be angry, bitter, but in fact he felt nothing but desolation.

An uneven step tripped him, jolting him from his thoughts. He clutched the damp stone wall to steady himself. *Concentrate!* His men and most of the castle's inhabitants were counting on him. He couldn't afford to let his mind drift, no matter how much Matilda had wounded him.

To focus his mind, he did what he had always done when pretending to be someone else. He shut all the painful memories and emotions away in a box in the back of his mind and locked it. It would remain closed until he had completed his task. All he had left now was Coed Bedwen. He couldn't afford to lose that too.

When they scrambled into the cellar, they found Godric waiting. Huw's heart lurched when he took in the deep lines scoring Godric's brow.

"What's happened?"

The stable master blew out a breath. "Nothing. It's just been an anxious wait." He held up a lantern. His hand trembled so violently the flame quivered, bringing the shadows to looming life. Huw was stirred with pity. Godric hadn't struck him as easily frightened. But then, how well did he truly know the man?

"Well, the wait's over." He prayed the need to act would ease Godric's fear. He would be no use to them if he froze. "Tell me the positions of Fitzjohn's men."

"Fitzjohn and one watchman are in the keep. There are four more at the gates and another four on the walls. Everyone else is asleep in the hall."

"Good. That's what I'd hoped." Huw drew his sword. "Let's go."

By prior arrangement, the party split up as soon as they entered the bailey. Godric led one group to the great hall, others went to cover the walls, while Huw led his group down to the gates. Pressing his sword to his side to stop the hilt striking his mail, he led them to the shadows behind the blacksmith's bothy. He held up a hand, halting the group.

"Remember." He lowered his voice to little more than a breath. "Whatever happens, we must open the gates. If you get the chance, take it." If they didn't let in Owain and the main force, they were doomed to failure.

He peered around the corner, looking for the watchmen. Unlike the guards at Redcliff, they were wide awake. They stood at their posts, up on the wall above the entrance, keeping watch on the approach road. If they were swift and quiet, Huw hoped he and his men could take the guards by surprise and overpower them before they raised the alarm.

He crept to the foot of the steps that led up to the wall. With silent gestures, he indicated which guard each man should attack. Then, taking great care to make no noise, he slipped up the stairs. After a rapid glace over his shoulder to make sure everyone was in position, he raised his arm. He lunged at his chosen guard, intending to strike his head with the pommel of his sword.

At that exact instant, a bat swooped over the wall. The guard turned his head to follow its movement. The red torchlight revealed his gape-mouthed horror when he saw Huw. He ducked under Huw's arm and seized him around the waist. They crashed down upon the walkway. Huw twisted away just in time to avoid landing beneath the guard.

He scrambled to his knees and heard the guard draw a breath. There was no time to think. Before the man could cry out, Huw flung himself upon him, pressing an arm to his windpipe. The shout came out as no more than a croak.

Gasping, Huw glanced around to see that all the other guards had been overpowered. Without shifting his arm from his captive's throat, he said, "Agree to surrender quietly and you won't be harmed. It's over."

The man's gaze fixed on a point over Huw's shoulder, before returning to his face. His lips curled. "I think not."

There came the clatter of several boots upon the stone steps. Before Huw could react, hands grasped his shoulders. They jerked him to his feet, spun him around. Other hands snatched his sword and tore his knife from his belt. He glanced round frantically for his men. Sweet Jesu, they'd be taken too. This couldn't be happening. He'd planned so carefully. Thought of everything.

A man stepped into the torchlight. Fitzjohn.

He sneered at Huw. "Did you truly think I would let Coed Bedwen be taken so easily?" He tilted his head toward a man standing in the shadows beside him. "Fortunately, I had help. I knew you couldn't have escaped alone, and as you'd been working in the stables, I worked out the most likely culprit."

Huw frowned at the dark shape. It couldn't be. It looked like...

"Godric!" he gasped. He strained against his captors, determined to land at least one blow upon the traitor.

Godric stepped forward, then dropped to his knees. Huw, in his surprise, ceased to struggle.

"Forgive me, my lord," Godric pleaded. "Fitzjohn

knows Alys is my sister. Said he'd kill her if I didn't reveal your plans."

Huw sagged. No wonder Godric had been shaking. He'd been terrified for his sister. Huw hated to think what he'd have done in a similar situation. "Peace, Godric; I don't blame you," he said. "I'm sorry for bringing you both into this."

He turned to Fitzjohn. "You have what you want. Promise you won't harm any more innocent lives."

"You're in no position to make demands. I might have Coed Bedwen, but I still need Matilda. Tell me where she is, and I'll consider it."

"Don't tell him," Godric cried, but Huw hardly heard him through the roaring in his ears.

Matilda. Devastation engulfed him. He'd lost everything. First Matilda and now all hope of regaining Coed Bedwen.

He hung his head and closed his eyes. His great-uncle had been right after all—he truly was worthless.

Fitzjohn gave a nasty laugh that grated down his spine. "Take him to the keep and erect a scaffold in the bailey. In the morning I'll show the people what happens to those who try to take what is mine. And after that there will be a wedding to celebrate." He sneered at Huw's gasp of denial. "Tomorrow night, your widow will be warming my bed."

Huw's captors shifted their grip for one moment. That was all he needed. He didn't hesitate—he would save Matilda from Fitzjohn even though he would most likely die in the attempt.

He flung his full weight at Fitzjohn and caught him squarely in the chest. The momentum of his leap carried them both over the edge of the walkway. For what felt like an eternity, all Huw was aware of was the wind whistling in his ears and the wool of Fitzjohn's tunic bunched in his fists.

Then they hit the ground, Fitzjohn breaking Huw's fall. There was a sickening crack. Fitzjohn jerked once, then lay still.

For a score of heartbeats, Huw lay still, fighting for breath. He gradually became aware of aches and bruises. With care, he tested each limb and found that although he would likely be black and blue in the morning, he had taken no serious hurt. He staggered to his feet and looked down at Fitzjohn. His enemy lay on his back, his neck at an unnatural angle, sightless eyes fixed open, reflecting the cold moonlight.

Huw wiped blood from his lips and looked up at the men on the wall. They all stared down at the ghastly body, making no move to fight.

"This ends now!" He shouted up at Fitzjohn's men. "Lay down your arms, and I guarantee no one else will be harmed. Those who wish it will be granted safe passage to England. Because Coed Bedwen is Welsh once more."

There was a harsh clatter of steel upon stone as one by one, Fitzjohn's men threw down their weapons. Soon cheers echoed from the walls as it sank in that Coed Bedwen had at last been returned to its rightful owners. Without needing any more orders from Huw, his men led away the prisoners and opened the gates for their king.

Huw sank down upon the cold steps and buried his head in his hands. He'd won Coed Bedwen. He'd finally achieved his wish.

It meant nothing.

He had won his castle but lost Matilda. Lost the one person who could give his victory any meaning.

As though his great-uncle was standing at his shoulder, he heard the words that had haunted him for years. *You* are *nothing.*

Only this time, Matilda's voice cut through. *What a vicious thing to say.* Which, of course, it had been. Only a mean-minded, heartless whoreson would say such a thing to a boy who had just lost his father. Not a man worth giving any credence to.

He looked at his men, all of whom had followed his command and taken the castle before the king could even bring reinforcements. Some of them saw him looking and raised their swords in salute.

He had done this. He had achieved what his father and great-uncle before him had failed to do. He had retaken Coed Bedwen.

He sprang to his feet, fists clenched. If he had won Coed Bedwen when all had seemed lost, then, by God, he would win Matilda.

At that moment Owain and his men, accompanied by the villagers, dashed through the gates. His mouth set in a determined line, Huw strode toward him. After all he had done for him, the king could surely spare men to help get the castle in a fit state to receive its mistress. He would fetch her at the earliest possible time and not a moment later.

He would fight for her love. And he was damned if he was going to lose.

Chapter Twenty

Matilda paced from the door of her uncle's great hall to the dais and back again. Fifteen paces. The same as it had been every one of the hundred or more times she had repeated the exercise this morning and each time she had done it over the past week.

She missed Huw. Ached for him. Mourned the loss of the only love she would ever know. But whenever she considered returning to him, the memory of the dream would return, leaving her sick and shaky. It was no good. The blood oath would always be there and sooner or later it would drive them apart. Yet how to overcome it? She still hadn't found a solution.

A door opened behind the dais and Gruffyth entered. "Come with me, Matilda. There's something I've been meaning to give you."

His tone implied it was something she would be pleased with, but she couldn't summon up much interest. She'd found it hard to muster enthusiasm for anything since she had parted from Huw. Nevertheless, she might as well see what her uncle wanted to show her. It beat walking another fifteen paces.

She followed him into his private chamber, to a table upon which stood a small wooden chest, painted with vivid swirls of red, blue, and green.

"This is something I've been holding for you for some years," Gruffyth said. "I was going to give it to you when you left, but you've seemed so lost since you've been here that I thought you'd like to know you do have some resources of your own."

He placed the chest in Matilda's hands. Matilda nearly dropped it, surprised at the weight.

"When my mother—your grandmother—died, she left some jewels to your mother. However, she died before I could send them to her, so I held onto them until I could find a way of giving them to you. Go on—open it."

Matilda fiddled with the clasp until she could swing the lid open. She caught her breath when she saw the gleam of gold and gems, as bright as the colors on the box. "I…thank you. They're beautiful. What should I do with them?"

"They're yours. It's up to you. Wear them…sell them…you decide. If there's anything you wish to buy, the value of these would more than cover it."

The only thing she wanted was Huw. And no jewels, however costly, could equal his value.

The value of a man's life. That reminded her of something Huw had said to her the night before retaking Coed Bedwen: *I don't need Comyn blood or a blood price.*

A blood price. Her pulse quickened. Maybe there was a way she could be with Huw.

"Uncle, can you tell me about…what is the word…*galanas*?"

Gruffyth frowned. "Is this to do with Huw?"

She nodded.

"I'm sure he doesn't hold you responsible, Matilda. I'd never have given permission for him to wed you if I thought he did."

"I know, but this is important. Please explain. Does it mean the killer or his family must pay a price to his victim's heirs to make restitution?"

"Broadly speaking, yes. The price set depends upon the status of the victim."

Matilda's heart stirred into life. "And would these jewels fetch the right price for Huw's grandfather?"

"It would more than cover it."

Matilda's hands started trembling so violently she had to replace the chest on the table before she dropped it. If Huw would accept it, then the blood debt would be paid. She and Huw could be together with no fear of his oath coming between them again.

Now she had the means to end the torment of being apart from him, she didn't want to waste a single heartbeat. "I have to go to Coed Bedwen. Immediately." She prayed it wasn't too late, that Huw hadn't given up on her. "Can you arrange an escort?"

"That won't be necessary, Gruffyth. I've come to take my wife back."

That voice! Matilda's stomach performed a giddy swoop. She spun around and pressed her hand to her throat when she saw Huw standing in the open doorway, silhouetted against the sunlight.

"Huw!" She stepped forward, then stopped.

Deep lines furrowed his brow. Her smile of greeting faded when he did not reply. She ached to touch him, but his face was stony. While he looked so cold, so remote, she couldn't bring herself to mention the blood oath again.

Huw held out his arm. "We're leaving now."

"Wait. What about my luggage? And I need to say farewell to my aunt."

"I'll send a servant for your luggage. I'm sure Gruffyth will carry your farewells to your aunt."

He took her arm. Matilda only just had time to bid a hasty goodbye to her smiling uncle and snatch up the box of jewels before he marched her to the stable, where his horse was waiting.

"I'm not dressed for riding."

"That didn't stop you before." Huw's gaze dropped to the chest. "What have you brought that for? I said I'd send for your things."

She clutched it tighter. "I'm not leaving without it." She couldn't explain. Not yet. She needed time to work out how to broach the subject. But when she did, she wanted to have the jewels with her. She would want to know there and then if he would accept them as a blood price. If he did, it would be assurance that he truly had let go of his blood oath. It was the only way she could be sure their love would survive.

Cursing its weight, Huw stowed the box in a saddle pack. He swung her up into the saddle and climbed behind her. With one arm clamped around her waist, he spurred his horse into a gallop.

The wind roared in her ears, and it was all she could do to hang on, leaning in the crook of his arm, just as she had done before. She leaned into his embrace. Talking was impossible, but she was in no hurry. If he refused to accept the blood price, this was the last time she would be able to take comfort in the warmth of his body, rest her head against his broad shoulders. Have his arm around her, making her feel safe. Conversation could wait.

At the speed Huw set, they arrived at Coed Bedwen in less than half the time it had taken her to make the opposite journey. However, he didn't ride to the castle. Instead he steered the horse toward the hill they had stood upon when they had first arrived in Coed Bedwen. When they reached the eaves of the woods, he slowed down and set the horse upon a narrow track that disappeared into the trees.

"What are we doing here?" She clung to his arm, still breathless. Whether from the ride or his nearness, she couldn't tell.

"There's something I must show you."

"What?"

"You'll see. Be patient."

The track followed a winding route, dodging around the silvery trunks of the birch trees. Overhead the heavy leaf buds were bursting open, decking the branches with glimmers of the palest green. Birdsong filled the air, a joyous clamor in complete contrast to Matilda's gut-wrenching nerves. This wasn't going how she'd planned.

"How far are we going, Huw? There's something I have to—"

Then a sharply sweet scent teased her nostrils. "I remember that smell," she said, feeling as though she had walked into a dream. "It's…"

Then they stepped into a clearing that was awash in a sea of nodding bluebells. Huw reined the horse to a halt and helped her dismount. She walked into the center, breathing deeply. Lost in memories of her mother.

"Oh, Huw—you remembered!"

"When I came here this morning and saw the bluebells, I took it as a sign that it was time to bring you back. To say what I've longed to tell you since we retook the castle."

Her heart thumped. "If it's about the—"

Huw held up his hand. "Hear me out. When I've finished you can have your say, but listen to me first."

He drew a deep breath. "Before our wedding, you told me Coed Bedwen was special to you because it was the only place that held happy memories. Then you challenged me to tell you why Coed Bedwen was special to me, and I couldn't answer. I didn't want to admit it then, but you had seen what I couldn't—I'd been so busy trying to fulfill my father's dream, I had no idea what *I* wanted. I couldn't see past my oath. And my great-uncle's words haunted me, made me believe that unless I fulfilled the oath, I was nothing. Worthless.

"When I met you, it wasn't long before I knew I could never harm you. But renouncing my driving goal in life gave my uncle's words more hold over me. The only way to prove him wrong, or so I thought, was to take back Coed Bedwen.

"Well, I've been here for a week, and I've been a blind fool. Coed Bedwen means nothing to me. I've never lived here, have no memories of the place. There's only one thing that can give it meaning, make Coed Bedwen special."

"What's that?" Matilda's throat was so tight she had to force the words out.

"You. I love you. If you give me another chance, try to trust me, we can make happy memories for the both of us. But…"

He paused, and his expression was so grave that a chill of foreboding crept through Matilda's limbs. She had been on the point of saying what was on her heart, but now she froze, mute, her heart hammering against her ribs.

Huw swallowed. "If you decide you still can't trust me, I promise to leave. I won't stay here, unwanted and unloved. It's time I formed a new purpose for myself—this time one of my own making. The deepest desire of my heart is to stay with you, protect and love you and guide the people of Coed Bedwen. But if you refuse my love, I'll leave Coed Bedwen in your control. I've heard rumors of another crusade to the Holy Land. I'll join that, just as you wished. I understand your fear of my blood oath, and I won't have you suffer anxiety on that account. I'll leave you in peace."

Tears pricked her eyelids. "Huw, I…I know I said I wanted Coed Bedwen for myself, but now… I couldn't face it without you. It was wrong and foolish of me to think I was better off alone. When you arrived at my uncle's, I was on my way to tell you just that."

Hope blazed from Huw's eyes. He slipped a hand around her waist and pulled her close. "Then you'll come back to me? Share my life?"

He stooped over her, his face so close she had to fight to urge to steal a kiss. But there was still one thing to be settled before she could make any promises.

"There's one condition."

He frowned, wary. "What's that?"

"The box I brought. Fetch it."

The furrows on his brow deepened, but he did as she asked. "What's in it?" he asked as he handed it over to her. "It feels like lead."

"Open it and see."

His look of shock when he raised the lid and saw the jewels inside would have made her laugh if her future wasn't in the balance. "These have come to me from my grandmother. They're yours. In payment of the blood price."

"Mallt, I can't take these. They're exquisite. You should wear them in honor of your grandmother."

"It's not negotiable. If you can't accept the blood price, then the debt still stands between us."

"But I told you the oath doesn't matter to me anymore."

"It matters to *me*. If you won't accept payment, then my grandfather's actions will always cast a shadow over our love. I would never be free of the fear that it would eventually destroy us, drive us apart. Please, Huw, take the jewels and end this."

The corners of his lips curved upward. "Our love," he repeated. "Then you admit you love me?"

She nodded. "More than anything."

"Say it."

"Tell me you'll accept the jewels, first."

"Then I accept. You've paid the blood price, and it no longer has any claim upon us."

The weight lifted from her heart. She felt light. Free. Giddy. Blinking back tears, she smiled up at him. "I love you, Huw. With all my heart. I'll never stop loving you."

He whooped, and before she realized what he was about to do, he seized her around the waist and swung her in a wide circle, jewel box and all. Then he dropped to the ground, set the chest aside, and pulled her across his lap.

She snuggled into his embrace, breathing in the scent of bluebells. Huw slipped his fingers under her chin and tilted her face up to meet his lips. His kiss was tender and reverent, but with the promise of passion to come. She curled her arms around his shoulders and poured all her love into the embrace, tasting the salt of her tears of joy.

Finally, Huw broke the kiss, and she rested her head in the crook of his neck. When he spoke, she felt the rumble of his voice against her cheek.

"If you insist on paying a blood price, then we must do this properly. The value of these jewels is far more than any blood price. We must ask the king to agree to an amount so you can keep the rest for yourself. He leaned over, and she heard the chime of gems striking gold, then she felt a cold weight settle around her neck. She looked down to see a wondrous necklace of gold and rubies.

Huw fastened it then leaned back to look. "It's no match for your beauty," he said, "but you must keep this for yourself. After all, I want my wife to have nothing but the finest jewels to wear at the feast I have planned."

"A feast?"

"Yes. To celebrate the return of my wife to Coed Bedwen. It will be even more lavish than our wedding feast." His eyes darkened, setting her pulse jumping. "Although it will differ from our wedding feast in one important respect."

"And what's that?" Huw's burning gaze made her so breathless she could hardly get the words out.

"I fully intend to bed my wife this time."

Her heart thumping, light-hearted with joy, she smiled. "It will be my pleasure." She pulled his head down and covered his mouth with hers, a pledge of her enduring love.

Then Huw pressed her down upon the bed of

bluebells and, enveloped in their sweet fragrance, proved to her all over again just how deeply he loved her.

A word about the author...

Tora lives in Shropshire in the United Kingdom. On childhood holidays her interest in history was fired by exploring castles in Wales and the Welsh borders, and she would make up stories about characters living there. When she started writing, it seemed only natural to turn to the settings that inspired her as a child. In her free time, when she can drag herself away from reading, she enjoys walking and cycling.

http://www.torawilliams.uk/

Printed in Great Britain
by Amazon